Life in Shadows

Elliott Kay

ISBN: 1532712553
ISBN 13: 9781532712555

To anyone who ever wished they'd have a book dedicated to their name.

This one's for you.

Congratulations.

WARNING

The four stories found in *Life in Shadows* collectively contain explicit violence, extended explicit sex scenes, explicit karaoke, profanity, rampant nudity, assault, murder, breaking and entering, belligerent urban wildlife, premeditated sexual promiscuity, vehicular assault, reckless endangerment, attempted kidnapping, attempted robbery, attempted ritual demonic possession, blatant violation of state regulations of adult entertainment, punching, kicking, cutting, stabbing, shooting, hair-pulling, name-calling, slut-shaming, cheap Halloween costumes, strippers, hipsters, poseurs, police, personal calls while on duty, arson, destruction of private property, lingerie, war criminals, break-up text messaging, lesbian demon seduction, accusations of Mary Suedom, poor workplace morale, premarital sex, nude calisthenics, immolation, false identification, ruthless exploitation of personal beauty, unsafe crowd control standards, vertigo, nude calisthenics, destruction of evidence, elitism, racism (don't worry, he dies), open relationships, workplace scapegoating, adult use of plumbing implements, fantasy depictions of witchcraft and paganism, at least one reincarnated ancient European warlord, and a girl-on-girl grenade fight.

All characters are over the age of 18, except the afore-mentioned reincarnation of an ancient European warlord. That gets sketchy.

CHRONOLOGY

Life in Shadows collects four stories set before, during and after the novels *Good Intentions* and *Natural Consequences*. These stories and the novels take place in the following order:

Authenticity: Spring
Naked Justice: Summer
Good Intentions: September
Halloween for Life: October
Natural Consequences: October / early November
Skin: Two weeks later

AUTHENTICITY

"Did you carve that adorable wand yourself, or did you buy it somewhere?"

Onyx stiffened. The question, asked from behind her with false warmth, interrupted her spell. The winged, seven-foot-tall gargoyle in front of her stared back with face-devouring rage. Onyx felt pretty much the same way. *Bitch did* not *just check my magic cred in a place like this*, she thought, yet she knew that some in this crowd would do exactly that.

The gallery held a couple dozen Practitioners. Almost every one of them saw the rest as a check on their own potential power. Grimacing, Onyx lowered her ebony wand and turned to face the inevitable games of "What's Your Practice (So I Can Mock It)?" and "Witches Aren't Real Sorcerers."

The middle-aged couple presented insincere smiles on unremarkable faces. Most of the attendees dressed nicely, if not quite formally. Onyx fit into that category with her long black frock coat, red top and dark slacks. These two went

1

above and beyond the rest. Everything about their clothes screamed excess, from his suit and her embroidered scarlet dress to their gloves and accessories.

No one else seemed interested in the conversation. Small groups of attendees stood here and there, talking among themselves or looking over the open crates, boxes, and the odd bits that didn't pack up so easily, like the gargoyle. At a glance, one might think the gallery was transitioning between displays. Everyone present, however, knew this for the much more somber occasion it was—though apparently the floor was now open to cattiness and petty sniping.

Beard with no mustache. What the fuck leads a man to make that choice?

"Do you have a problem with my wand?" Onyx replied flatly. Though her dark curls and young, pretty features gave her a soft image, she was ready to parry and thrust if necessary, be it with words or magic. If neither of those worked, she could always try stomping with her knee-high Doc Marten boots. She already felt like skipping straight to that option.

"Oh, you're no problem at all. I only ask because it has such a busy style," the woman explained. "A wand is more effective if the user creates it herself, but I suppose there are sometimes reasons to buy from a crafter instead. Especially if you're only starting out. Besides, smooth contours and bulbs like those would probably only come out on a lathe. It's very…Hermione."

The young witch blinked. Her wand looked like nothing of the sort. It had a different shape, style, and even a completely different color. Still, arguing over that was pointless. Harry Potter references eliminated any possibility that the woman wasn't mocking her. "You two came all the way out to Seattle to cosplay as people who grew out of high school?" Onyx gave them an approving nod. "Good job on the threads. Maybe work on the characterization a bit more."

She turned back to the gargoyle. *Gotta be tourists. Locals would be way more subtle with the passive-aggressive elitism.*

"I guess what we'd really like to know is why you have it out," said Beard-With-No-Mustache. "Were you not told the rules of this engagement?"

"She has it out because she got permission," said another woman. She wore a subtle, dark suit and kept her long, black hair pulled back into a ponytail. Her lovely light brown face bore little makeup. In contrast to Onyx's sparring partners, her silver jewelry was minimal and understated.

"We were told there would be no casting."

"As a rule, no. One minor spell of perception, requested properly, in advance? Yes. I made an exception."

The pair of visitors took in the same frustrated breath. "And what is the proper form of requests for exception, Ms. Oakwood?" asked the woman. "Is there some custom? I'm sorry, we're proper hermetics. We're not up on Native etiquette."

The hostess's dry tone offered no forgiveness for the implications. "She asked politely. Using words. She was fine with being told no."

Beard-With-No-Mustache barely avoided rolling his eyes. "We didn't mean to offend. Sorry we aren't familiar with the most politically correct behavior. Come on, darling." He tugged his companion along with one hand on her wrist.

Onyx turned her blue eyes to meet the hostess's gaze. "I didn't mean to cause any problems."

"You didn't cause anything. They decided to make fools of themselves. 'Native etiquette' my ass." She rolled her eyes. "They see my complexion and hear where I'm from and they assume I'm some shamanistic type all about spirits and nature. And I am, but I also use a wand and even a Tarot deck sometimes. I trade with Chen's circle in the International District, too. Never heard them complain about 'Native influence,' but I'm sure Archimedes and Hypatia there would be mortified by all the cultural contamination."

"Wait. Are those really their names?"

"That's how they were listed on the invitations. They're from Olympia. As far as I know they're a circle unto themselves. I'm sure their birth names are much more prosaic... Onyx."

"Hey, I was an Onyx years before I was a witch," chuckled the younger woman. "Online poetry posts in middle school totally count. I don't care what anyone says."

Her hostess laughed. "I'll take your word for it."

"With a pitch like that, everyone always does. No one ever wants to look into the bleak darkness of my thirteen-year-old heart." Having felt out of place since she arrived, Onyx was glad to find someone with some warmth and a sense of humor. So far, this hadn't been a social occasion. "I'm not that paranoid about my identity. Plenty of mundanes know me by Onyx, too. It's fine."

"Well, for the record, you can call me Kate. But those two can keep calling me 'Ms. Oakwood.' They can cross the street so they don't have to share the same sidewalk with me, too, for all I care." She tilted her head thoughtfully. "You're with the redhead, right? Leather jacket, mostly in black?"

"Yeah. Molly. Gotta be around here somewhere. She's the one who got the invitation," Onyx explained. The shift in topics drained the mirth from her voice. "I met Elizabeth a few times, but that doesn't feel like it was enough to say we were friends."

Kate's smile remained, though it turned sad. "Elizabeth wouldn't have said so." She gestured to the others in the gallery. "I'll grant not everyone here is a friend. Some came as a formality or out of self-interest. But if we've ever had a community in Seattle, Elizabeth was at the center."

"Yeah, we're not all that plugged in," Onyx admitted. "Molly met a few other Practitioners while working in Elizabeth's shop, but she didn't make any serious connections. I don't know anyone."

"Most of the Practitioners here belong to one of a few groups. You could say the same thing for the city as a whole. We've got a couple of pagan Believers from different circles. Their sanctuaries are outside Seattle proper, as you'd expect. A couple of guys from my circle are here. You could call us a Native tradition if you're really into labels. Jin over there is with a group from the International District," she continued, nodding toward an Asian man in a suit studying one of the many large tomes laid out on one table. "The biggest group in the city is the Brotherhood of Apollo. A couple of them are here tonight."

Onyx lowered her voice to a whisper: "Would they be the stock broker types?"

"That's them. They're recruiting, too. If you're with a group of any size, like mine or Jin's, they won't get pushy. Loners and smaller circles get the hard sell. Let me know if they give you a hard time."

"Thanks. I appreciate it."

"Anyway, you wanted to look over the gargoyle, right?" Kate asked.

"I did, yeah." She turned back toward the stone monster. "Little distracted."

Onyx raised her ebony wand, holding it sideways and bringing it down in front of the gargoyle's face. Rather than speak words of magic, Onyx merely relaxed, focused, and breathed deeply. She lowered, raised, and lowered her wand once more. It turned in her fingers to point toward the gargoyle.

Her eyes widened. She saw faint wisps of dull, darkened colors around the statue. None of them remained long, nor did they show up as brightly as the natural aura of a living being. The fact that she saw hints of an aura at all surprised her. Ordinarily, she could learn much about a person's nature from reading such colors and images. Here, she couldn't keep track of any of the constantly fading colors long enough to make out much.

Reaching into a pocket of her coat, Onyx pulled out a single bay leaf. She concentrated on minute details in the gargoyle's face: the curl of its snarling lips, the energy in its eyes, the wrinkles of its furrowed, angry brow. She pointed to the gargoyle with her wand, murmured in Greek, and then held the bay leaf to her ear. When she finished the words of the spell, she crumpled up the leaf.

Rather than giving her the soft sounds of a bit of healthy greenery, it crackled as if she'd stepped on it during a dry autumn day. Onyx stepped backward with wide eyes. "Woah."

"Not an appealing result, I take it?" asked Kate. She didn't seem particularly disturbed by the younger woman's reaction.

"Yeah. That's...really not right."

"What do you see?"

"It looks like a person," explained Onyx. "Only not. Like it's got all the trappings of a soul except...broken. And it's all so negative. I mean even complete assholes aren't this bad."

"You're not wrong. If you want an inanimate object to move and act on its own, that spark of life has to come from somewhere."

"Wait, this thing—there's a *soul* in there?" Onyx looked back to the statue in surprise.

"What's left of one," Kate explained. "Elizabeth didn't know for sure who created it. She said the gargoyle fell into her possession a few years before she left Europe for the US. All of her documentation was second or third-hand.

Apparently, this is some pre-Enlightenment prison for somebody whose crimes were so awful that all the other options weren't punishment enough. Most gargoyles are the ordinary statues you see on buildings or whatever, but this isn't the only one of its kind."

"That's awful," said Onyx. "How...how did Elizabeth know she could trust that documentation? I mean how did she know if whoever's trapped in here was really a bad guy at all, let alone deserving this? Everything in there is ugly, but... how could you *know*?"

Kate shrugged. "She didn't. Apparently, she never got the thing to move or speak, either. She only knew it had the potential. But it's all that's left of someone who died a long time ago," Kate pointed out. "Elizabeth didn't know if that soul was a good person on the wrong side of a bad guy or vice versa. She didn't know how to release it, other than destroying the statue. Who's to say if that's a mercy? Once you destroy something, it's gone." She smiled faintly. "As far as I know, one thing magic *can't* do is turn back the clock. I find that comforting."

"Ugh. Still. I get not letting magical artifacts loose in the world, but carting something like this all the way over from Europe when you don't even know how to use it? Or if it even works at all anymore?" Onyx couldn't get rid of her frown. "I'll suffer for a principle, but this is way past my limits."

"Ladies and gentlemen," called out a man in a suit at the entrance to the gallery's second large room. Onyx wondered if Jin was as relaxed as he appeared, or he was simply good at navigating hazardous waters. "We're about to start. If you could join us in the other room, you'll find your names on the seats arranged for you."

"That's my cue." Kate offered Onyx a slight grin and gestured to the gargoyle. "With any luck, this guy won't be your problem." She walked over to the doorway to join her fellow host, leaving Onyx on her own again.

Though no one rushed for the doorway, Onyx noticed the shift in tone of conversation and the body language of the others in the gallery. The guests wouldn't linger for long. Onyx left the angry gargoyle to find Molly, idly considering the appropriate payback for being abandoned at what turned out to be a largely anti-social event. At that thought, she couldn't help noting Archimedes and Hypatia's location and checking to see if they were looking her way.

Great, she thought. *One nasty exchange and now I'm tracking them when I should be ignoring them. Acting like they don't matter while I pay close attention in case of another blow-up. Fucking high school all over again.*

Onyx eventually found her partner in a side room filled with the gallery's usual artwork. Molly's short, spiked, fire-engine red hair made her easy to spot in any crowd. At the moment, though, she was in a crowd of only two—that being the "You Can't Make Me Dress Nice Even for This" crowd. Molly's perpetual Goth-casual black pants, band t-shirt, and leather jacket had found a match in a handsome black man wearing a rugged brown trench coat over a half-buttoned dress shirt and wife-beater.

"...shop on Aurora, just north of the park," he said to Molly as Onyx entered. His deep voice and strong Jamaican accent made as much of an impression as his image. "I don't work the counter, though. Ask whoever's up front who you can talk to about custom work, and be discreet. They'll know you're there for me."

"Good to know. Thanks. Oh hey, you," Molly said as Onyx joined them. "Sorry I ditched you. Got tied up in one conversation and wound up in another here. This is Hector. He's a...craftsman. Hector, this is Onyx, my girlfriend."

"Nice to meet you," said Hector, offering his hand. He didn't come across as warmly as Kate, but the gesture still marked him as less standoffish than most of the other attendees. His handshake suggested as much power in his muscles as in his voice.

"You're a craftsman? What do you make?"

Hector smirked at the choice of words. "Guns. Bullets. Knives. Special toys for special people."

"Oh." Onyx hesitated. The answer brought up any number of possible implications. "By special, do you mean Practitioners?"

"Them or the sort of people with their problems."

"So we're not talking about ritual tools, then?"

"Oh, I can do ritual stuff, no problem. But I'm more about practical applications."

Again, Onyx found herself at a loss for words. Her first thoughts about him held firm: strong, polite, and not at all warm. "Wow. I wouldn't think that guns would be in demand in these circles."

"You'd be surprised. People learnin' to work magic usually learn to defend themselves along the way. That don't mean everyone's good at it. The right weapon might do you better in a fight than a spell, and for a lot less effort depending on what you're packing. Guns are like spells that way. You get what you pay for."

"That's a good question," Molly spoke up curiously. "What's the going rate for a magic gun?"

"Depends on the kind of gun and the kind of magic, but I guess you could say it's always expensive. If I'm short on cash, I charge money. Most of the time, with clients like mine, I'm more likely to charge something else. Favors, you know? Trade in kind. Some Practices leave you swimming in cash. Others ain't cool with that sort of thing. Mine doesn't allow for conjurin' up the dollars."

"Neither does ours," admitted Onyx. "Can't say it's much for guns, either, but we've never really had the need. Kind of outside my experience."

"And may it ever be so. Bit of free advice, though: don't count on it." His gaze flicked past the two young women to the other room. "We should probably move on. Don't wanna be rude to our hosts." He nodded to excuse himself before slipping past the pair.

Alone in the smaller gallery room, Onyx looked at Molly and found a mischievous grin. "We do not need a gun," said Onyx.

"We don't *need* one, no."

"Molly."

"You don't know what he can do with his."

Onyx groaned. "I knew the double entendres would turn up."

"I'm just sayin'," Molly grinned. "Seriously, you missed most of the conversation. He made some points I hadn't considered before. He's a nice guy."

"Molly, that is not a 'nice' man," Onyx warned. "That's a guy who *uses* the stuff he makes. And I'm pretty sure we can't afford whatever he'd charge, money or otherwise."

"I know, I know. He was nice to me, at least. Most everyone else here is kinda cold."

"I hear you. It's like you said when the invitations came. Sharks in these waters."

"Yeah. That's the *other* reason I didn't want to come. Tough enough to accept that she's gone, but even if I have to do that…" Some of Molly's stress broke through her façade, along with some of her grief. "Why did she want all this? I thought public readings of a person's will only happened on TV."

"I don't know." Onyx slipped her hand in Molly's. "Anything I can do?"

The redhead glanced through the doorway, then leaned in to kiss Onyx on the lips—hardly more than a peck, but heartfelt. "Everything you already do. Every day."

"Sweet, then I'll keep stealing all the covers in bed," Onyx quipped as she started for the door.

"Keep that up and you're gonna wake up with the neighbor's pet snake curled up against you one morning," warned Molly.

"You'd never put Steve in that kind of danger and you know it." She managed to control her grin as they entered the other room. This was a somber occasion. Private banter to help Molly keep it together was one thing; openly joking around in front of others would be in poor taste.

Most of the guests had taken their seats when Molly and Onyx arrived. Once again, they found some of the gallery's regular art on the walls, but the floor had been cleared to make room for folding chairs arranged in simple, comfortably spaced rows. Onyx spotted name cards for herself and Molly on a pair of seats on the right side of the middle row. Many chairs remained empty. Given the number of guests, she guessed that Kate and Jin wanted to give the various factions and individuals plenty of space.

In front of the seats stood a lectern and a small desk holding various folders and envelopes. Kate took up the spot behind the lectern with Jin at her side to assist. They waited patiently for everyone to sit before they began.

Onyx still didn't know most of the crowd. She guessed that the nicely-dressed and otherwise normal suburban-looking group in the front row might be some of those Believers Kate mentioned, and made some other guesses from there. The pair of men from the Brotherhood shared the middle row with Molly and Onyx. Most of the rest sat either alone, like Hector, or in pairs, like Archimedes and Hypatia to the right and in front. It let Onyx keep an eye on them. *Damn it, I'm doing it again. They're just snotty. It's not like they're supervillains.*

She suspected that the men in suits sitting to either side of the audience might be from Jin's group from the International District. Something about their demeanor suggested they were working rather than merely attending. She'd seen the man and woman at the back of the room with Kate earlier, and figured they were from her circle up north. The two sets certainly seemed to be positioned to act as plainclothes security. She didn't mind the presence. Not after Molly's warning about sharks.

"Thank you for coming," said Kate. "Elizabeth knew all this would be unusual. She asked us to read this brief statement:

"'*Dear friends and associates,*'" Kate read, "'*Let me start by apologizing for any discomfort these arrangements may cause. Please understand that this is in the interests of peace and goodwill. We are all aware of the tension created when so many Practitioners share the same region. This gathering is only happening after trusted friends have verified that I am gone through natural or purely accidental causes. I want to leave behind no doubts. No one need avenge me. No one need see my death as a reason to look over their own shoulders. I dearly hope Seattle's Practicing community will continue its history of peaceful coexistence.*

"'*In keeping with that concern, I wish to avoid any rumors, suspicions, or conflict over my estate. The bulk of my mundane assets have been handled through other arrangements. My shop and my finances are spoken for. However, my property of a more sensitive nature must be placed in capable and trustworthy hands.*'"

Kate paused to glance around the room. Onyx did the same. She saw curious looks and a few frowns, but heard no objections. Kate continued.

"'*To Harold Weiss or the current proprietor of the Circle's End bookstore, I leave all consumable ritual materials in my home, including any invested crystals, candles, powders and so forth.*

"'*To Jin, I leave my collection of East Asian writings, charts, and maps.*

"'*To the Brotherhood of Apollo, I leave my former residence on Queen Anne Hill, along with its keys, warding charms, and legal property titles.*'"

Onyx looked to Molly as Kate continued. The redhead shrugged. "She lived here for seventy years," whispered Molly. "Lots of time to build up property. And secrets."

"She's sharing them with great people," Onyx complained quietly so no one else would hear.

"I trust her," replied Molly. "Trusted. Whichever."

The dark-haired witch squeezed her hand. "Trust."

Molly frowned sadly. "Yeah."

"'*To Hypatia and Archimedes*,'" Kate continued, "'*I leave my gargoyle statue. To Hector King*—'"

"Excuse me," piped up Hypatia, raising her hand. "Is there no other note there for us?"

Kate shook her head. "No. '*To Hector Kingston, I leave the crafting tools and books from my workshop…*'"

Onyx barely held back a snort and a grin. Again, she squeezed Molly's hand. "We both trust her," she amended softly—and then saw Hypatia scowl at her. The young woman had little time for the death glare. Her attention was pulled away almost a second later.

"*'To Molly, I leave my Book of Shadows.'*"

Though Kate continued on with the reading, and though no one spoke out, Onyx noticed immediate interest from the rest of the small audience. Heads rose. Whispers in the crowd ceased. Hypatia, Archimedes, even Hector looked over to the pair. Molly turned to Onyx with wide eyes and a half-dozen unspoken questions or objections on her lips: Elizabeth kept a Book of Shadows? That wasn't even part of her Practice. Did it mean to her what it meant to them? As studied and experienced as Elizabeth was, would she use that term lightly?

And above all: Why me?

They missed the next couple of bequests. Someone got Elizabeth's property in Kirkland. Someone else received her wands, a poignant and personal gift of great value. To Kate, she left her large house in Snohomish, which Onyx had seen once and thought beautiful. Like the house given to the Brotherhood, it surely held occult significance if it turned up on this list. No one could know straight from the reading of her will which of Elizabeth's bequests held great power and which ones were simple if pretty or pricy keepsakes.

Nothing left Molly or Onyx envious. Not after the gift left in her name. By definition, the book would contain Elizabeth's most important spells, rituals, and personal writings...if it meant to her what it meant to their own Practice.

"*'My friends, I have nothing else to give but my sincerest wishes for harmony and peace,'*" read Kate. "*'I was not the first Practitioner*" here. As I have watched the city grow, so too have our own numbers. I have seen conflict. I have also seen cooperation. I dearly hope for a future of the latter. Thank you for all you have given me.'" Kate folded the paper and added, "I also want to thank you for your patience. Most of the items listed are available here. Jin and I will distribute and let you all be on your way."

Some attendees rose. Others lingered in their seats to speak in hushed tones. Archimedes fairly launched himself out of his seat to speak with Kate and Jin, trying but failing to keep his voice low. "Is there any documentation to go with the gargoyle? Something to explain what it is and what it does? And how are we expected to transport that thing ourselves?"

Kate and Jin offered the same polite smile. "Elizabeth listed nothing else in your bequest, no," said Jin.

"You okay?" murmured Onyx.

"Guess we'll find out," replied Molly.

"Ladies and gentlemen," spoke up one of the Brotherhood representatives. He was tall and broad-shouldered, with an almost suspiciously good-looking face. "If I might beg a moment of your time while you're all here? As our hosts noted, we so rarely gather in numbers like this."

The request put a pause on everyone's movements and conversations. Onyx saw silent wariness in many of the faces in the room.

"My name is Victor Saxon. I'm a member of the Brotherhood of Apollo. My friends and I want to first offer our condolences on the passing of Miss Van Dalen. She was a luminary of our kind. We also want to echo her wishes for harmony, and to that end, we want to extend to you all an invitation.

"We all know that the number of Practitioners in a given area limits the power any one Practitioner might attain. We also know that forming a circle mitigates this dilution of power greatly. Here in Seattle," Saxon continued, gesturing to the full gathering with his hands spread wide, "that drain grows significant. Every loner, every partnership is another drain upon the rest.

"The Brotherhood of Apollo welcomes many traditions of magic. We assure tolerance and freedom of Practice. We offer fellowship, support, and protection."

"I didn't hear 'equality' in that list, man," came Hector's deep, accented voice from across the room. He stood listening with his hands in the pockets of his trench coat. "Is your Brotherhood a circle, or more like a pyramid?"

"We're certainly more structured than some coven," Saxon answered with a chuckle. "We're all beholden to the same rules. Unless you're asking if we're a town hall democracy? We're not that. The Brotherhood has leadership and some hierarchy based on merit, but newcomers can rise quickly. We have no tyrants. And as a single circle, even as our numbers grow, the power of this region is not diminished. In that, we all benefit equally."

"What does all that cost?" asked Hector. "Don't tell me all this is free."

"A small contribution of your time, and some of that only for social gatherings. Your time and your willingness to defend your brothers and sisters should the need arise."

"With no restrictions on behavior outside your circle?" Jin spoke up. He still stood beside Kate at the lectern. He held a completely neutral expression and tone. "Surely the Brotherhood follows rules to prevent the abuse of ordinary people?"

"We police our own as far their actions affect our brothers and sisters," Saxon answered. "It's better than leaving every Practitioner to their own devices, wouldn't you say? But we wouldn't be so arrogant as to tell anyone how to live or how to manage their power. How our members handle their own affairs outside the Brotherhood is up to them. I'm surprised to hear that you and yours might be interested, Jin. Surprised, but pleased."

Jin's gaze never wavered, though his lips turned into a slight, grim smile. "We are not. Thank you."

"Can't blame me for trying," Saxon conceded. "I'm happy to speak with anyone else who might be interested, as is Mr. Gold here. Thank you for your patience."

With that, the audience resumed its general exit. Some waited near the lectern for Archimedes to settle down so they could ask their own questions. Onyx caught another narrow-eyed look from Hypatia. She blew it off to focus on her partner. "What now?"

"Let's get out of here until this breaks up a little," Molly decided, tilting her head toward the door. "I don't want to stand in line."

They moved back into the gallery, taking up a spot by one of the bookshelves clear of the doorways. "I didn't expect to see this many people here. Makes me wonder how many are in the Brotherhood. And how many Practitioners are there in Seattle all together?"

"These aren't all exactly Seattle people," Molly noted. "Kate's circle is from north of Everett, and one of those pagan groups is kind of out in the sticks east of here. I don't think either of them are part of the 'drain' the Brotherhood guy is talking about."

"Competition is a better word."

"Yeah. I mean we never feel it because we never reach that high. 'Course, that sort of asks what the Brotherhood is doing that they need so much power, y'know?" Molly tone made her thoughts on that issue plain, and Onyx agreed: it couldn't be anything good.

"You might hit that limit with some of the things in that book Elizabeth left you."

"The book she left us," Molly corrected. "She knew that when she wrote down my name."

Onyx didn't argue. She took Molly's hand again. "Might never have met you if I hadn't wandered into her shop."

That brought a grin to her partner's face. "You weren't wandering. You knew what you were looking for in there."

"I wasn't looking for a hot redhead."

"Bullshit. Everyone is looking for a hot redhead."

Onyx snorted and leaned her head on Molly's shoulder. "Okay. You got me. Anyway." She looked up at the others filtering out of the other room. A few individuals, accompanied by someone from either Jin's circle or Kate's, moved to different boxes or shelves in the gallery. "Did you need to talk to anyone else here?"

"I'm ready to bail as soon as we can. Are they cleared out already?" Molly asked, turning back to the other room.

"Not quite," answered Saxon as he came through the doorway. His friendly smile remained. "Sorry if I'm intruding. That sounded like it might be part of an open conversation. Molly, is it? And...?"

"Onyx," answered the other young woman. She noted that Saxon was alone and wondered if his companion was already fielding pledges to his fraternity. "Are Kate and Jin still tied up?"

"Yes. I don't think it'll be long." His eyes turned to Molly. "That's quite a bequest she left you."

"Hey, you guys got a house in a nice neighborhood," Molly pointed out. "Real estate in this town isn't getting any cheaper."

"And yet I doubt you'd be interested in a trade, though I'm happy to make the offer," he ventured.

"Wouldn't dream of it."

"No, of course not. Can't blame me for trying. I didn't come out to ask about the book, though. But if it's not too forward, Molly, are you by chance a hermetic like Elizabeth? I didn't think she ever took on any apprentices."

Onyx gritted her teeth. *Round Two of What's Your Practice?* she thought.

Molly handled the question with more humor than Onyx could manage. "Is that a forward thing to ask? We don't get out to a lot of wizard parties."

"You should definitely come to ours, then. We have plenty."

"I'll bet. No, I'm not a hermetic. I didn't apprentice under Elizabeth, either. I worked in her shop for a couple years. She wasn't hung up on lines between Practices."

"No, she wasn't. It's probably why she kept a Book of Shadows. So if you're not one of her students, how did you come into your own Practice?"

"Saw a bunch of freaky shit while working at a Renaissance Faire. You have to camp out overnight at the big ones, y'know? Those people keep it friendly and safe for all the customers, but once they close down for the day it's all green hair and nipple rings."

For the first time, Saxon's friendly smile wavered. He seemed genuinely unsure of how to take that. His eyes glanced to Onyx. "It's true. I've seen it," she said.

He summoned up a small, good-natured laugh. "Fair enough. I don't mean to pry. But I'm serious about the invitation. We'd love to have you both. I'm fairly sure a couple of our members are the body-piercing sort themselves. Like I said, we welcome all types."

"I think we'll have to decline," said Onyx. "We're private people. But the courtesy is appreciated."

Saxon offered a business card. "The invitations still stand. Don't say I never tried." Molly accepted the card so he would go away, and then smiled politely as Saxon moved off to other conversations.

Rolling her eyes, Onyx took on a sarcastic, mocking tone. "*'Hey, can you join my club? By the way, we all share books. Can I borrow the one you just got?'*"

"That's what I figured," said Molly. "C'mon. Let's go collect and get out of here."

They had to pause for another moment as Archimedes and Hypatia exited the audience room with Mr. Gold following closely behind them. The well-dressed couple still looked thoroughly put out. "What the hell is their problem?" Molly asked once they were out of earshot.

"They've got a debilitating case of Entitled Asshole Disease," grumbled Onyx. "I talked with them earlier and wish I hadn't."

"That gargoyle statue would be cool if we had a place to put it."

"No. No, it wouldn't. That thing is made of wrong. I'll tell you later."

"Molly, Onyx, thank you for waiting," said Jin as the pair stepped up. He reached over the desk to shake their hands. "I'm sorry we couldn't meet under better circumstances."

"No worries," said Molly. "Thank you for doing all this. Seems like it's a little awkward for everyone."

"A kind choice of words," noted Jin, "but accurate."

"So is the book in the other room?" Molly asked. "Do we need to pick it up somewhere?"

"Not at all." Kate opened up one of the desk drawers to produce a large, leather-bound book closer to an encyclopedia in size than a personal journal. Its worn, buckled brown cover bore simple geometric decorations, but no words. Several envelopes and loose papers poked out from its pages. Kate held her silence long enough for Molly to take the book

23

and turn it over in her hands. "She left you a private note tucked into the first pages," Kate said. "It's something she asked us not to mention during the reading. She said to start with the note."

Onyx heard a shaky breath from her partner and put her hand on Molly's shoulder. "Thank you," said Molly.

"One last thing," Jin spoke up again. Onyx noted the low tone of his voice and the way his eyes took in their surroundings. "Do not leave the same way you arrived tonight. I am not sure everyone will honor the agreement of safe passage."

He said no more. "Thanks for that, too," said Onyx. Jin nodded to her, his concerns plain in his dark eyes, and then stepped away to speak with another guest. Kate offered only a quick farewell.

Molly held the book in both arms as she and Onyx walked out. Both women kept a wary eye on the others in the gallery. One of Jin's associates helped a guest sort through some books on one of the shelves. Saxon stood with Archimedes and Hypatia near the gargoyle. The over-dressed couple seemed receptive to Saxon's overtures, though nothing looked like a done deal. The other guy from the Brotherhood lingered near the entrance while seemingly looking over something on his cell phone. Onyx thought that was a little too convenient.

She didn't see Hector anywhere.

"What do you think?" Onyx asked.

Molly leaned in. "I think a warning like that means a lot. Especially from either one of those two, let alone both of 'em."

"Sure. I mean, what do we do now? We came in your car. Ballard to Shoreline is a hell of a walk."

"Buses are still running. Or we could go to one of the bars and call a cab."

"Buses and cabs put us in a vehicle with other people," Onyx pointed out. "So then it's a question of whether we're safer in a crowd or if we're putting other people in danger."

Molly's eyebrows rose. "You think we're at that point already?"

"I think Elizabeth's will wasn't as much of a plea for peace as it was a warning." Onyx looked less at Molly as she spoke than their surroundings. Her partner did the same. Being face to face allowed each to cover the other's back. "Look, I've never been in a fight with other Practitioners, y'know? Hopefully I'm only being paranoid, but remember what Saxon said about the Brotherhood's rules for dealing with normal people? Jin knew the answer before he brought it up. That wasn't a question. Jin was making a statement."

The other woman let out a heavy breath. "Whatever's in this book isn't worth putting someone we don't even know at risk. Or you," she added, catching her partner's eye. The look she received in return stopped her from taking that thought any further. "Okay, okay," she relented. "In this together."

"Damn straight."

The front entrance opened, drawing their attention. A well-built man in a dark suit and gloves entered, heading straight for Hypatia and Archimedes, though he held off rather than intrude on their conversation with Saxon. Onyx needed to watch for only a few seconds to decide he must be their chauffer or bodyguard, if not both. She also noticed Hypatia's frequent glances in her direction. Molly spoke up again, bringing Onyx back to their main problem.

"Okay, public transit's out. Cabs are out. Walking is out. We could go into stealth mode once we're out of here, hole up in a hotel room or something nearby and go back to the car in the morning. Hate to spend money like that, but how long is anyone gonna look for us?" Then she frowned. "But if we're gonna do that, we're still going back to the car."

"We didn't exactly get a rock star parking space," said Onyx. "I mean we're a couple blocks away."

"Yeah," agreed Molly. "Fucking Ballard nightlife. What I'm saying is maybe we're overthinking this. Maybe we just take a long ninja-walk around the neighborhood and come at the car from another direction?"

"Ninja-walk?"

"It's more fun to say than 'sneaky.' If anyone follows us out of here, we have to shake 'em before we get into a car, anyway."

"I'm game." Onyx let out a heavy breath. "We haven't exactly practiced this sort of thing much."

"No time like the present to learn, huh?"

To their credit, they learned quickly. Onyx looked at the reflections in the gallery windows as they left rather than turning to the crowd. She saw Hypatia's unfriendly glare and Mr. Gold's quick look up from his cell phone as they came to the door. Molly kept the book tucked close to her chest with one arm like a wide receiver carrying a football. Once they were outside, she pulled her wand from the interior pocket of her leather jacket and slipped it up her sleeve of her other arm.

Onyx's car waited a couple blocks away to their left and around the corner. Instead of going that way, the pair turned right when they hit the sidewalk.

Overcast skies didn't offer any rain to tamp down on visibility. Trees rising along the wet sidewalk were only now regaining their greenery with the first weeks of spring. Old Ballard offered mostly brick buildings, none more than three stories tall, but felt a little closer in than other neighborhoods in Seattle.

"Nightlife and crowds or dark and quiet?" asked Onyx.

Her meaning was plain enough. The gallery put them only one block up from Market Street, where bars and restaurants were still open. In the other direction lay houses and the ever-encroaching condo developments threatening to consume anything that didn't fall under an historic registry. "Witnesses tamp down on magic power," Molly considered, "but they don't prevent old-fashioned muggings. Think we're better off with dark and quiet."

They picked up the pace. Only a block away from the gallery, both young women chanted words under their breath, one speaking in Greek and the other in Hebrew. Their footsteps faded into silence. The zippers and buckles of Molly's clothes stopped jingling. The next streetlight up blinked out a few seconds before they came under its arc.

Onyx could still see her breath in the chill night air, but she could no longer hear it.

Molly let out a couple of quick, high-pitched whistles. It broke the silence, but Onyx understood the value. A few steps later, Molly gave her best crow call. It wasn't bad.

"Calling in the whole crew, huh?" Onyx whispered.

Her girlfriend gave her a sidelong look, along with a low, warning feline growl clearly not meant for her. Then Molly frowned and looked over her shoulder. "Don't think I'm gonna bother calling out any dogs," she murmured. "They mean well, but they aren't subtle."

"Probably only little rat dogs that fit inside a purse in this neighborhood, anyway." Onyx grinned. "Be nice to have something mean on our side, though."

Molly considered it for a second, then managed a couple of squeals so soft but high-pitched that Onyx was impressed she could manage it at all. "The hell is that?" Onyx asked.

"Trash pandas. Fuckers you have up here are mean."

"Oh, what, Arizona raccoons are sweet and cuddly?"

"I don't think I ever saw a raccoon before I left Arizona," Molly thought out loud.

The pair fell silent, walking quickly down the sidewalk of a quiet, narrow residential street. Trees and parked vehicles lining the street offered some small degree of cover, but that seemed equally as worrisome as it was comforting. Anything that might hide them could hide a stalker, too.

They listened carefully as they walked. They watched the path ahead, watched to their sides, and looked back over their shoulders many times. Onyx fought down the urge to hold Molly's hand. They would both need their hands free in the event of trouble, and her partner already had to hold onto Elizabeth's book.

Not for the first time tonight, Onyx considered that she'd never been in a serious fight in her life. A few childhood shoving matches in school, sure. One time things even escalated to slaps, hair-pulling, and a few badly-thrown punches. The self-defense class she took after that offered only the barest basics. Mostly the instructor focused on ways to counter or escape an attacker, hurt him enough to make him think twice, and then run like hell.

Once she started on the path of witchcraft, Onyx learned protective magic, but only a few spells that could cause harm. Most of it wasn't flashy. Her study of auras led her to the worst spell she knew—one that could easily inflict emotional turmoil and a crippling headache. While it could do far worse harm if she really pushed it, Onyx couldn't conceive of a situation where she'd want to hurt someone that badly, let alone through such intimate means. If things were that bad, she could always hurl a little fire. She didn't need military-grade flamethrower power to scare off serious trouble.

Past that, Onyx turned her studies to simple things that helped her and Molly through everyday life. If she had a specialty, it was in matters of perception, not fighting. Yet as she and Molly made their way between parked cars and half-built condominiums, her magically sharpened sight and keen hearing only seemed to make the trees and buildings loom taller and the shadows draw closer.

Her brow knit together. Even as a child, shadows and dark spaces never frightened her. If monsters could hide under the bed, so could she. Onyx turned her gaze to the rooftops. *This is my element*, she asserted silently, and rejected any thought of how silly or naïve that might sound. *I like it dark. Nobody gets to turn that against me. Nobody.*

It was then that she heard the first crow call out, two blocks behind them, quickly joined by another. The calls didn't last—one caw, then another, and then nothing. She heard another caw from across the street. "Someone behind us and some*thing* above," said Molly. Her voice carried an uncharacteristic tremor. "I can't understand what that means."

They picked up the pace. Crows called out again down the street behind them. Molly glanced over her shoulder and promptly pulled Onyx off the sidewalk, almost yanking her behind a trailer-sized dumpster outside one of the construction projects. For Onyx, the wide-eyed alarm on Molly's face spoke volumes. She'd never seen her partner so frightened. Come to think of it, she'd almost never seen Molly show fear.

Onyx heard her own breath shorten before she felt it, and then she heard another thing: footsteps. Many footsteps, coming from down the block where she could no longer hear the warning of crows. She didn't dare poke her head around the corner of the dumpster. The cars nearby, however, offered her a better option. Onyx reached out toward the nearest car with one open hand and whispered, "*Tavo alYadi.*"

The rear view mirror obeyed the gestures of her fingers, turning and tilting to show her the street behind them. Given the spells she'd already cast to sharpen her senses, Onyx could make out the shapes in the mirror perfectly well despite the distance. They didn't amount to more than silhouettes and shadows outside the streetlights, but she saw more than enough of them to steal her breath away. That wasn't a couple of people stalking them. It looked more like a mob.

Molly had her wand out as she looked left, right, and up ahead for some avenue of escape. "There's nowhere to go," she hissed.

The fear in Molly's voice did more to scare Onyx than the shadows or the noises. Between the two of them, Molly was the rock. She was the one who always held that things would be okay and who never backed down from anything. Onyx forced herself to take a deeper breath. Shadows shouldn't scare her, and *nothing* should have scared Molly.

Onyx trusted her senses. She trusted her instincts, too. She couldn't see who was fucking with them, but she could see through their bullshit. Their fear was legitimate. It shouldn't be *this* bad.

The large dumpster that concealed them stood outside a half-built condominium. The building stood three stories tall, taking up almost half the block and protected only by a chain-link fence. White house wrap with blue product logos made up most of its façade. It didn't even have a front door yet. "Let's hide in there," Onyx suggested.

The redhead practically cringed. "We can't! We don't know what's in there!"

"Molly. We are not afraid of a fucking Ballard condominium."

Another crow called out, this time joined in its warning by the yowl of a cat somewhere Onyx couldn't pinpoint. Molly's attention snapped to the taller set of condos on the other side of the street. "There," she gulped. "Something's there."

Onyx saw nothing. "Okay. So we go the other way." Her partner shook her head, breathing rapidly and somehow unable to speak. Onyx squeezed her arm. "You're a bad ass, Molly. You're the biggest bad ass I know. Anything that finds us is gonna wish it hadn't. Open that thing up and let's go."

The pleading look in Molly's eyes pained Onyx, but the redhead seemed to gather her nerves again under her lover's firm stare. She pulled a loose key from one pocket of her leather jacket, closed her eyes and murmured out the words of the spell almost like a prayer, and then threw the key toward the gate on the fence. It hit with a light, high-pitched ringing that seemed all the louder for the silence that the pair tried so hard to create. The disruption paid off as the chains holding the gate closed visibly sagged and the padlock fastening the links together fell to the ground.

She looked back to Onyx, still afraid but seemingly ready to move. "They'll see us," she warned.

The other witch looked around for a solution. Parked vehicles lined both sides of the street, stretching around the corner up ahead. Her supernatural vision revealed the subtle red flash of one car's active alarm. The construction lot offered the other half of the equation. Onyx reached out with the same spell that tilted the rear view mirror on the car nearby to pick up and hurl a loose hunk of concrete at the BMW parked down along the next block. As soon as the concrete went flying, she looked to Molly and hissed, "Go!"

Flashing lights, high-pitched tones, and a honking horn erupted in an automated tantrum as the pair darted from cover. Fighting down her fear, Molly paused as soon as she was through the gate to let Onyx through, then closed it shut again. She didn't bother with the chain, let alone the lock, but closing it at least eliminated the most obvious sign of their passing. The pair heard the rush of footsteps in the dark street. They plunged into the condominium through its doorless entrance and immediately crouched in the shadows.

"This isn't gonna work," whispered Molly. Even in the darkness of the partially-built hallway, Onyx could see the fear on the redhead's face. "They're coming for us."

"Molly, don't let your fear win," hissed Onyx. "You're bigger and badder than—Molly!"

She rose, shaking her head and stepping backward. "There's too many of them!"

As she spoke, the pair saw movement outside the fence. The mob slowed to a walk as it came into view with little noise other than footsteps and many unintelligible whispers. The crowd seemed entirely male, though Onyx couldn't make out anything more than shadows and silhouettes.

Molly took off down the hall, quickly coming to the building's main stairwell and vaulting up its concrete steps. Onyx chased after her. Though the redhead's fear gave her speed, Onyx could rely on the spell she'd cast over her vision to help her through the dark and incomplete building.

She made the connection as she followed Molly up to the third floor: if she could see fine in here, why couldn't she make out the crowd's features? Even with the clouds, the trees, and all the other little factors in play outside, the street still offered more light than the incomplete building.

At the top of the stairs, Molly paused to look for somewhere to go. Once again, she found little more than hallways still lacking in drywall or mounted doors. "Molly, wait!" Onyx hissed again. It didn't stop the redhead. She rushed out of the staircase and down the nearest path to the back of the building until Onyx added, "Don't leave me!"

That stopped her. Molly turned back, suddenly confronted by a concern that even her terror couldn't override. It was one thing to flee with Onyx right at her heels. Abandoning her lover was unthinkable. "Onyx, c'mon!" she whispered when she saw the other young woman going toward the empty window frame facing the street outside.

Onyx hustled to the portal, noting the absence of the sort of racket her boots would normally make on this floor. Their flight up the stairs had been similarly silent. It proved that their spells worked properly. Even their voices wouldn't carry. Whoever and whatever followed them couldn't be tracking them by sound.

She dropped low as she came to the windowsill, peering over the edge while showing as little of herself to any observer outside as possible. The space immediately outside the building remained clear. She saw muddy ground, crates and boxes of construction gear, and a chain link fence with its gate still latched. No one came past the fence. The mob of men lurked under nearby trees and in the shadows of parked vehicles. They all clung to the darkest places available.

A hand tugged at her shoulder. Molly tried to pull her away from the window, gripping both her wand and as much of the fabric of Onyx's coat as she could. "C'mon," she repeated.

Onyx held firm to look over the mob carefully. She'd tracked Molly through the pitch-black staircase thanks to the spell over her vision. Her spells of perception worked fine. So why couldn't she make out anyone's features in the crowd below?

One spark of doubt brought on others. Hadn't the mob been running before? And now they walked and lurked quietly? Onyx found that even stranger than their obscure features. Whoever was following them had to have recruited the mob from the nightlife nearby. That much seemed plausible. Magic could make speech compelling, or it could whip emotions up into a frenzy, or maybe both. But to instill this sort of control over a whole crowd? This sort of discipline?

"Shit," Molly breathed, tugging again. "They're gonna get us."

"They aren't real," said Onyx. "Molly. They aren't real. It's a trick. It's an illusion."

"No, it's not."

"Yeah. Yeah, it is. Those aren't real people. They don't even have faces."

Molly's eyes, wide with fear already, practically popped right out of her head. "Ohmygod what the hell kind of spell takes away someone's fucking *face*?"

Onyx barely managed to choke down her laughter. Even if the mob was an illusion, its presence still proved someone was after them. "I'm saying they're made of shadows or something. They can't hurt us. Look, they'd have come in here by now, right?" She pointed out the window again. "They'd have come in here when we started running. I don't think they can do that because they aren't real.

"This fear isn't real, either. Something's making us scared, Molly. It isn't natural. It has to be magic."

"But we're warded," Molly pointed out. To her partner's relief, her voice carried a little less fear and a little more logic even if she stated objections. "Shouldn't that protect us?"

"Wards don't always block everything. It's never a guarantee. You taught me that." Onyx reached out to squeeze Molly's wrist. "C'mon, babe. I hate seeing you like this. You're the gutsy one, not me."

Molly watched the shadows outside. They moved and whispered, but didn't approach. "Someone's fucking with us," said Molly.

"Yeah."

The crows called out another warning outside. Molly looked up at the sound. "It's in the air," she said. "They don't know how to describe it, but it's in the air, and it's big."

"Like another animal?"

"It's got wings, anyway." Molly's breath steadied out. Her voice returned to something close to her usual confidence, too. Another crow call turned Molly's attention from the street to the ceiling. "Over this building now."

Illusions and animals, Onyx thought. *At least they're hitting us with stuff we know how to handle.*

Then the roof caved in.

The pair jerked away from the collapse—only a few feet in diameter, but still loud and frightening enough to pull a shriek from Onyx and to leave Molly falling onto her backside. A dark form broader and taller than any man they'd ever met shook the floor as it landed amid the broken wood and other debris, blocking their way around the railing that led to the stairs. It immediately swung one forearm against Onyx, catching her in the ribs like a baseball bat only much thicker. The impact sent her stumbling toward the open window. She barely managed to get her left arm and shoulder up against the window frame before going right out of the building.

Without her partner's enhanced vision, Molly saw only a hulking, silent silhouette looming over her. The full terror of earlier moments rushed back all at once, compounded by the sight of an attacker that couldn't possibly be human. Molly didn't consider her options; she reacted with the first practical step available. She swung her wand out in an arc over her shoulder, ending with it pointed at the monster while blowing at it as hard as she could.

The winds summoned through her wand roared through the open window behind her. The spell had the added benefit of blowing Onyx back out of the portal, but Molly didn't even know her lover had been there. Her spell concentrated the air into a single irresistible blast of force against her attacker.

The dark figure threw out its arms to steady itself as it staggered back from the impact. Powerful hands broke the banister on the stairway and smashed through wood framing and drywall to stop its backward momentum. Each step sent a tremor through the floor. Molly's spell pushed her attacker back a few yards, but from its stance she guessed that she hadn't hurt or stunned it at all. The air didn't last, either. As soon as the rush of concentrated air ended, the figure took another floor-shaking step forward.

Orange light flashed through the hallway as a small blast of fire shot over Molly's head to strike the attacker in the chest. Once again it seemed unhurt, though the flash of Onyx's spell at least allowed both women to identify their attacker. The gargoyle from the gallery stepped forward again, ignoring Onyx completely. Its face and unmoving eyes seemed fixated on Molly.

Every step the thing took seemed to make the floor bounce. Molly didn't have time to think twice. She tried again with the same spell, channeling more sudden wind into immense blasts of force, only this time she drove that force into the floor at either side of her in time with the gargoyle's footfalls. It all happened quickly. With the first step that came in tandem with her spell, Molly felt herself almost lifted off her butt. She felt the same sensation again as she threw the spell again with the enemy's next step, only this time it came with a loud, awful cracking and tearing sound.

"Molly!" Onyx yelled as the floor gave way under her partner and the monster. The break ended a few inches from her boots, leaving her with room to stand but no chance to reach out and grab Molly.

If the other witch cried out, the noise of the floor crashing into the second story overwhelmed her voice. The resultant cloud of dust stung Onyx's eyes and sent her into a coughing fit. She fought through the irritation to breath and vision. It was only one floor below, she told herself. Hardly any distance at all. "Molly!" she called again.

"M'okay," grunted the most important voice in her world. "We're okay, right? We're okay." She saw Molly right where she'd been before, only about ten feet lower, pulling herself up from that same seated position on the floor with Elizabeth's book still tucked under one arm. Not far enough away for comfort, Onyx saw the gargoyle getting up off its back. "Shit, it's still alive!" Onyx warned.

One of its wings had broken off in the fall. Another cracked off as it rose. It showed no sign of feeling pain from this development. Apparently animated statues didn't have much of a sensitive nervous system.

"Aw fuck!" said Molly as she got to her feet. "My wand snapped!"

Onyx thought quickly for some way to help Molly. Her earlier blast of fire had been stupid, she now realized. She could have lit up the whole building while doing no harm at all to the gargoyle. Self-recrimination didn't solve her immediate problem, though: *How do you put down an enemy made of stone?*

She needed a jackhammer, or a missile launcher, or maybe a speeding bus. She had no such weapon on hand, just her wand and a repertoire of spells for enhancing her senses, wards, stealth, and lots of helpful domestic bullshit. Onyx blurted out words in Greek to lay a curse of misfortune on the thing for lack of a better option, but she doubted it would slip on any banana peels in this building.

The gargoyle blocked Molly's route to the staircase. Back on its feet once more, the thing moved in complete disregard of whatever spells the redhead threw at it. Onyx didn't even know what Molly was trying. Her mind focused on her own options. She doubted illusions would help here. She'd already tried fire. The only other dangerous spell she knew attacked the psyche, and this thing didn't—

No. Wait. There's a soul in there, Onyx remembered. She pointed her wand and focused her will, looking again for those faded, ugly colors that made up the aura she'd seen earlier that night. Molly's blast of wind hit the thing in the chest again, weaker now that Molly had no wand to help channel her power. The spell only slowed the enemy rather than pushing it back, but that gave Onyx vital seconds. A single wisp of dull red rippled over the gargoyle's shoulder. Onyx seized on that formless bit of color, imagining herself grasping it in one hand and crushing it mercilessly.

The gargoyle fell to one knee. One arm flailed around for something to hold onto, only to break the wooden banister separating the hallway from the stairs. Its other arm reached out to steady itself on the floor. Lacking vocal cords or moving lips, the thing couldn't cry out, but Onyx felt echoes of pain and anger along the connection her spell established between herself and the last bits of the soul inside her target. She unwittingly groaned on the thing's behalf.

Molly looked up to her lover in surprise as Onyx drove the gargoyle to its knees. "Is that you?"

"Can you get around it?" Onyx managed to ask. The stress of her spell came through in her voice. It was all she could do to focus on the spell and ignore the pain in her abdomen. The gargoyle had not left her unharmed.

Molly didn't answer, opting to watch their enemy rather than distract her partner. She still held Elizabeth's book close to her with her left arm. Debris covered the floor, making it difficult to maneuver, and Molly didn't want to underestimate the monster's reach. Even driven to its knees, she knew it might still have the wits and strength to reach out and grab her if she came too close.

Then the gargoyle bowed its head. Molly ran forward. She had only a few yards to cross before reaching it, but that at least let her build up a little steam. Rather than going for either side of her moving obstacle, though, Molly planted one foot on the gargoyle's broad shoulder to launch herself straight over it. The gap in the ceiling offered her plenty of clearance. Molly escaped the gargoyle's reach before it could thrash about in reaction. Though her landing wasn't graceful, she stayed on her feet and absorbed her momentum with a few steps further down the hall.

She looked back up through the gap in the ceiling at her partner. "Okay, now what?"

"Huh?" Onyx huffed.

"I thought you had a plan!"

"Fuck if I know what to do!" Onyx gasped. The spell threatened to drain her physically as she tried to chase around the fleeting bits of the gargoyle's consciousness and crush them out. Each shred of success filled her with loathing. She was half-convinced that killing it was as much an act of mercy as violence. That didn't make the experience any less ugly. "Find a sledgehammer or something!"

"Those are for wrecking houses," said Molly, "not building—gah!"

She didn't see him come up the stairs. The man in the black suit had Molly's wrist twisted around her back in the blink of an eye. He pushed her up against the nearest wall. "Either of you says a word of magic and she dies," he said, pressing a pistol against her head with his other hand. "I know how magic works. You drop the book, and you," he said, looking up at Onyx, "let the gargoyle go. Now!"

Onyx winced, looking from the gargoyle to the man she'd seen with Hypatia and Archimedes before leaving the store. "Molly?" she asked.

"Steve!" Molly replied.

Onyx blinked. "Wait, Steve?"

The driver shrieked without a shred of dignity. His gun went off as he fell back, but the bullet flew up into drywall and wood framing rather than into Molly. One second, he had the situation in hand; the next, he was on his back fighting against a snake attached to his inner thigh.

Molly kicked him hard in the face, stomped on his ankle for good measure, and scooped up his gun as soon as she saw it on the floor. "Holy shit," she grunted. "You carry around a fucking Desert Eagle? Seriously?"

"Aagh shit get it off me!" wailed the driver.

"Oh, hush, it's already off you," said Molly. It slithered close to Molly's boots. "Seriously, you run around with this in your coat? I mean I only recognize like four different guns, but Jesus. Talk about a sign of crushing inadequacy."

The driver plainly didn't care about her opinions. He crawled away from her and the snake at her feet, still clutching his wounded inner thigh. "Oh fuck what the fuck is it poisonous?"

"Oh yeah. Burmese python? Totally poisonous," Molly outright lied. She turned the gun on the gargoyle. "Sorry, buddy. Turns out I've got the right tool for this job. Unlucky break for you."

The big pistol kicked fiercely as she expected. Molly's experience with guns was limited to trips to the shooting range and renting guns with her uncle, but she knew how to hold it properly. The same spell that silenced her footsteps and the rustling of her clothes muffled the boom of each shot, though it still put out as much noise as a hammer banging away on a board. Molly emptied the magazine into the gargoyle, shattering stone and kicking up a cloud of dust and gun smoke. By the fifth shot, the statue lay in big, broken hunks on the floor. Molly devoted the remaining shots to breaking up the biggest pieces further, then switched her grip on the empty gun so she could shake her aching right hand. "Ow," she complained. "Onyx? You okay?"

The other witch sat against one hip on the broken edge of the third-story floor above Molly. "Think so," she answered wearily. "I don't feel good."

"Babe, we gotta go."

"You gotta help me!" wailed the driver.

"Oh, shut up, you're not gonna die," Molly grumbled.

"I'm not?"

"Not right away, at least."

"Oh god!"

"Can you get down?" she asked Onyx.

"I think…yeah," Onyx decided. In truth, she had her doubts about doing it safely, but she didn't have much choice. The gap in the floor separated her from the central staircase. Grimacing at the pain all along her midsection, Onyx got to her hands and knees to look for a good place to drop.

"Hang over the side, I'll help you down," Molly offered. She stepped forward with her arms out.

"That's no good. Just stay clear." The pain across her ribs warned Onyx against straining her core muscles any further than necessary. She knew her knee-high Doc Marten boots weren't built to absorb this sort of impact, either, but she decided she'd have to suck it up. Onyx sat on the edge, feeling broken bits of masonry and rebar scrape against her thighs before she pushed herself over.

Her landing went about as well as she could expect. She knew how to take a fall, but Onyx still felt a sharp jolt of pain in both ankles before she rolled into the impact. The debris on the floor didn't exactly give her a soft landing, either.

"Shit, are you okay?" Molly asked.

"Guess I have to be." Onyx picked herself up and tested her feet. Though they both hurt like hell, the pain was bearable and she could stand. "Long as we don't have to run for the car, I think I'll be good," she said. As Molly helped her up, Onyx came face to face with the very worried victim of a venomless snakebite.

"You gotta help me," he pleaded.

Onyx ignored him. Molly offered her arm, but Onyx shook her head. "Don't want to stretch anything right now." Along the way to the stairs, Onyx noticed the scaly passenger draped around Molly's neck. "You brought Steve?" she asked, gingerly heading down the first steps.

"He wanted to come," said Molly as if that explained everything.

"What, did you go next door to ask?" She knew they should keep quiet, but it wasn't as if any remaining enemies didn't know where they were. At this point, talking felt more reassuring than silence. Molly seemed to feel the same way.

"No, he got loose again. I found him outside our place when I got home from school. I'll take him back to Angelo's apartment in the morning. Serves that jackass right if he spends the night freaking out about it. He's moving out at the end of the month, anyway."

"Poor guy must be freezing."

"He was wrapped around my belly all night. Figured I could use the extra hug where we were going. And the extra security."

Onyx winced as they hit the bottom step. "Supposed to get a security blanket, not a security snake."

"It worked out, didn't it?"

The pair paused at the end of the stairs. Onyx saw and heard nothing as she looked out through the front entrance. The gate lay open and the illusory crowd seemed to have vanished, but otherwise they saw nothing different from when they'd arrived. They shared a grim look, needing no further words to assess their situation.

Onyx still had her wand, along with two aching ankles and whatever happened to her ribs. Molly had an empty pistol and a snake. They had no choice but to face whatever awaited them head-on.

They made it to the sidewalk before one more confrontation arose. Archimedes stepped out from behind the closest SUV parked on the street, covered slightly by the overhanging branches of a fir tree. Hypatia stepped out around the other side of the SUV to block them from continuing on down the sidewalk. Both of them held wands at the ready.

"Let's not drag this out or make it any worse for you than it has been," said Archimedes. "Hand over the book and walk away."

"Tsk tsk tsk," Molly clicked out in quick, calm disapproval. "Not the kind of peace Elizabeth wanted."

"Elizabeth wanted responsible stewardship over this city and the region, too," said Hypatia. "That's not something that comes from letting amateurs run around messing up the place."

"Amateurs? Oh for fuck's sake," grumbled Onyx. "You couldn't hang onto your gargoyle for ten minutes before doing something stupid with it. We're not giving you Elizabeth's book."

"You can give it or we can take it," said Archimedes. "That's the only choice you have here."

"Tsk tsk tsk," repeated Molly, her attention focused on Archimedes.

Onyx stared at him, too. An observer without such sharp eyes might not have noticed the way his wand shook. "You seem nervous about this," she observed. "Both of you. Have you even done anything like this before?"

"No concern of yours," said Archimedes. "We're under no obligation to explain ourselves to a couple of random girls playing at being sorcerers."

Onyx heard Molly growl oddly. She knew enough to cover for it. "We're witches, dumb ass," she said quickly. "We already went through your toy and your goon. Don't make us go through you, too."

"Hypatia," said Archimedes, "have we given them enough of a chance?"

"I suppose we have," answered his companion.

"Tsk-tsk-tsk!"

The bearded man's brow furrowed in confusion, but he didn't wonder what Molly was chittering about for long. Grey, furry, angry shapes dropped down on him from the trees. The pair of raccoons bit and clawed him viciously, sending him stumbling around in a screaming panic. He dropped his wand as he tried to swat them off.

"Fred!" blurted out Hypatia. Molly didn't hesitate. Her broken wand would no longer do her any good. The brass knuckles she kept in her jacket, however, could still do their job. Hypatia didn't track the redhead quickly enough to dodge her charge or her swing. With a single punch, Molly laid Hypatia out on the plot of grass running along the sidewalk.

"Get off! Get them off me!" yelled 'Archimedes.' He, too, laid in the grass and mud, though he was far more animated about it than Hypatia.

"Sure. One second," said Onyx, who then promptly stomped on his wand. The move aggravated the pain in her ankle, but it was worth it to hear and feel the wood snap under her heel. "Hsst! Go away, guys!" she ordered. Though she didn't have Molly's ability with animals, the pair of raccoons leapt off of their bloodied victim and scampered off on their way. Onyx pointed her wand at the bloodied man at her feet, waiting until he looked up at her.

The quiet sound of a footstep off to her left preempted her from casting a new spell. She hobbled back from Archimedes with her wand up at the ready to face the newcomer. Saxon looked surprised at her reaction. "Good ears," he conceded.

Onyx glanced around at the path behind him. She thought she saw someone else further away, sticking close to the shadows and trees rather than taking the sidewalk. Whoever it was, they relied more on cover and technique than magic and didn't come out where she could see them. "So are you following these two?" she asked Saxon as Molly stepped up beside her. "Or are you pushing them?"

Saxon gave the pair a sad smile. "If you had taken up my invitation, I'd be here to protect you. I'd be obligated, even. The Brotherhood looks after its own."

"But screws anybody else, right?" asked Molly.

"As I said, we're not here to regulate how Practitioners handle their own affairs. Only how they relate within the Brotherhood, and our relations with a few recognized circles." He shrugged. "You don't belong to any such circle."

Saxon brought his hands together at waist level in a casual stance. If he hid a wand or some other implement, Onyx couldn't see it, but she noticed the odd way he folded his fingers.

"So independents don't count?" Onyx frowned.

"No. No, I'm afraid two Practitioners don't make up a circle according to Brotherhood policy. We're not under any obligation to aid or protect outsiders. We are, however, obligated to offer at least some aid to our aspiring members." He nodded to the pair of sorcerers laid out behind Molly and Onyx.

"Then pick them up off the ground and go," said Molly.

"I'm afraid my obligations go a little further than that." His hands snapped up with electricity arcing between his fingers, flashing bolts of lightning at the pair in the blink of an eye. Onyx had her wand up in time to counter, drawing the energy directly toward the ebony shaft. Saxon flashed her a grin. "Better than I expected," he conceded, though his ready stance hinted at more to come.

"Mista Saxon, man," called out a deep voice behind him. Saxon spun around quickly, lightning still crackling between his hands. Two loud gunshots from only a few yards away split the night air. The first caused Saxon to jerk back a step. The second, accompanied by a flash of sparks from the gun's barrel under a nearby tree, put him on the ground.

Onyx glanced at Saxon only once. The bloody mess of his torso assured her he wouldn't get up again. Somehow that scared Onyx more than anything else that had happened. Despite the danger and violence she and Molly had already suffered, despite the fact that Saxon had thrown a probably lethal spell at them both only seconds ago, Saxon's death raised the stakes beyond anything Onyx had ever experienced. It was one thing to face mortal danger. Seeing someone die was another entirely.

She didn't know how to process this. And she didn't have time.

Hector stepped out of the shadows with a smoking, sawed-off double-barrel shotgun in his hands. Onyx realized he'd probably stood in the same spot where Saxon hid when

Hypatia and Archimedes first confronted them. She wondered if he, too, had the same motives.

"What the hell," exclaimed Molly, "is it Jump Everyone from Behind Night?"

Hector popped open his shotgun to reload it. "You can see why it's a classic move. Shit works."

She released a heavy breath. "Well, thanks for the assist."

"Like I said," Hector began, opening up his weapon to reload it, "sometimes a spell does the job, sometimes a gun does it better." He held up a pair of shotgun shells in his hand before putting them into the barrels. "One with rock salt to take down defenses and wards. One with lead for the regular job. Too many assholes learn magic and think they never need Kevlar again, y'know?"

"Why did you follow us?" asked Onyx, trying to hold an even tone. She wanted to join Molly in skipping straight to gratitude. After all they'd been through tonight, she knew better.

"I didn't like the way this one looked at you two after the reading," Hector explained, gesturing to Saxon with his gun. "Saw him split off from his friend after helpin' those other two peacocks get their new toy moving. Figured I'd see if he was up to something. Looks like he was."

"You saved our asses," said Molly.

Hector shook his head. "Don' read too much into it. I like you two, sure. Thing is, 'like' don't account for much in my book. This is self-interest."

"Aw, I dunno," Molly ventured, cracking a grin. "Looks like maybe a little altruism to me."

"I'm only *altruistic* when it don't cost me nothin'," explained Hector. "Conversation an' advice is free, right? So I'll give you that much, no problem, especially when you're nice to me. Keeps things friendly. But Molly, don't ever expect anything more than that. Not from me, not from nobody, especially in this life we all lead."

Again, he gestured to the dead man on the ground. "This asshole an' his buddies think they can push any Practitioner around if they ain't part of a big enough club. He's even okay with jumpin' other Practitioners comin' straight out of a neutral gathering, you know? That means eventually he'll come lookin' for me, too. I helped you out, sure. Maybe you'd have come out on top on your own. I'm glad it worked out for you, but I came out here to take care of a problem before it took care of me."

With his weapon ready again, Hector steadily walked around the pair of witches. Onyx kept her guard up, watching him carefully and ready to retaliate if he tried anything. She wondered if he held the same suspicion of her, and couldn't blame him if he did. Regardless, Hector moved past them both to stand over Archimedes as he tried to get Hypatia to her feet once more.

"The question now is whether or not I've got two more problems to take care of preemptively."

Torn up and frightened, Archimedes vigorously shook his head. "Y-you'll get no trouble from us. We're done here. W-we'll ju-just be on our way."

"Unh...ow," Hypatia moaned as she stirred.

"Mr. and Mrs. Arch?" called a voice from the condominium lot. The driver in his now dust-covered black suit limped out into the open. "Is that you? I heard shooting."

Archimedes winced. Hector grinned. "I'm guessin' if your man there could'a done somethin' for you, he'd have done it already, right?" Hector glanced over at the driver only once to see him standing there indecisively now that he understood the scene. Then he turned back to the matter at hand. "Cops gonna be here soon," said Hector. "Real soon."

Onyx wondered whom his observation was supposed to benefit. "You don't have to kill them," she said.

"You sure about that?"

"Woah, yeah," agreed Molly. "Hector, they tried to mug us, sure. There's a long way between that and murder."

"Same question: You sure about that?" Hector asked. "You don't know how far they would've taken things for that book. Or to keep Mista Saxon there happy."

Onyx looked from the tense scene to Molly. The driver didn't seem to know what to do about it, either. She limped a little closer, then stopped as she noticed something on the ground. "Don't do it, Hector." She bent over to retrieve the broken bits of wood. Molly walked with her, ready to lend a hand if she needed it. Though she appreciated the unspoken offer, Onyx managed on her own. "If we wind up regretting it, that's our problem. We'll take the risk."

Hypatia shook off the cobwebs in time to see Onyx drop two broken bits of wand in front of Archimedes. Then the younger woman leaned in closer, holding her own wand up for the two to see.

"Yes, I made it myself, and yes, it was done on a lathe. I took wood shop in my senior year just so I could make this. Assholes." With that, she kept walking and didn't look back.

Molly, on the other hand, looked over her shoulder with a grin. "Y'know, Hector, if this wasn't out of the goodness of your heart, you could've told us we owe you."

Police sirens drifted in along the breeze. Hector shook his head. "I'll add it into the cost if you ever need my help again. Nice meeting you." He glanced at the cowed driver standing nearby. "Might want to get these assholes outta here before you have to talk to some cops, man," he warned before he walked off in the other direction.

Eventually, Onyx put one hand on Molly's shoulder for support. However their enemies had trailed them, it wasn't a trick available to ordinary police. They knew their magic would let them escape notice as the patrol units sped by. They didn't worry about Hector or the others evading detection, either. It wasn't their problem. The walk back to the car provided more than enough of a final challenge for the night.

They found Onyx's used Chevy undisturbed where they'd left it. Onyx surrendered the keys to Molly and settled into the front passenger's seat. Molly entrusted her with Elizabeth's book before walking around to the other side.

The car's engine reassured Onyx almost as much as the presence of the driver. "You're pretty bad ass, y'know," she said.

"Pot, kettle," Molly replied with a grin. "And never doubt Steve or the mighty trash pandas."

"No. Never again."

Street lights flashed by. They found little traffic at this hour. The ride home started out quietly.

"So what's in the book?" asked Molly.

"You don't want to wait to open it yourself? She left it to you."

"Nah, I told you. She knew leaving it to me meant leaving it to us. It's fine. Open it up. There's a letter or something anyway, right?"

Onyx unfastened the clasp with care. She'd forgotten Kate's mention of a note, but found it tucked into the book immediately behind the cover. The first line on the folded sheet of paper left no doubt about its audience.

"'*Dearest Molly and Onyx,*'" she read aloud.

"'*You have surely asked yourselves if this book is a true "Book of Shadows," as I do not follow your Practice nor share your faith. You will find as you read through these pages that it is the genuine article. These are spells, rituals, and entries transcribed from my personal journals over the years that I would share with no one else. In truth, I share it now only because I am gone. Even that has not been an easy decision. I hope this expresses the trust and affection I feel for you.*

"'*My dear friends, I wish I could have left you virtually everything. I disbursed my estate for fear that any individual or sole group who received it all would become a target of greedy and ambitious rivals. I chose to do so publicly to prevent anyone from going off in search of some hidden treasure hoard. Inevitably, someone will still* try to uncover the "real truth" of my will. They will be disappointed to learn that everything is as it was listed. That is why I did not disguise this gift as something it is not.

"' You have by now heard my plea for peace in Seattle, read to yourselves and others. I am not so naïve as to think that plea will be heeded. This book is the greatest single share of my power and knowledge. I hope it prepares you well. Seattle's Practitioners and others who live in the shadows are still keeping largely to themselves. We still know peace. I don't believe it will last. Sooner or later, the knives will come out.'"

"Yeah," sighed Molly. "Now she tells us."

NAKED JUSTICE

"Please don't make me shoot you," breathed Kevin. "Please don't make me shoot you. Please oh please, motherfucker, don't do it…don't…"

Standing behind the driver's side door of their patrol car, Tyrone Johnson couldn't hear the mutterings of his partner on the other side of the vehicle. Both men already had their Glocks drawn. "Turn off the car and keep your hands visible!" ordered Tyrone over the patrol car's loudspeaker.

They had the Bronco boxed in. It sat in an alleyway, blocked by a freight truck parked up against a loading dock. Tyrone had pulled the patrol car up in the middle of the alleyway, leaving the Bronco with nowhere to go. The guys at the dock moved for cover as soon as they saw the guns.

Dark grey clouds released a constant drizzle. Rush hour had just started. All of downtown Seattle's streets behind and beyond the scene were already thickening with people leaving their offices. Sirens wailed in the distance, but it was anyone's guess if that was back-up or just some other call.

Both uniformed officers waited. Water slid through Kevin's inch-tall spikes of dirty blonde hair, across his thin, toned forearms and down the light blue fabric of his uniform shirt. He waited and hoped.

The Bronco's engine didn't turn off. Instead, the reverse lights blinked on.

"Shit," the partners grunted under the squeal of the Bronco's tires. Both men flung themselves to the alleyway's walls as the pickup rushed backward into their patrol car. Kevin flattened up against the nearby bricks just in time to avoid impact. The Bronco didn't hit quite straight on, but rather at an offset of bumper-to-bumper that sent the patrol car skidding back and to its right to slam up against one wall. Pressed against the alleyway wall, Kevin felt the bricks shudder with the impact. The violent gambit gave the Bronco enough space it needed to escape the alleyway.

Along with the crash came gunshots. The Bronco's driver was busy at the wheel, but the passenger next to him had nothing better to do than try to kill cops. He reached out through his open window with his handgun, firing wildly at Kevin while screaming something. The officer ducked, but his life was saved mostly by the shooter's abundant excitement, lack of training and a bad angle.

Kevin didn't suffer from such habits of ego. Friends might argue that he was similarly free from the afflictions of common sense. He rushed around his wrecked vehicle, chasing the retreating Bronco as it hurriedly backed out to the street. As soon as he had a clear shot, Kevin put two bullets through the windshield on the passenger side. His Glock punched holes through the glass that were immediately surrounded by blood stains.

The vehicle kept moving. So did Kevin. The conflict spilled out into the street when the Bronco turned out of the alleyway and rammed its already damaged rear end into an oncoming car.

Kevin ran up to the Bronco, stopping himself against its hood with his free hand while he fired off two more shots. Even at such close range, there was plenty that could cause a man to miss.

He didn't.

The Bronco sat still, its rear bumper now stuck up against another car and its driver slumped over to one side in a bloody mess. The engine idled. Cars around the vehicle ground to a halt while pedestrians looked on in shock.

"Kevin!" Tyrone shouted, hurrying out of the alleyway. His leap from the side of the patrol car had taken him off of his feet. It made him only a few heartbeats slower. Blood trickled down from a gash on his head. "Kevin, you alright?"

Kevin tried the passenger side door. It was locked, but the window was down. He reached inside to get the door open, then hopped in over the bloody, expired occupants to throw the Bronco into park. He lingered just long enough to pull the keys out of the ignition.

Neither occupant would ever move again.

Kevin slipped out to find his partner waiting for him. At the Bronco's rear, a stunned and frightened couple came out of their Honda Civic to look at its smashed front end. The sirens drew closer.

"Hey, man," Tyrone repeated calmly, "you alright?"

"I'm okay," Kevin nodded.

"You can put your weapon away," Tyrone said.

Kevin blinked, glanced around, and nodded. He holstered his pistol as he stepped back from the vehicle. Third Street was already a mess of honking horns and shocked witnesses. Tyrone paused to clap his hand on Kevin's shoulder, looking his partner in the eyes to make sure he was still there with the rest of the world. A moment later, Tyrone turned to take control of the immediate scene.

Kevin looked up to the cloudy early summer sky. The drizzle quickly picked up into full rain. Not for the first time, his light blue Seattle Police uniform—itself barely two years old—was covered in blood.

He turned thirty-two that day.

———

"You're uncle's hot, Molly."

"Oh, Jesus," Molly grumbled, pulling the car off 105th onto the darkening side street. "How much of this am I gonna hear out of you?" She looked good tonight, her fire-engine red hair cut short and spiked just the way she liked it. Her torn-up VNV Nation shirt was almost a work of art, and it was finally warm enough to go without jackets or long-sleeve shirts.

"Probably a lot," confessed Onyx, "because your uncle's fucking hot." She sat in the side passenger's seat of Molly's beat-up old car with her hands folded in her lap and her dark curls dangling down in front of her face. As usual, she went for darker yet more girlish clothes of black silk and lace. She made for a very pretty Goth.

The pretty redhead's eyes narrowed. "Never any parking around this place anytime after eight," she muttered. "Feels like it's still late afternoon, too. Sun stays up later than a—"

"I'll bet he fucks like an *animal*," Onyx mused. "All fierce and powerful and possessive, y'know?"

Molly stopped the car in the middle of the narrow residential street. Her head turned to stare at her girlfriend with daggers in her eyes. Onyx said, sheepishly, "I'm just sayin' I bet it runs in the family."

"I'd better never hear a firsthand account," replied Molly. "Things I don't want to know about my blood relatives. Ew. And let's not bring up the rest of my family, okay? Kevin's the only one who didn't bat an eye over me being pagan or being into girls. Seriously, any one of my relatives who didn't freak when I came out about being one flipped over me being the other. Kevin's the only one who supported me."

"I could keep my mouth shut," Onyx teased.

"You do not get to fuck my uncle!"

Onyx sighed. "Fine... not even a little bit?"

"No! Jesus!" Molly got the car rolling again, soon finding a spot to park. "Look, if we want a guy to play with, let's find one together and go in on it together, okay? And that means no relatives!"

Onyx stared at her lover as Molly turned off the car. "Wait, really?"

Molly looked up at her and shrugged. "Do you want to?"

"I don't... I don't know. I mean I never really thought about it."

"You thought about my uncle enough, you sick-minded tramp," Molly smirked.

"Well, yeah, but I didn't really—I mean he's got eleven years on me, right? I mean... wait, are you serious?"

Molly sighed, slipped a hand up around Onyx's neck and brought her in for a soft, reassuring kiss. "We can talk about it later. You've never gone all the way with a guy and I know you're still curious. I'm open to pretty much anything that doesn't ever involve letting you go. Or my uncle. Ew."

Onyx was floored. "Wow."

"Later though, okay? We've got a birthday therapy thing," Molly said, nodding toward the bar.

"Yeah," Onyx agreed sweetly. She shouldered her purse and exited the car along with Molly, taking her lover's hand as they walked up the residential street to the bar at the corner. She gave it an affectionate, meaningful squeeze as they walked in silence.

Molly smiled and enjoyed the moment.

"Seriously, I bet he's just like a sleek jungle cat—"

"Oh, God."

"—and all you can do is just *lay* there under him and *take* it and *love* it."

"You are not allowed to fuck my thirty-two-year-old uncle."

"I'm not gonna! I'm just saying somebody should."

"Onyx, you do realize that he's a complete goofball, right?"

The younger partner shrugged as Molly reached for the big brass Chinese dragon handles on the heavy wooden door. "That could be sexy," she countered. Then she heard the music, and what technically passed for singing.

"I said you'll pay for this mischief,
"Oh, in this world, or the next.
"Oh, then he fixed me with a freezing glance,
"And the hellfires raged in his eyes…"

Onyx looked on at the full-grown adult on the karaoke stage throwing goat horns as he wailed into the mic without the least concern for dignity. He even wore a fake '80s hair metal wig. "I'm gonna quote you on that later," Molly warned.

"He said, 'you wanna know the truth son?
"'Lord, I'll tell you the truth!
"'Your soul's gonna burn in a lake of fiii-eyaaaaahh!'"

"Um." Onyx struggled for words as Kevin straddled the mic stand. "He's more or less in tune." Then she winced. "Mostly."

———

"You missed my first number," Kevin said, hugging Molly tightly as he joined her and Onyx at the bar.

"I did? What was it?"

"*Wanted Dead or Alive*."

"I'm amazed anyone else is still here," Molly chuckled.

"Hi, Onyx," he grinned, releasing his niece.

"Happy birthday, Kevin," smiled Onyx. Her porcelain skin rarely betrayed any shyness or embarrassment, but now she blushed uncontrollably. The two hesitated as if unsure of whether a hug was appropriate or not, and after a nudge behind the back from Molly, he went for it anyway. Onyx's eyes went wide over his shoulder as his arms briefly came around her.

"Can I buy either of you a drink? Uh. You can drink, right?" he asked Onyx.

"About two months now," she confirmed. "But it's your birthday. We were coming to buy you a couple."

"Sounded like you might need it, Officer Murray," added Molly.

"You already heard?"

"Yeah. First a little news blurb, then I started digging. Wound up putting two and two together," Molly explained. They took up seats at the bar. Molly noted that Onyx put

Kevin in the middle rather than leaving it to Molly, but gave it no more than an amused, accusing eyebrow.

"Right, so, the Kung Pao here is pretty good," Kevin said in a deliberate shift of topic. He held the menu out to his niece and another to her girlfriend. "The fried rice is a total waste, though. Crab Rangoon's okay."

"Kevin. Tell us."

Kevin frowned, dropping the menu. "Tyrone and I spotted a Bronco that matched the description from a home invasion robbery last night. Five guys killed an old lady and put her grandson in the hospital."

"I read about that."

"Yeah. So we followed the Bronco into an alley and lit 'em up. With the lights, I mean. We got out of our car. Tyrone told 'em to shut the car off. They tried to run us over and shoot us instead. Smashed our car, almost killed us. I shot 'em both in the face. Had to run out into traffic to get the driver before he ran someone over."

"Tyrone's okay, though, right?" Molly asked.

"Oh, he's fine. He's mad that he fell when they tried to roll over us. Probably would've been a lot more shots fired if that alleyway hadn't been so slippery. I'm lucky I didn't crack my skull myself."

"Is he going to join us later?"

"Nah. His girlfriend's kid is playing the Dentist in '*Little Shop*' tonight. This isn't my first birthday or my first shooting, but how many opening nights do you get in high school?"

"That's a great role," Onyx smiled.

"It is."

Molly took time to order up three Irish car bombs. "Three shootings in two years on the force," she said finally.

"Shockingly, I heard that more than a few times this afternoon."

"What're they saying?"

Kevin shrugged. "There was a security camera in the alley. All the physical evidence is there. If this isn't a justified shooting, then there ain't no such animal. But I'm still a cop who's been in three shootings in his first two years, on a force where lots of the other violent incidents aren't as clean-cut as mine. Justified or not, it adds up, y'know?

"Plus there's all the other shit that didn't actually involve shooting anyone," he continued, "but use of force is still use of force. I mean they deliberately call me out to help with warrants on guys they know are violent, they stick me in the most violent precinct in the city, and they wonder why I've got so many use of force incidents in my jacket? Not once have I been the one to initiate. Not once."

"Rookie of the year on your first year, though, right? Didn't you get some awards this year, too?"

"Not sure if I get to keep all that if they have to bounce me."

"Yeah, but you said yourself, all the evidence is on your side, right?"

"Sometimes it doesn't matter. The department's in so much hot water with all the stuff that really *does* stink over the last couple years that it might not matter how right this was. Like I said, it adds up."

Molly paused. "Do you think it was right?"

"Well, I don't feel *good* about it, if that's what you're asking."

"I didn't ask that."

"Why not?"

"Don't need to. But do you think it was right?"

Kevin took a deep breath and let it out. "I don't know what else I was gonna do."

"Nothing else you could've done, aside from let them go. Which is what you signed up *not* to do." Kevin shrugged. Molly leaned over a bit to press the point. "Those two shitbags and their other three friends—who are still out there some-where, but now at least they're shitting their pants—those guys all murdered an innocent woman last night and put her grandson in the hospital, and that poor kid gets to live with the memory. They tried to kill you and your partner. They probably would've killed others. You did what somebody had to do. Just like with both of the other fuckheads you shot."

Kevin looked at her, then turned his attention to Onyx. "This birthday party's cheerful, huh?" he asked her.

"We like you," Onyx said with a sweet smile. She even batted her eyelashes at him.

"Their dumb luck for running into a Mary Sue like you, anyway," Molly added.

"A Mary—wait, what?"

"A Mary Sue," Onyx grinned up at him. "She's saying you're so awesome it stretches suspension of disbelief."

"Yeah, I know what it means," Kevin fumed, turning from Onyx back to Molly. "I am not!"

"You are, too," she teased calmly.

"I'm not a Mary Sue! And I'm not a fictional character!"

"You're a total bad ass, you did well in school—"

"You're really hot," Onyx put in.

"—you've got an awesome cat…"

"Okay, first off, it'd be Marty Stu for me."

"Eh, whatever," Molly replied dismissively. "You're not hung up on gender bullshit."

"Okay, if I was a Mary Sue, I'd be able to actually communicate with my cat for real instead of just pretending I know what he's thinking." Kevin took another gulp of his drink. "And I'd have a hot girlfriend. And a unicorn. And a magic sword or something."

"You do have a—wait, what about Meredith?" Molly asked. "What happened with that?"

"Went back to her ex last week," Kevin frowned. "Didn't I tell everyone?"

"Ugh. The useless drunk guy she left for running up her credit cards? How ugly was that?"

"Wouldn't have been ugly at all if she hadn't tried to take Attila with her."

"Attila? Really? I'm surprised you didn't shoot her, too."

"Well, like I said, it got ugly, but that wasn't me. Attila let her know whose cat he is in no uncertain terms."

"Sounds like a crappy recipe for a birthday," said Onyx.

"Yeah, well. Like I said, I've had worse. I'm home, I'm not in a hospital and I don't have any funerals on the calendar." He held up his shot of whiskey, clinked it against theirs when they followed suit, and poured it into his Guinness. "Cheers," he smiled, and took a long pull.

Onyx had hers down first. "So what happens now? With your job?"

"Now? Two days of nothin'. Mandatory paid administrative leave after a shooting. I wrote all my reports and statements, got my ass-chewings and my sympathetic talk from the chaplain and yet *another* appointment set with the same lame trauma counselor from my other shootings, and that's it. They don't want to hear from me for two days. At all. I could practically turn off my phone."

"Wait, you're supposed to sit at home and stew on it?" Onyx asked.

"Yeah. Keeps you from doing anything crazy while you're still rocky from the incident. Lets you focus, gives the department time to figure out if you really did fuck up and you shouldn't be trusted with a squirt gun. I'm supposed to get my mind off of it, but all I'm gonna do is sit around thinking about how I killed two guys on my birthday. What gets your mind off that?"

He stared at his empty mug with a sigh. "Worst part is, Tyrone and I were supposed to go talk to kids at a middle school tomorrow. Do a big summer safety thing, be all Officer Friendly and stuff. But I can't do that when everyone knows I'm really Officer ShootsYourAss."

Molly tilted her head curiously, glancing at Onyx. Her lover knew most of her looks by heart. It wasn't telepathy, but it was close enough. "So there's no reason not to sing yourself hoarse, throw your dignity to the wind and get hammered tonight, right?"

He shrugged. "Gotta be coherent enough to get a cab home," he thought aloud. "Never needed dignity for that." He frowned and patted his pockets. "Not sure I even brought any with me in the first place."

"We'll take care of you," Molly offered, gesturing for the bartender.

———

Onyx honestly hadn't planned on groping her girlfriend's uncle tonight, let alone this much. As she and Molly helped him out of the car, putting one of his arms around each young woman's shoulder, Onyx wound up putting her hand against his chest, his side, and even his ass, all without any malicious or mischievous intent. They had to get him inside his townhouse, after all.

He felt exactly how she expected: toned and fit without being bulky. Once again, Onyx decided that the women comprising Kevin's string of short-term, dysfunctional relationships must have been nuts. Then again, the fact that he'd had to take restraining orders out on more than a few of them seemed to make that obvious.

"You don' hafta do this," Kevin slurred. "You c'n leave me on the doorstep. I'll jus' take a nap there."

"It's totally not a problem," Molly grunted. Despite the physical strength that she was usually happy to show off,

Molly found the task of hauling Kevin inside tougher than she expected. It was less an issue of dead weight than it was of balance and direction. He was trying hard to help. Too hard.

"Nnnnnno, really," he went on, "I've slept outside lots'a timesh. I was a soljer, y'know. Didjou know that? When you were still jus' a kid."

"I know," Molly said. "I remember. You sent me letters from Afghanistan."

"Ssssuch bullshit," he grumbled. "But yeah. An' I remember you bein' jus' a little girl when I was in high school. You used to play with—"

"You're done!" Molly commanded him loudly. "You're done. Finished. No more of that."

"Okay, okay, sorry," he smiled at her, then turned to Onyx. "Sssshhhhh."

Onyx turned her head and blinked away the fumes. She knew Molly wanted to get her uncle good and smashed for some specific reason, but as yet that reason hadn't been made clear to her. She staggered on, glad she had opted for her Doc Marten boots rather than anything with fancy heels tonight.

Molly dug around in Kevin's pocket for his keys. She and Onyx kept him upright as they tried the door, needing only three tries before she found the right one to open the lock.

The simple, two-story townhome was dark. A staircase rose only a few feet beyond the front door, with the kitchen opening up immediately to the right. Onyx heard a thunk at the kitchen countertop. "Aw, kitty," she announced.

"Awww, kitty," Kevin slurred. He straightened himself enough to pull away from the ladies, slipping behind them to put his arms out on the countertop around the cat. Molly found the light switch, illuminating the room to reveal a healthy, almost muscular grey and white cat. The pattern of his fur made Onyx immediately think of snow tigers.

He was also, from his demeanor, quite skeptical. Kevin petted him with one hand, both elbows propped up on the countertop. The cat reached out to press one paw against his cheek.

"This is a nice place," Onyx observed. "Comfy."

"Prol'y gonna haveta move soon," Kevin complained. "Lan'lady's gonna have a realtor come over an' assess 'r something." He let out a sigh. "This sucks. Lost my girlfriend. Gonna lose my place. Might even lose my job." Attila then stood up, flicked his tail and walked out of reach. "Lost my cat," Kevin added.

"He's just being a cat," assured Molly. "Hey, Attila. We're putting Kevin here to bed."

"He's gorgeous!" declared Onyx.

"Yeah, he is," Molly agreed with a huff. "Me and that cat are pretty tight."

"He's my buddy," Kevin nodded.

"He's keeping his distance from you tonight, you drunk," Molly said. She slipped around him, looking through his cabinets until she found a glass and filled it with water from the tap. "Drink," she ordered, holding it out to Kevin.

He let out a sigh. "Okay," taking it and downing it as instructed. "'m not gonna have a hangover," he said. "Drank a lotta water at the bar. Took some aspirin. 'm sure I'll be fine."

Molly leaned in to Attila and shared an affectionate head-butt. "You and me gotta talk later, 'kay?" she asked. The cat let out a neutral meow. Molly scratched his head, then turned her attention back to the matter of her uncle. "Up the stairs. I know you can make it on your own. Go. Wait, no, gimme the glass. Okay, now go."

Onyx followed a staggering Kevin and an uncharacter-istically bossy Molly up the stairs, waiting patiently for her explanation. Attila remained in the kitchen, watching with inscrutable eyes.

"No no no," Molly said in the bedroom before Kevin could collapse on the bed. Her voice took on an unnaturally firm, serious note of command that surprised both him and Onyx. "Not sleepy time yet. Shower first."

Kevin swooned a little. "Okay," he mumbled before he walked into the bathroom, seeming steadier and yet more lethargic than before. He closed the door behind him. Then he opened it again and leaned out, wincing as he did. "Hey Molly," he whispered in a conspiratorial tone, "your girl-friend's hhhhhot."

Standing in the corner outside Kevin's line of sight, Onyx clamped her hand down over her mouth.

"I know, Kevin," Molly said.

"I'm just sayin'. You *totally* gotta hit that. Like, a *lot*."

"Shower!"

"Okay, okay, sorry I stink," Kevin rambled as he closed the door again. The sound of running water could soon be heard.

Molly turned around with a mischievous grin on her face. Onyx was waiting with her arms folded across her chest. "What the hell are we doing?" she asked.

"We're giving him something else to think about."

"We couldn't just take him out to lunch tomorrow or something?"

"No," Molly said. "We're doing this. Help me grab all the sheets to his bed. Everything but the bottom sheet."

"...why?"

"Because it'll be funny," Molly said, yanking the comforter off of Kevin's bed.

"What's funny about taking his bed sheets?"

Molly didn't answer her right away. Opportunity interrupted her. "Oh. Hey, Attila," she said, dropping down to her knees as the cat wandered in. He leapt up into her arms without hesitation. "Attila, we're gonna steal all of Kevin's clothes! Wanna help?"

The cat looked at her, and then around the room, acting for all the world like an entirely normal cat. As far as Onyx could see, there was nothing odd here happening at all. People talked to cats as if the critters could understand all the time, but everyone knew that was ridiculous.

Everyone except Molly.

Attila meowed again. Molly grinned widely. "C'mon," she said to Onyx, "we've gotta work fast."

Onyx stared at her lover with disbelieving eyes. She knew Molly was a prankster, but this was beyond anything she'd expected to see—let alone participate in.

Minutes later, the two stood at the bottom of the stairs with Kevin's clothes hamper, his blankets and even the box of clothes clearly marked for Goodwill at their sides. The drawers from his dresser and the hanging clothes from his closet were already in the car.

"OK, you get the clothes he just took off in the bathroom. And the towels, too."

"What?" hissed Onyx. "You've gotta be kidding me!"

Molly's huge grin impacted her credibility as she said, "I wouldn't kid about something like this. We need the bath towels, too, or he could walk outside with one wrapped around him."

"How's he gonna dry off?"

"Leave all the hand towels," Molly snickered. "Anyway, you gotta go up there and get 'em before he gets out of the shower!"

"Me?" Onyx fairly shrieked. She lowered her voice to a hiss when Molly shushed her, but didn't lose her intensity. "Why the fuck do I have to go up there?"

"Because I don't want to risk seeing my uncle naked in the shower!" Molly hissed back. "You're the stealthier one, anyway. Now go! I'll start moving the rest of this into the car."

Onyx struggled for a counter-argument, but failed. Deep down inside, she had to concede this was hilarious. And fun. She looked to Attila for support. "This is crazy, isn't it?"

The cat didn't respond. "He doesn't see a problem with this," Molly said. "Go."

Onyx threw her a glare, then turned away and started up the stairs. She paused to say over her shoulder, "You're sending me into a room with your naked uncle."

Molly shot a glare right back at her. "I'm gonna screw you until you can't even remember me having an uncle," she threatened.

Onyx grinned. "Awesome," she said, and rushed up the stairs.

The sound of the shower reassured her as she entered the bedroom. Onyx crept up to the bathroom door, nudging it open carefully and looking inside. Sure enough, Kevin had only half-closed the shower curtain. She had a great view of his naked backside.

She bit down on her fist. Despite her relentless teasing, she wasn't *that* hung up on him. But he was awfully nice to look at: a nice face and body, intriguing scars, the paratrooper tattoo behind his shoulder and that adorable ass. He was a great topic to tease her lover over.

Onyx thought about the bad run of luck he'd mentioned downstairs. Some of that had been the alcohol talking. Kevin generally wasn't one to mope or feel sorry for himself. Still, she couldn't help but pity him a little. She felt a slight pang of guilt for the prank she was pulling, too. It wasn't remotely enough guilt to overcome her amusement or change her mind on the whole thing, but she opted to try to make up for it.

She whispered the words of a charm for luck, concentrating her thoughts on Kevin as she softly sounded out the incantation. One could never really know if such a spell worked, since luck was always subjective. Who's to say what trouble might be avoided by staying home and doing nothing? Perhaps not getting hit on the head by a meteor on Thursday was luck and one simply didn't know any better.

She finished her plea to the universe, then slipped inside, gathered up his pants, his shirt, his socks and underwear and the larger towels off the rack—and took another gleeful look at his glutes before she made her escape.

Kevin awoke to Attila pushing head-first under his arm. Satisfied that his human was now cuddling him, intentionally or not, Attila settled back down again. Kevin gave a little smile. Attila was a good cat.

Kevin lay on his belly with his head hanging halfway off the side of the bed, which, now that he was partly awake and considering it, seemed a little odd.

Sensory information pushed his brain along. He wasn't cold, but he wasn't exactly warm, either. He must've kicked off all the covers. Kevin shifted and realized he was utterly naked.

The sun was up, but that meant nothing. It was probably only five-thirty, if even that. The problem with Seattle summers was the ridiculous length of the day; sleeping late became a challenge because the sun went down so late and came up again so goddamn early.

He wasn't late for work, though. No, it wasn't that. His alarm didn't go off. Plus, he remembered now, he wasn't supposed to go in anyway. He was on leave. He'd shot someone yesterday. Two someones. Right.

The bar. Shit. Molly and Onyx. Hopefully they had left before he took off all his clothes and fell on top of his bed naked. After the shower. Right. He vaguely remembered that part.

He must have been really drunk, too, because he remembered using the hand towels to dry off, as if he couldn't find his regular towels. That was stupid. How drunk do you have to be to lose your bath towels in your bathroom?

He risked turning his head, not quite lifting it off the mattress, to look at Attila. The cat's eyes were already closed, but his ears twitched in obvious disapproval of any disturbance. It was a necessary experiment. The movement did nothing bad to his brain. "Well, 'm not hungover," Kevin mumbled. "That's good."

Attila had nothing to say in response to this. He never did, and it would freak Kevin the hell out if that ever changed, but Kevin talked to him anyway.

"I gotta hit the bathroom," Kevin muttered. "Sorry, buddy." He fumbled and crawled upright, leaving Attila to once again fuss around for a comfortable position on the bed. As he staggered to the bathroom, he stepped on a damp hand towel, and then another. "Must've been really fucking drunk," Kevin mused as he staggered into the bathroom. His eyes hardly opened during the whole process. They even remained closed as he washed his hands. It was the unexpected difficulty in drying them that forced him to look around.

There were no bath towels at all. None on the rack, none on the floor, or hanging over the shower curtain rod. "What the hell?" He shuffled out into his bedroom again, picked up one of the hand towels to dry his hands off, and then noticed how out of place things were.

His closet was open and largely empty. The drawers were missing from his dresser. The realization that he might have been robbed woke him up instantly. Kevin's eyes took in the whole room. His wallet was still on the dresser, as were his keys, but his phone was gone. He rushed to the closet, found his uniform belt still hanging there with all his equipment. His gun safe was undisturbed. The dirty clothes hamper was gone, though. So were his spare bed sheets. What the fuck?

A moment later, Kevin found the note taped to his doorframe. It was a simple, folded-over piece of computer paper with his name on it, written in black pen.

"*Dear Kevin: You said you needed something to get your mind off yesterday. Hope this helps. Your clothes, towels, sheets, laptop and phone are safe with us. We checked to make sure you have plenty of food. We'll play answering service for you if anything comes up and we'll be back late tomorrow evening with your stuff. Chill out, play video games and watch some porn or whatever it is guys do when they hang around the house alone and naked. Love, Molly and Onyx.*"

His eyes flared. He looked around his room again twice to make sure he wasn't dreaming. His bed contained only pillows, a bottom sheet, and a cat who looked up at him like he might be crazy.

Kevin flew out of his bedroom and headed downstairs. Maybe they were still there. Maybe that was the prank. Screw it; if they wanted to see him naked, then here he was, naked, and if he saw a single solitary camera he'd take it and—

No. Nobody home. The place was completely quiet. The drapes were drawn shut. The lights were all off. Kevin stood naked in his silent, peaceful home. Naked and alone.

Except, that is, for the cat. Attila followed him downstairs and headbutted his ankle with a purr to remind Kevin that as long as he was up, he could always replenish the food dish.

———

He cooked his breakfast naked. On a normal working day he didn't have time for this, but he had about as much to do today as he had clothes to do it in. He threw together toast, scrambled eggs, and thick bacon, catching more than a few tiny drops of spattering hot grease on his naked chest and stomach along the way. It wasn't as if he had an apron. Even if he did, Kevin doubted he would go so far as to wear an apron with his naked ass hanging free in the back. Not without someone to impress or at least amuse, anyway.

He ate naked, too, sitting at his small dining nook table wondering what he was supposed to do with himself today. Well, he could do *that* with himself, of course, but what about the rest of the day? Obviously he wouldn't be hitting the gym.

Kevin tried to at least knock out some naked calisthenics. Stretches were no problem. Sit-ups were fine. Push-ups were a little weird, what with his dangling junk hitting the floor again and again, but whatever. He realized, finishing up his reps, that jumping jacks were right out.

He showered and shaved, taking his time with both, though he wondered why he bothered with the latter. It seemed like something to do. Drying off with only hand towels was a bit of a pain, but he didn't feel like dripping dry.

He straightened up the living room. Unloaded the dishwasher. Cleaned up after breakfast. Stood and stared at his home again. Naked.

"Fine," he said to no one in particular, and then to the cat who sat on the couch staring at him, "fine!" He stomped over to the couch, picked up his Playstation controller and fired up the console. "Whatever."

He remembered, then, that the console connected his television to the internet. He could get email after all, at least... but then what? Email Tyrone and ask him to bring over some clothes and have to explain this? Or one of his other friends? Send a nastygram to Molly and give her even more of a laugh than she was already having?

Kevin stared at the screen, growled, and kicked the cursor over to his video game. There were aliens to kill. He could always save the galaxy again.

Naked, this time.

———

"So this guy has the highest record—the highest record, bar none—of use of force of any cop in the city of Seattle for the last two years running."

Kevin wiped away the last of the spots on the stove top, glaring at the old clock-radio on his counter. "*Somebody's* gonna have the highest record," he grumbled. "That's kinda how numbers work."

"Let that sink in, people: he's been a cop for all of two years, and in those two years he's racked up a higher count of injuries and deaths inflicted on our citizens than any other cop!"

"Yeah, and I go home and open a beer and celebrate it every day. Naked."

"And now we've got two more dead at his hands. Two suspects out of five, right? The cops believe there are five guys in this home invasion murder-robbery ring, but now they don't have anyone to question, because Officer Murray has to go off and shoot both of them!"

"Oh, fuck you!" Kevin snorted, glaring at the radio. Attila hopped up on the counter. "No, not you, buddy."

"You know what he did on his first night on patrol?"

"Watched my training officer get his car stolen by high school kids while serving a noise complaint at their party?" Kevin asked over the rhetorical answer of the other guy on the radio.

"No! No, he punches out this woman in a nightclub, one Cassie McClintock—"

"After she stabbed me with a four-inch knife!" Kevin said, throwing the sponge over his shoulder. "Jesus, I wasn't even talking to her when it happened!"

"So, why's he still out on the streets?" asked the program host.

"Technically he's not right now," pointed out another, more reasonable guest. "He's on administrative leave after yesterday's shooting."

"They do that to give everyone time to circle the wagons and protect each other," said the first guest. "They did it with Sergeant Machado—"

"Actual douchebag," muttered Kevin.

"—Officer Levy—"

"Racist douchebag," Kevin nodded.

"—who didn't shoot anyone, but the arrest was still considered violent enough to warrant a similar response, and they did it after that pursuit that led to a fatal crash involving Officer Fenwick."

"Reckless, racist douchebag," said Kevin to the radio. "Those are all bad cops! Why are you lumping me in with them?"

"But we should point out," said the host, "in Murray's case, or cases, all of his shootings have been against armed suspects who fired other shots. The department released dashboard cameras and other video."

"Yes!" agreed Kevin. "And there's video this time, too! And witnesses!"

"They haven't released it this time."

"Argh! It hasn't even been twenty-four hours!"

"But just for the sake of argument, let's say this time, once again, the suspects were armed and they did shoot at him as reported. Even so, with three shootings in two years and these other incidents, doesn't that say something about his practices? Doesn't that leave us to question the approach that gets him into these situations? Why are all these people attacking this one cop?"

Kevin reached over Attila to turn the radio off, interrupting the man's statement. His now-clean kitchen was filled with blissful silence. "That was a mistake," he said to his cat. Attila let out a meow that may have been an agreement, or perhaps instead just a reminder that there were salmon treats in the cabinet above him.

His mood remained dimmed by the radio show. Public radio usually had better call screening than that. He was surprised the host didn't jump in after the blood money crack. Ultimately, what he really wished for was a chance to defend himself in public, but he already knew from experience that it wouldn't likely happen. He also knew what would happen if he publicly objected to being lumped in with those other officers.

"Starting to wonder if this job was a mistake, too, buddy," he confessed.

———

"He killed Al and Don, man," growled Dick, leaning in with his fists on the table. "Fucking shot both of them in the face. In the *face*, man."

John looked back at Dick with a scowl. It was hard to eat his McNuggets and his fries with someone in his face like this.

"I know, Dick," he said. "Everybody knows, alright? Whole world knows. All over the news. What the hell do you want to do about it?"

"Let's fuckin' smoke him, man!" Dick banged his fist on the small motel table, rising up to pace around the room. He ran his hands over his balding head. Like the others, Dick was a big man, with tattoos decorating any of his skin not already covered by his jeans and Harley t-shirt. "I mean this is bullshit! Someone murders two of our brothers and what do we do? Scurry out of town and hide out in this cheap dive like a bunch'a pussies?"

"We are not killin' a cop, Dick," John replied firmly. He was thinner than Dick, and younger, too, with piercings and tattoos to spare. "We've got enough heat on us as it is, or Al and Don wouldn't be dead in the first place. We go smoke a cop and they're never gonna let up on us across the whole fuckin' state. We wouldn't even be safe in fucking Portland or Vancouver, either. Have to clear out of this whole fuckin' part of the country!"

"We were planning on doing that anyway," said Carl, who sat on the bed with his laptop. "That was the deal, right? Handful of jobs, then we sell off all the junk, buy some new bikes and head off to SoCal? I remember that being the plan."

John let out a long sigh. "Well then why aren't we sticking to that?"

"Because Al and Don had most of the cash from the last job, remember? That's why they were downtown in the first fuckin' place. And so now we've gotta do more jobs just to come out to where we were before, and we weren't even quite done yet."

"Man, all those goals we had were set between us," countered John. "We made all that shit up. It's up to us to change it."

"Why would we change it when we know we'll need that money? Anyway, we know we'll have to do more jobs. Only this time we'll be doing it with people knowin' we're down two of our guys. We run the risk of people trying to stand up to us. Play hero. Fuck everything up and make an even bigger mess."

Carl turned his full attention on John. "I'm not letting two of our brothers die without any kind of payback. Are you saying we should? What if it was me or Dick got killed? Would you leave that alone, too?"

John chewed on it. In truth, he would, but he couldn't afford to actually tell them that. "No," he lied. "It's not that, it's just—don't we run an even bigger risk of getting caught?"

"Not if we change up our M.O.," Carl said. "We change up our way of doing things. Operate in different hours. Make sure the clues point in confusing directions. They'll know it was us, but they won't be able to prove it."

"Fine," John sighed again. "But how do we even find him? I mean all we know is his name after all the news stories, but that don't help a whole lot. Ain't like a cop's gonna be stupid enough to have his name in a public directory."

"A cop wouldn't," Carl agreed, "but someone who isn't a cop yet might. The internet's an archive, my friend," he smiled. "And they teach you all kinds of good job skills in prison these days."

———

Friday morning was much the same as Thursday. Kevin cooked breakfast. Ate. Exercised as best he could given his circumstances. Showered, shaved, cleaned up the kitchen and plopped down on the couch for some quality time with his Playstation and his cat.

Attila sat beside him, cleaning his fur and occasionally looking up at Kevin as if waiting for something Kevin was supposed to say.

"I don't know what to do now, buddy," Kevin told him, weaving his car through this obstacle and that on the big screen. "They might kick me out. Maybe I should go on my own. But after all the trouble I went through to get this job, I can't see quitting. Y'know?"

Attila went back to his work.

Kevin played through another couple of levels, marginally entertained but mostly bored. He had to admit that a day and a half after the shooting, he felt a little less shaken by it. Time made a difference. Then again, maybe Molly's prank created a productive mental distraction. None of it really did anything about any of his problems, but time helped put things into perspective.

What he really wanted now was a chance to go out and do something about the rest of his troubles. There was bound to be some manner of further fallout for the shooting, regardless of how justified it might be. Too many people looked only at numbers and not context, at least when it suited their agenda. He couldn't blame them for that agenda—hell, he agreed with a lot of it. That didn't mean he wanted to be an unintended victim of it all.

Kevin completed another level. The screen went dark as the Playstation reloaded new data for the next one. Seconds passed with no change. Kevin wondered if the system had frozen.

He heard the metallic flump and clank of his mailbox outside through his open front window. It offered a new distraction. He hadn't even checked the mail yesterday. Amazon owed him packages. There might be a magazine or two out there. Bills, too, probably, and junk mail, but it was contact with the outside world. He looked at the clock. Today was supposed to be the last day of school, but it was still in session at this hour and most people would still be at work… he wondered how risky it might be?

At the very least, he'd be able to tell Molly truthfully that her nudity-based incarceration project hadn't completely held him for the full two days.

Kevin hustled upstairs to the study and looked out its window. Cars rolled up and down the major street of Aurora Avenue a couple blocks away, but nothing moved on his quiet side street. No pedestrians. No bicyclists. Nothing except the postal van, already crawling up and away from his place. Were it not for his unclothed predicament, he'd never be able to stay in on such a nice, warm, sunny day.

He came back down the stairs without wasting his chance. His mailbox stood with several others on the sidewalk only a few yards from his door. Parked cars all along the street offered plenty of cover even if someone did drive by—and what were the odds that it'd be anyone who knew him and would call in a complaint? He peered through the small window of his door again. Fuck it.

He unlocked the door, opened it, and slipped outside. Someone small and furry slipped out, too, right between his ankles. "Attila, no!" Kevin called, but it was too late; his grey and white housemate was out and gone, already trotting down the steps and out to the sidewalk as if he was as entitled to an early afternoon stroll as anyone else. He looked back to Kevin and meowed once as if to ask what the big deal was about walking around naked, considering he did it all the time, and then turned and walked off to his right.

"Shit. Not again. Not now." He threw the deadbolt on his open door to make sure there'd be no chance of it accidentally locking on him and then darted out after his cat. Kevin didn't trust the neighborhood enough to let Attila out. The cat blithely strolled up the sidewalk while Kevin ducked behind one car after another in pursuit.

"Buddy, c'mere! Attila! Dammit, cat!" he hissed. He went for a grab. Missed. Went for another, and missed, and this time Attila darted under a car outside of Kevin's reach. "Attila, don't do this to me," he said.

Attila meowed. A pickup truck rolled by, moving toward Aurora. Kevin stayed low.

It stopped right in front of his house. Kevin glanced over his shoulder at the jacked-up blue vehicle, thinking little of it until a man in a denim jacket, jeans and a ski mask stood up from the back with an AK-47. The driver leaned out of his window with a pistol, too, and even the passenger side door opened with a third masked man, also armed with an AK. All three leveled their weapons at Kevin's townhouse.

The roar of gunfire that followed drowned out every other sound. The shooters emptied their weapons in a matter of seconds. Glass shattered and wood splintered all over the building's façade. More than a few rounds struck the homes on either side of his. Kevin didn't believe his neighbors were home, but couldn't be sure. His heart went into overdrive.

A moment later, the guy in the passenger's side slipped back into the truck. The shooter in the cargo bed crouched back down again. Kevin made his decision before the pick-up got rolling again. Like Molly said, he hadn't signed up on the force to let bad guys go.

He ran forward, having somewhat more of a plan than he had clothing, but that didn't mean much. He hoped dearly that Attila would have the sense to find his way home again. Molly would take good care of him if Kevin didn't make it out of this alive, which seemed entirely likely.

Potholes in the road prevented the driver from flooring the accelerator in their escape. Kevin managed to catch hold of the tailgate with his left hand and put his right foot up onto the bumper before the pick-up left his block.

The shooter in the cargo bed spotted him immediately. His eyes nearly bugged out of his head as he leveled his AK at Kevin and pulled the trigger, but he'd already spent all his ammunition shooting up the townhouse. The gun denied his wishes with a loud "click."

Kevin nearly slipped off the bumper. His left foot dragged on the pavement for only a split second, but that was enough to cut into his skin and leave him bleeding. Kevin threw his hurt foot over the tailgate and then launched himself the rest of the way in, coming down on the shooter with a resounding right cross to the face. The man fell back against the passenger window.

Suddenly panicked at things not going according to plan, the driver slammed down on the accelerator and turned out onto Aurora Avenue.

Satisfied that the unreasonably loud noises had passed, Attila emerged from his hiding spot to look around. The street no longer held any appeal for him. He padded back up to the townhouse, finding the door wide open and debris everywhere. Attila trotted inside, sniffed around, and moved off to the kitchen, picking his way through fallen wood and glass.

On the floor of the kitchen, amid shattered bowls and plates, was the bag of salmon treats that Kevin normally kept in an overhead cabinet out of the cat's reach. Attila recognized the scent immediately and tore into the bag.

Later, Attila found the drapes over the sliding glass door to the back porch had fallen after the curtain rod had been struck by a bullet. With the glass no longer obstructed, Attila found a nice, warm patch of sunlight on the living room carpet he could lounge in. He padded around, sniffing the air again. The open front door and all the shattered windows made for a pleasant cross-breeze. Attila curled up for a nap.

All in all, Attila had a pretty nice afternoon.

———

"This whole street used to be hookers and dealers all up one side and down the other," Sergeant Claudia Esposito explained to the rookie beside her. "All the way from Shoreline down to the north side of the bridge into Queen Anne. The Woodland Park zone gave you a break from it, but as soon as you were out of that area, bam. More mess, more skeezy people. This area has come a long way."

Officer Angela Weir gave a nod, listening to her attentively. She was a little intimidated by the sergeant. Claudia was confident, tough and businesslike. The two had met before, with Claudia serving as one of Angela's unarmed combat instructors at the academy. The sergeant was also pretty, with the sort of smooth golden skin that women would kill for, and her boyish haircut didn't make her look masculine.

"Yeah, I remember from when I was in college," Angela said. "Growing up in Kent, I didn't come out here a lot, but the couple times I did and wound up on this road, I thought it looked pretty sketchy."

"It's a good word for it. Still not the greatest in the city, but—" Claudia suddenly held up her hand and slowed the car. The sustained roll of popping noises came straight through the patrol car's open windows. Then it stopped.

"Think that was off to the right up here," suggested Angela, gesturing out her window.

Claudia frowned. "We better go check that out," she said, pulling off to the far right lane and making ready to turn. "This close to the Fourth, we get a lot of kids playing with all the stuff they buy off the reservations, but—woah!"

The blue pick-up truck swerved out into traffic right in front of them. They saw two people in the cargo bed. One wore denim. The other was shirtless. Both flailed and grabbed hold of the truck's sides for dear life. Claudia hit the accelerator and went into pursuit. "You know how to call it in?" she asked urgently.

"Yeah," Angela nodded, reaching for the radio. "Yeah, I can. I just—"

Words failed her. She looked on as the two men in the pick-up both rose to their feet, readying punches for one another. The guy in the denim jacket and ski mask threw a right hook, only to have it blocked and countered by the... naked guy?

Naked. Stark, raving naked. Fit, trim, focused on his fight, and turned out to give both women a prime frontal view as he fended off his opponent.

"Okay," Angela faltered, "maybe I don't know how to call that in."

"Holy shit," burst Claudia, "is that motherfucker Murray?"

———

Block. Backfist. Jab. Balance balance wwwwooooah!

Preferring not to fall out of the truck, Kevin flopped onto his back in the cargo bed. His opponent did likewise, slumping once more into the corner closest to the passenger cab. The guy reached into his jacket for something. Kevin didn't want him to have it, whatever it was, so he launched out his foot in a horizontal stomp that plunged into the guy's belly.

Kevin heaved himself at his opponent, throwing his elbow at the guy's head. He caught nothing but metal for it and winced at the pain. They rolled around together, wrestling for a dominant position.

"You're under arrest!" Kevin yelled.

"Get offa me you naked fuck!" the other retorted.

The shooter had a greater advantage in weight and size, but he wasn't quick to adapt to the shifting environment. Kevin slipped out of his grasp, wound up crouching over him and grabbed just enough of the ski mask to pull it out of joint, covering the man's eyes. That made it easier to follow up with a crushing punch to the face.

They heard sirens. Kevin glanced back to see the cop car following them. On the one hand, it was a relief, and on the other he doubted it would do much of anything for him. The guy in the cargo bed was still trying to kill him.

So were his buddies. Kevin heard the passenger cab's back window slide open, and looked just in time to see the passenger pointing a gun out at him. He slapped it away, heard it go off, and then grabbed for the hand holding it and yanked it out. Kevin twisted the gun down hard, breaking the passenger's finger when it didn't come out of the trigger guard fast enough.

"Carl," yelled the driver, "kill that fuck!"

"I can't!" shouted the passenger in obvious pain, "he grabbed my fucking—oww!"

Kevin wrenched the gun free from Carl's hand. He tried to turn it around in his own grasp, burned his hand on the hot barrel and heard Carl shout, "John, take him out!"

He almost had the gun at the ready, but the two seconds he needed to accomplish it were two seconds too many. With his ski mask on straight again, John all but tackled him against the passenger cab. Again, they wound up struggling for a better position.

The pick-up kept swerving. More sirens came on. None of it helped Kevin at all.

Then the driver hit the brakes to avoid trouble. Kevin and John were both pressed up against the passenger cab by their momentum. The fallen pistol flew up beside them as well, clattering around on the cargo bed right by Kevin. John reached for it, leaving himself open.

Kevin drove his bruised elbow up into John's throat, holding onto the passenger cab with his other hand. He pulled back and did it again as John tried to recover, shoved him back, then finally had room to throw an uppercut right into the bigger man's jaw. John lurched back. Kevin kicked hard.

The pick-up sped on while John tumbled over its right side and out onto the street with the gun. The police cruiser closest behind swerved around John and maintained pursuit. The one behind it stopped for the fallen man.

"Dick," shrieked the passenger, "shoot him!"

"I can't!" yelled the man behind the wheel. "I'm driving! Shoot him yourself!"

Kevin held onto the passenger cab for dear life as the driver swerved ever harder in a vain attempt to shake him. "Pull the fuck over!" Kevin bellowed into the cab in the most intimidating voice he could muster.

"Fuck you, freak!" shouted the driver.

The passenger said nothing. He had his AK loaded up again and, though he had to manage it left handed, tilted it up over his left shoulder and tried to shoot it out the back window.

Kevin flattened himself against the floor of the cargo bed with a completely undignified yelp, then realized there were smarter ways to handle this. He reached up, grabbed the wooden handgrip just behind the barrel and yanked hard. It flew free from its owner's hand. Carl gave another yelp and promptly slammed the rear window shut again.

Kevin got his hand into the trigger, angled the barrel upward at the rear window and fired, smashing out much of the glass. The short burst scared the hell out of the truck's occupants, but Kevin had no intention of shooting the drivers of a moving vehicle on a busy street. He reversed his hold on the weapon and shoved it into the cab with all the force he could muster.

Carl's head bounced from the butt of the AK into the dashboard and then back up again. Kevin didn't wait to assess; he slammed Carl in the head a second time. Carl swooned and doubled over in his seat.

Down to one opponent now, Kevin decided to try again. "Seattle Police!" he shouted.

"Where's your badge!?" Dick countered.

"Stop the fucking truck now!"

"What're you gonna do? Shoot me?"

Kevin held on through further violent swerves, fuming with rage as he tried to think of something to do. He looked over his shoulder at the pursuing patrol car and recognized Claudia and the new gal, Angela, through the windshield. A motorcycle cop was up near them, too. Further in the distance was a state patrol unit. They were on into the green area of Aurora, headed south between the zoo and Woodland Park. Traffic was much lighter here. There weren't even any oncoming cars; the guys working the speed trap must've blocked off Aurora northbound at the bridge already. That was pretty quick.

He looked into the passenger cab again. Shooting the guy didn't seem to be much of an option, but he had one other idea. He smashed out the remaining bits of framing in the center of the rear window with the rifle and brushed away the last of the glass. It was an incomplete job, but two seconds was about all he could spare on it.

With his left arm low to protect his crotch, Kevin threw himself into the passenger cab. He flopped into the small seat space between the driver and the unconscious passenger, sucked up the cutting and scraping of the remaining shards of the cab's rear window and the battering arm of the driver to get his free hand on the parking brake.

The resultant squealing lurch nearly caused the truck to overturn. Kevin fell further in, smashing his head into the truck's stereo and floundering face-down in the cab. The pick-up swerved and turned, coming to a halt at an angle that straddled two lanes.

Bailing out of the truck, Dick pulled out the pistol tucked his belt. He backed away, leveling his gun at the naked freak who'd fucked up everything.

Kevin looked up to see the weapon. He had just enough time to wish he'd come up with a better plan before he heard the gunfire.

The hail of bullets fired from two pistols back behind the pick-up truck tore through Dick. Round after round tore holes in his flesh after another until he was a bloody mess on the pavement.

Sergeant Esposito and Officer Weir approached with their pistols still drawn and still smoking. Claudia had her weapon pointed at the truck. Weir kept hers trained on the fallen man beside it. They found Kevin hanging upside down in the passenger cab, one foot still dangling out the back window. An unconscious man in a ski-mask sat slumped forward in the passenger seat.

"Murray, you okay?" Esposito demanded.

"Owwww," Kevin moaned. His body was covered in grime and blood from a hundred small scrapes and a few not-at-all-minor cuts. His hands covered his groin. "Can you find me some pants?"

———

Two full days of complete nudity was, Molly decided, one of her best ideas ever. She couldn't remember ever having so much sex with Onyx, apart from their first few days of serious romance... and the first couple weeks of living together... and, well, assorted pagan holidays. Still, the constant undercurrent of intimacy and availability couldn't be beat.

Onyx had challenged Molly—practically demanded even—to take what she'd dished out to her uncle. That Molly would doubtlessly have a better time of it, what with a live-in lover and all, wasn't the point, Onyx claimed. She had to make up for this. Perform penance. Balance the scales. Whatever.

Ultimately, the two were reminded of how crazy they were for one another. They saw one another naked frequently enough, but that was casual nudity and this was an actual *event*. The context changed everything. Molly couldn't let Onyx's pouty ass or her sweet, taunting breasts go by without wanting to put her mouth on them. Onyx was similarly mesmerized by Molly's legs, by her chest, and her knowing grins.

The two lay in bed together, on their sides, heads buried between one another's legs in a long, aimless bout of lovemaking. Molly and Onyx reveled in the give and take. When one whimpered and laid her head against her lover's thigh, weakly succumbing to the other's kiss, there was no sense of unfairness or of anyone not holding up their end of things. There was only further indulgence.

It was Molly's turn to enjoy this time, giving up in the struggle and admitting that Onyx had gotten the better of her. "I'm not... wow," Molly sighed. "I don't know when I'll be ready to retaliate."

"Poor baby," Onyx smiled. She pulled away from Molly, heedless of Molly's small whimper of complaint as she shifted around. The kisses she trailed along Molly's belly and up towards her breasts more than made up for it.

"So in love with you," Molly droned, "you don't even know."

Then the phone went off. It was neither Molly's nor Onyx's, but the one sitting on the nightstand beside the bed with the unfamiliar ringtone.

"I should get that," groaned Molly.

Onyx took her mouth off of Molly's breast long enough to say, "So get it."

Molly grumbled. She reached for the phone, picked it up and hit the answer button. "Kevin Murray's phone," she said, "but this is not Kevin Murray."

"Ah, yeah, can I speak with Officer Murray, please?"

Molly let one hand fall down onto the long dark locks of the hot girl making out with her breasts. They shared a wink. "He can't come to the phone right now, can I take a message?"

"Yeah, this is just Joel Chang from the Times, and I wanted to get Officer Murray's comment on the pursuit and shooting he was in a few hours ago? And the attack on his home? I'm told he's been released from the hospital already, is that correct?"

Molly's eyes snapped wide open. "What!?"

———

The police tape did nothing to deter the two women, nor did the damage to the front of the townhouse. All the cops who'd been on the scene marking down every little thing had taken off before darkness fell. Molly and Onyx picked their way through the barriers of yellow tape and fallen debris to the closed, bullet-ridden door.

"Not what I had in mind when I cast that good luck charm," Onyx thought aloud.

"Swear to God," Molly murmured, "if anything happened to him or to Attila I'll never forgive myself."

"Molly, it's not your fault psychos with guns did psycho stuff," Onyx said. "The reporter guy said Kevin's out of the hospital already. I'm sure he's fine."

"Still," Molly said, finding the key to Kevin's apartment on her chain, "I need to know everything's okay."

"You really think he'd even be here?" Onyx asked.

"Well, I don't want to try to deal with that stupid desk jockey answering the phone for the non-emergency numbers again," Molly grumbled. "He was no help at all and—Attila!"

The cat wandered up to her as if nothing was wrong or out of place. He leapt up into her arms. Molly held him tight. "Oh, kitty, I was so worried!"

A light shone on them from up the stairs. Molly and Onyx looked up into it out of reflex, then found themselves squinting at the bright source. "Who are you?" asked a deep but feminine voice.

"I'm Molly Murray," came the answer. "My uncle lives here. Who are you?"

"Oh. Hah!" the woman laughed. She pointed her flashlight to the ceiling. The couple at the entrance saw her short, dark hair, her bare shoulder, and the gun in her other hand, now pointed safely at the floor. "Are you two the ones who stole all of Murray's clothes?"

"Who are you?" Molly blinked.

"Sorry, I'm Claudia. I work with Kevin. Kind of. Not in the same precinct. Anyway, he's cool. He's up here. But he's in the bathtub right now. Oh, hey, did you bring Kevin's clothes back?"

"...yeah?" Onyx ventured. "They're still in the car." In truth, they had never been offloaded to begin with.

Claudia paused, looked over her shoulder, then back down at them and hissed, "Can you bring 'em back tomorrow, maybe? Or Sunday? We're kind of both on two days' leave now 'cause of what went down today with work. Mandatory psych thing."

"I..." Molly faltered. "I think we can do that."

"Awesome. I'll tell him you came by and I sent you away. It'll drive him nuts. Thanks!" With that, she slipped back into the bedroom and turned the flashlight off. The townhouse was completely dark again.

Onyx stared up the steps into the shadows. "What was that?" she asked.

Attila meowed. Molly scratched his head. "Probably another crazy woman. Kitty says they all are."

Onyx gave him a few pets for good measure. "Guess we should go, then?"

"Yeah," Molly huffed. "I do not wanna hear the sound of whatever's goin' on upstairs."

HALLOWEEN FOR LIFE

The shower wasn't enough. He should have slept more last night. He should have put Serena off. Most guys would think it crazy to turn such hot sex down for any reason, and Jack would generally be inclined to agree, but things had been like this for the last few nights.

Jack almost fell asleep while shaving in the bathroom mirror. He cut himself twice. He hardly even noticed the second cut until the blood dribbled down his thick wrist and marred his "Dirty Deeds Done Dirt Cheap" tattoo. Jack stared down at it with red, blurry eyes and wiped the blood away.

He kept shaving. He had to make this meeting. Even now, he hadn't decided what he would tell those assholes from the State Department. Maybe he'd tell them the truth. He already had immunity. But then again, maybe he'd decide, *fuck those guys, we didn't do anything wrong*. Lethal force was always part of the tool bag. Uncle Sam knew that when he hired Jack's company. Hell, once upon a time, the government approved.

The brats probably would've grown up to blow up some bus stop in Israel or something, anyway, he thought.

Fuck their investigation. His company was paid to do a job and they did it. They kept their client secure and safe— maybe pissing his pants, but safe. What more did they want?

Jack kept shaving away his blond stubble. His eyes drifted to the "Big Red 1" tattooed on his muscular left shoulder, leading his thoughts back to the Army and days when he'd seen the world in brighter colors. Once more, Jack reconsidered. He had immunity. People just wanted closure. The guys from State didn't make it personal. Maybe he should spill and let them close this whole case? He didn't owe anything more to his former employers.

They couldn't get him on shooting the Arabs. Couldn't get any of his fellow contractors. Could they get him on anything else? Maybe he should talk?

He was tired. Really tired, though in a good way. He certainly couldn't complain.

Finished with shaving, Jack washed his face one more time and stepped out into his bedroom wearing only a towel, his battle scars and his tattoos. His suit was laid out on the bed.

So was Serena.

"Baby, do you have to go yet?" she asked. The black bed sheet only covered her crotch and the moving hand between her slender, inviting legs. Jack's eyes drifted up to her full, enticing breasts and the brown hair that cascaded down her naked shoulders. Serena grinned like she already knew she would win this round.

"Christ, there's something wrong with you," Jack huffed, shaking his head. He looked down at his suit. Everything was there except his boxers. Where were his boxers?

"Yeah, there's something wrong with me," replied Serena in a voice that could make a porn star blush. "It's this emptiness inside. Only you can fill it, lover."

Once again, Jack went to war, only this time it was entirely internal. Turning her down seemed insane. It should also be reasonable at this point. Hadn't they fucked all night already? He had no idea when they'd finally stopped, but he sure didn't get nearly enough sleep. She clearly liked his money and his luxury apartment. She knew how he made his money. He'd already explained to her how important this meeting was in ensuring he could make more.

He looked her up and down again: the legs, that sweet spot between them, those tits, those eyes. She felt so good. Making her come felt so good.

"You don't wanna leave me," the beauty smiled. She lifted one leg and pointed with her toes at the tent formed in the towel around his waist. She could get him up like nobody else he'd ever been with. It was a talent. Like magic.

Now that he was up and ready, and wasting it seemed foolish. "Serena, I gotta go do this," Jack reminded her, trying to be assertive. She liked it when he was assertive. Liked it when he pulled her hair. Made her moan. All that… *Wait. No. Stop thinking that shit,* he told himself. "I don't show up to this meeting, they'll subpoena my ass."

"So let 'em," Serena pouted. "Won't change what you have to say. Or not say. Fuck 'em, right?" Her lopsided grin returned. "Or better yet, fuck me."

He took a deep breath. She knew all too well how he loved it when she talked dirty. "When I get back."

"C'mon, baby." She beckoned with one hand while the other continued to toy with her flesh under the sheet. "You don't even need to warm me up." Her voice dropped and her words slowed enticingly. "We can be quick. Just for fun. You can fuck me, and when you're at your meeting with all those assholes, you can think about how you're the only guy there who's gotten laid before lunch, or if any of them have someone like me waiting for them at home."

She knew how to make him forget his fatigue. Hot sex, no lengthy foreplay, just get in and get off and bail until later. Serena pointed at his groin with her foot again. "Somebody looks ready to me," she taunted him. "If you don't, you know you'll be sorry."

Jack snatched up her foot to pull her toward him on the bed. "Guess that's a good point," he said. He took up her other leg, too, spreading them around his hips as his towel fell to the floor. The pleasure of penetration banished his concerns of fatigue. *God, she really is ready.*

"That's my man," she said, her lip curling with animal lust. "My big, strong killer. Take me, baby. Take—nnh! Yeah!" Serena grunted as thrust into her, taking every advantage of her readiness. She played her role to the hilt, displaying her naked beauty for him while he pushed into her again and again. Her breath grew audible, hitting notes of passion and surrender.

She knew how he liked it and how to keep him from going anywhere. She knew how to get him off, and how to keep his full attention, and how to wear him down.

Jack would never make his meeting, or any other, ever again.

———

"It's not that I enjoy falling down the stairs, you know. It's just that I like to see you nice young people. The fall gets me down to the ground floor faster."

Shannon allowed a brief smile at the old man's joke as the blood pressure pump on his arm came to full inflation. She slipped the diaphragm of her stethoscope under the inflated pad and listened. The ambulance leaned left and then right, zooming its way through streets that were just open enough to allow them constant movement. Its siren wailed.

"How can you even hear anything in all this racket?" asked the old man's grandson. He looked a bit cramped sitting beside the gurney. Today, Paul wore a simple polo shirt and slacks. He had come from the golf course. The last time Shannon's ambulance had to come for George, Paul came from work in a tailored suit.

"I've had lots of practice," Shannon answered. She wanted to tell him off, but this was obviously neither the time nor the place. All she could do now was swallow her irritation and ignore him as much as possible. She had given up on calling him 'sir' after the second encounter, where he complained about his father getting an ambulance from a "private EMT company" rather than "real paramedics" as if he understood the differences.

On one hand, Shannon appreciated the obvious concern Paul had for his aging grandfather. On the other, she didn't care for his tone when he spoke to her or her partner. He was too quick to act like he had some supervisory authority over her.

"I know what that's like," smiled George. "I used to drive a tank, back in the war. Everyone would ask how I could hear things over the engine, but I could. The lieutenant... he liked to say I could tell what might be wrong with the engine just by listening to it."

"You should listen to the staff at the home, Mr. Upton," Shannon told him. "No more walking near the stairs when you feel dizzy. You're sure that's all it is?"

"Yes," George nodded. "Only a little dizzy sometimes." He fell silent, looking at her for a long moment as she listened for his pulse, and watched the dial, and counted. "You have hair like his wife."

"Hm?"

"The lieutenant's wife. French girl he met in Paris. She was a librarian. Married her right in the middle of the war. Redhead, like you. Kept it tied back tight, like yours. Skinny, but it was Paris in the war and there wasn't a lot of food to go around for a good while there, you see. And she wasn't carting old men out of retirement homes or anything. But oh, she was so pretty..."

The ambulance rattled again. "How'd that work out for them?" Shannon asked. "The marriage?"

George didn't answer right away. Shannon noticed his eyes stopped tracking for a moment, but then he closed them again. "He died," George said. "Took a bullet for me outside the tank. Right at the end of the war." His voice diminished. "All this time I've had... all these years, because of him."

This wasn't right. Shannon watched him, listened, and quickly realized what bothered her.

"I'm sure he'd be glad to know how things turned out for you, grampa," assured Paul. "Don't worry about that now."

Shannon no longer paid attention to the conversation. She couldn't hear the thump of his pulse in the stethoscope anymore. *Oh no,* she thought. "George?" Shannon dropped the stethoscope. "George, are you okay? Can you hear me?"

"What's wrong?" asked Paul.

"I need that," she grunted, pointing at an equipment bag behind him. "Move. Ian!" she called to the driver. "Ian, he's gone cardiac! Right here in the wagon!"

"Aw, you're kidding me!" her driver snapped.

"What's that—wait, right now?" Paul demanded.

Shannon had the defibrillator out of the bag already. She suspected it wouldn't do any good. George was old and infirm. Shannon had done this job long enough to know a done deal when she saw one. Still, he was a fighter, and so was she. Shannon wouldn't give him up without a struggle.

"Ian, haul ass!"

———

Serena loved her life. She loved the glamour, the adulation, the intrigue, the wicked pleasures. She loved playing different roles for different partners, and loved to reveal her naughty, dirty girl core. She loved the raw power invested within her in all its facets. She absolutely loved to be lusted after.

She also loved the sex.

Her current partner, Jack, was a good one. He had a strong, animal lust and responded beautifully to the right strokes to his ego. Jack fucked her selfishly, which spoke to his nature. It worked out perfectly for Serena. She didn't mind his selfishness at all, and in fact did all she could to encourage it. To his credit, Jack also liked to get Serena off—mostly for the ego boost he derived from hearing and feeling her climax, but it still meant more pleasure for her.

His motivations mattered little to her. Her partner delivered in bed, and that meant everything.

Jack took her from behind, pulling back again and again with one hand on her hip and the other clutching a fistful of her hair. He didn't hurt her. He *couldn't* hurt her, not with all his considerable strength, but Jack didn't know that.

He had been back there for a long time, relentlessly pounding her in search of satisfaction. Serena made sure Jack knew she loved every minute of it. She didn't want him to quit. The longer this sort of thing took, the more satisfaction and happiness she received in the end.

His endurance had finally reached its limits, though. His thrusts slowed and his breath grew ragged. The only thing about him that refused to weaken was his cock, and he was too out of sorts to think critically about that, or about how many times he'd gotten off without a rest. He never stopped to consider how unnatural it was.

Yet he couldn't give up. Couldn't stop. She felt too good to stop, and she knew it. She had him fully enthralled. Serena felt his pace ease up, and smiled, and gave a small, taunting whine. "So close," she said. "Fuck, I'm so close."

Jack rallied. It wasn't much, but his hips crashed forward into her again, still slow but at least with more force. She knew how to keep this cycle going. He didn't want to get her off out of consideration for his partner so much as out of his own sense of pride. Serena gasped, "Yes! Oh yes more!" in time with his hips, until his body trembled to a final release.

It was every bit as good for her, too. She couldn't deny that—not honestly, anyway, and there was no need to lie. Serena's eyes rolled back and her voice rang out in moans of genuine pleasure.

He all but hung by that hand in her hair, using it to keep himself up. She could support him easily like that. She was far stronger than she looked.

"I gotta stop," he wheezed. Jack's eyes drifted around lazily. Were it not for the hand in her hair and the irresistible pleasure of remaining coupled with her, he'd have collapsed. "Baby, I gotta... I gotta stop..."

"No, Jack, no, ssshhh," Serena counseled. She rose upright on her knees, reluctantly disengaging from him to turn around and face him. "I'll take it from here, Jack," whispered Serena. "I'll take it from here. You just lie back."

With her partner settled onto the bed, Serena swung her leg over his body and straddled him in reverse, facing his feet rather than his face. She found his cock still ready for her, and brought it into herself with another whimper of pleasure. "Enjoy it, Jack," Serena said as she began to rock against him. "Enjoy me. Enjoy it while it lasts."

———

"They can't have asked us to stick around here for anything good," Ian muttered. He stood beside Shannon in the ER waiting room, taking up one small stretch of wall away from the patients, the victims and their various companions. The cell phone and paper Starbuck's cup in his hands kept him mostly distracted, but he could still spare enough of his attention to complain.

"We did everything we could," shrugged his ambulance partner. Shannon didn't look up from her clipboard full of paperwork at him as she spoke.

She had two years on him. They got along fine as co-workers, though never became particularly close. Like Shannon, Ian signed on with the company straight out of his

EMT certification tests. Like Shannon, he did a bang-up job with the company. Like Shannon, he came in with ambitions of working his way through college to a better-paying medical career.

Unlike Shannon, he hadn't actually gone back to school yet. He didn't carry the burden of increasing student debt compounded by their crappy pay. Still, he'd been with the company long enough to know when trouble brewed.

"How long do we wait?" he asked. He looked around the waiting room, noting that it was as busy as one would expect on a Monday morning. Adults waited. Children cried. Almost every seat was filled. None of the remaining empty chairs looked appealing, given who the immediate neighbors would be.

"Dispatch said to wait until we were released," Shannon muttered for the second time. "If they need us to cut loose, they'll let us know."

"Just sayin'. We could be out there doing stuff."

"Not sure there's that much for us to do if they're willing to leave us at the hospital's mercy." Shannon glanced down at the game of Tetris he played one-handed on his phone and considered checking her own, but felt that might look unprofessional. Bad enough that Ian did it in plain view. It seemed like a silly thing to worry about, though, given the wait they endured.

Then she became aware of the heavyset emergency room doctor as he walked up. Shannon thought he might be about her same age, though his tired eyes and the deep bend to his lips made him look older than he probably was. Too many hours on duty could do that to even a young doctor. "Are you the two who brought in George Upton?" he grumbled.

Shannon glanced at his nametag. "Yes, Dr. Woerner," she said. "How'd he turn out?"

"He's dead," Woerner replied.

Shannon grimaced, but nodded. She had done this for several years now. This sort of thing happened, especially with patients in their nineties. She had done all she could.

It still ruined her day. Every time.

"He hung on all this time?" Ian asked.

"No. I've been with other patients I couldn't leave waiting," snapped the doctor. "You're both perfectly healthy, so I figured you would wait. I know how to prioritize appropriately. It's more than I can say for either of you."

"I'm sorry?" Shannon blinked.

"You two want to tell me how you turned a simple slip-and-fall transport into a clusterfuck like this?"

"Wait, what?" Shannon worked to control her voice. "He had the cardiac in the wagon while I checked on him. Doctor, we know what we're doing. I'm a nationally-certified paramedic and—"

"Not for long," the doctor interrupted. "I've got my copy of the paperwork. You can explain this to your bosses before you're suspended, Ms. Abrams."

"Suspended for what?"

"*I* didn't lose that patient, Abrams." His finger came up at her chest. "*You* did." With that, the doctor stormed off.

"What—what the hell?" Ian burst when his jaw came off the floor. "Is he off his rocker or something? We did nothing wrong!"

"Off his rocker or suffering from having his head up his ass," Shannon concurred.

"I mean, did you do anything wrong?"

"No." She shook her head. It wasn't her first ambulance ride. She worked to resuscitate the patient the entire way to the hospital, going above and beyond anything expected of her by the book. She did nothing out of bounds for her certification level.

"Because that guy's gonna claim we fucked up!"

"He's gonna claim I fucked up," Shannon corrected. "All you did was drive the bus."

"Jesus. This is really shitty," grunted Ian. Shannon noted that his anger had suddenly diminished into mere annoyance. "Hey, I'm gonna go hit the bathroom and then we can get out of here, okay?"

"Sure." Shannon watched him leave and let out a sigh. It really would all come down on her head alone. The whole thing was baseless, of course; the doctor had no case. She hadn't seen the guy here before. He was probably new. Given his youth, she wondered if this was the first patient he'd lost. Yet she'd still wind up having to deal with it, and her supervisor wasn't exactly known for his backbone.

Glumly, Shannon waited for Ian to get back. Boredom got the better of her. She pulled her cell phone out of the pocket on her pant leg, turned it on and looked for messages.

She found a single text from Brad. Shannon opened it up, hoping for some sort of encouraging word from her boyfriend of over a year.

"I hope I'm not an asshole for breaking it to you like this," read the text, "but it's just not working out anymore. There's just no spark. I think we should both move on."

———

Serena's voice mingled with the weak sighs of her partner as they came together yet again. Her shapely ass ground against his hips while her hands busily worked the outer flesh of her sex, drawing out her orgasm well beyond his. Her body gleamed with sweat. Jack's grew ever paler.

"Oh, I knew you'd be a fun job, soldier boy," the beauty declared as the last spasms of climax subsided. She didn't let him go, nor did she take any time to rest. Instead, she rocked against him once more, still fucking him despite his breathless pleas.

"Can we stop a second?" Jack begged weakly. "Please. Gotta rest. Can't... can't do more."

"But it feels so good, doesn't it?" Serena smiled. She didn't need to look at him to know how he'd react. "You want it, don't you?"

"Yeah. Yes," he admitted. "Fuck yes. I just... I can't... I can't..."

"I can. Don't worry. I'll keep this party going until you're all finished off, Jack." Her grin became malicious. "You should've gone to your meeting."

"Wh… what?"

"I said you should've gone to your meeting. Maybe you could've confessed your crimes there. But if I was going to let you do that, I wouldn't be here in the first place."

"Hhhhuh?"

"Oh, c'mon, Jack. Big bad warrior like you. Guys like you should know trouble when they see it." She inhaled sharply, riding out electric sensations between her legs. "Should've seen it in me."

"No. Let go," he said through cracked lips and a dry throat. "Lemme go."

"I will, Jack. I'll let you go. Right to your eternal reward." The mere thought made her shake. "Oh, it's gonna be so good… for me. Maybe not for you. But you know that now, right? Can you feel it?"

Jack's eyes fluttered open again. Now he saw the broad, black wings, and the tail, and the reddish hue of her skin. It made her no less sensuous, and did nothing to diminish the pleasures of being sheathed within her, but Jack's heart beat faster.

"Oh fuck, baby, you've got at least another hour in you. I knew you'd be a stallion. Most of the guys I fuck aren't nearly this in shape, but you're a fighter. You're a champion. All those people you murdered…mmh! They knew it, too, didn't they? Before you died? Unh. I'm not… usually into… challenges… but oh, fuck, have you been worth it."

His weak, trembling hands reached for the nightstand.

"Aw, I took the gun out of the drawer while you were in the shower, Jack," Serena taunted. "Paranoid fool. Sleeping with a gun by the bed. But oh, fuck. Such a good cock." Her hands came between her legs to touch his shaft as she rocked back on it. "All the gun you need, right here."

Jack's fear pushed him to try again. The nightstand was empty. He reached back behind his head, hardly able to feel anything by touch while overwhelmed by the pleasure of Serena's flesh, but he had to try. His hands fumbled back behind the pillow for the other pistol on its holster hanging below the headboard.

He was about to come again. He was close. So close. For the first time since he'd met Serena, he managed to deny himself. His life was at stake.

Jack pointed the gun at her back. It shook in his trembling hand. Holding it up seemed all he could do. The final pull of the trigger was almost more than he could manage.

The bullet struck her at the base of her skull. Serena immediately flew off of him and landed face first against the dresser across from the bed. The pistol fell from Jack's weak hand. He tried to cough, but couldn't muster the energy. His eyes fluttered open once more. The danger was gone. He knew that much, at least. He could rest now. Rest.

Serena rose with rage burning in her eyes. Jack's eyes snapped open again before the flames erupted from her mouth, engulfing him and his bed. He had no energy left with which to scream as he died, taking years of violent sins with him.

Almost as soon as the last wisp of flame left her mouth, she regretted it. She'd acted out of pain and anger. It was reflex. Sloppy. Stupid. The fire spread quickly, igniting the wallpaper and the sheets. "Aw, shit," she cursed at herself.

Serena looked toward the door for an escape, then the window on the other side of the room—and saw the gleaming halo and white wings of a young-looking beauty in a simple white dress as she stepped in straight through the windowsill.

"Well, fuck me running," the angel scowled. "I *thought* I smelled skank in this neighborhood."

———

"Please don't call her that."

"No, seriously, he's gotta have some skank," Ian said. He drove along with one hand on the wheel and the other holding his burrito. "I mean if he's ready to dump you for her after dating you for a year and he does it over text? That means he's got somethin' he doesn't want to own up to in person. If you think there might be another woman, then there probably is."

"Okay, but if there is somebody else, you don't have to call her a skank," mumbled his partner. For the first time in memory, she had her phone out in the ambulance, busily keying in commands. "I don't even know who it might be. I don't know what's going on with them. And it's not like we had moved in together or anything."

"Seriously? Shannon, she stole your man! She's a skank!"

"Seriously, Ian. Stop it," said Shannon. "That's a shitty thing to say about anyone and I don't need to hear it. Brad chickening out on me is one thing. It doesn't make any sense

121

to be mad at her if she even exists when he's the one who's pulling all this shit. She didn't do wrong by me in any way that I know about. She might not even know he had a steady girlfriend, or he might have lied about me and made her think dumping me was healthy for him. So leave her out of it, okay?

"Nobody 'steals' anyone," she continued. "He's an adult. He makes his own decisions. If he's not interested enough to stay with me, then I don't want him."

"Fine," Ian shrugged. "Jeez. Sorry."

He drove on in sullen silence. She knew he was waiting for an apology for her snapping at him. It wasn't forthcoming. Shannon could be firm and loud in an emergency, but she rarely rebuked him or anyone else with the company. She was always shy at parties. Quiet. Not withdrawn, but certainly introverted. A rebuke like that only came out when someone struck a nerve.

She hadn't even let anyone know she had a boyfriend until the Christmas party last year. Now she had lost him, and felt more annoyed than heartbroken. She realized the heartache would come later. For the moment, her biggest problem was the guy looking over her shoulder as she tapped at her phone. "Changin' your relationship status on your profile, huh?"

"No," answered Shannon. "I never post that kind of stuff. I'm tempted to close the whole stupid account except for all my family out of state."

"So what are you doing?"

"I'm trying to figure out how to make it stop sending me updates when people send me something or tag me."

"Why's that?"

"Because he changed his status and people are bugging me about what's wrong."

"Seriously? He did that already? Shannon, this fuckin' guy—"

"Is out of my life now, okay?" Shannon sighed. "Let it go. I'm better off without him. I'll find somebody new sooner or later." She looked out the window, wishing she could step right out the door and out of this conversation.

"Well, you're a pretty gal, right? I mean I don't want to get awkward, but you are," Ian pointed out. "I bet you get asked out a lot, right?"

"No."

"Really?"

"I think I project it or something, but…" Shannon let out a sigh. "I *hate* dating."

———

Serena hated being thrown through drywall.

She crashed through the plaster and flimsy wood in a mess of dust and splinters and continued straight through the coffee table in the living room, too. The naked succubus flopped to a stop at the foot of the entertainment center.

"Oh, you stupid demon *asshat*," ranted the angel in the bedroom. Through the hole in the wall, Serena saw the angel swiftly pulled the burning bed sheets and pillows together into a bundle. Jack's lifeless, charred head and shoulders flopped up into view for a heartbeat as the angel gathered him up with the rest.

"What did I say? What did I fucking say to the last two fuckers I sent back to Hell with their heads shoved up their asses?" She moved out of view, presumably heading for the window to throw the bundle outside where the flames would provide less danger to the building. The wall still burned, but the angel clearly meant to remove what fuel she could before dealing with that.

Serena shook herself. She ached all over, but it would take more than this to put her down for good. That angel could do it, though. She knew exactly who she faced. In the last few weeks, every demon in Seattle and far beyond it had heard of Rachel.

She hated feeling afraid, but she felt it now. Going toe to toe with an angel of such power was suicide. Unfortunately, Serena knew full well that she'd never get away if she simply turned and ran. She needed much more of a head start than she would get out of the distraction made by a simple apartment fire.

The succubus dove for a small closet facing the living room. Hidden behind hanging coats and suits stood a tall, locked box of some of Jack's favorite things. The lock on the metal box couldn't keep Serena out. Sharp talons grew from her fingertips to provide all the cutting power she needed.

"I said, 'No more of you fucking dingleberries in my city!' That's what I told 'em to tell all of you!" Rachel continued to rant as she came back into view. She had curtains in her hands now, using them to beat at the flames still growing across the bedroom wall. "Other people live in this building, you stupid bitch! How the fuck am I supposed to put this out? Piss on it? I don't have that kind of plumbing!"

She snapped the curtains at the wall again. "You still out there?" Rachel asked. The angel looked over her shoulder. "I haven't forgotten about y—"

Serena pitched the grenade through the hole like a shot putter. Her timing was perfect, as was her aim. Jack was not remotely the first dangerous man she'd slept with. She'd learned all sorts of useful things from her lovers over the centuries.

The grenade exploded in mid-air less than a foot from Rachel's back. Smoke obscured Serena's view, but the succubus didn't waste time assessing the damage. She pulled the automatic shotgun from its case, hidden behind more hanging clothes.

Clothing. She would need clothing, too. A succubus had great powers of illusion, but power was finite. Having a little to work with would make things easier. Even a coat would do. With the Saiga shotgun locked and loaded, Serena kept the weapon trained in Rachel's direction while she grabbed a long black trench coat off of a hanger.

In the bedroom Rachel coughed as she got to her hands and knees. Her head felt like it had been used as the ringer for a cathedral bell, and for that matter so did the rest of her body. She recovered quickly, but even she wasn't invulnerable.

Rachel blinked away her disorientation. At least the blast had blown out most of the flames.

She couldn't have this here. People lived in this building. Protecting them took priority. Bad enough that the succubus had started a fire. Rachel hadn't expected her to escalate from that to explosives. She got off her knees just in time for the second grenade to land at her feet.

"Really?" she grumbled before the grenade blew. It lifted her with enough force to bang her up against the ceiling. Gravity immediately brought her crashing through the smoldering remains of the bed.

"Fucking knock that shit off!" raged the angel. She briefly reverted to the natural intangibility of the angels, rushing up through the wreckage of furniture and going straight through the wall to launch herself at her opponent. She couldn't remain intangible and land a blow, though, and her foe knew it. As soon as she came through the ruined wall, the shotgun blasts erupted at point blank range.

Rachel screamed more in anger than pain, though she felt plenty of that, too. A mortal body would have been shredded; hers would be severely bruised when this was over. Still she came on, bringing a furious left hook into Serena's side. The punch took the succubus off her feet and sent her flying over the bar separating the apartment's living room and kitchen.

She stormed after her opponent. Serena's mouth let loose another storm of fire the instant Rachel came into view. Every tongue of flame that didn't strike Rachel ignited something beside or beyond her: the countertop, the wall, the carpet. Rachel staggered back under the assault. The Saiga pounded her again with more shots, driving her back another few steps farther.

Serena held down the trigger. She saw blood and smelled burnt flesh. Even angels had limits. Perhaps, Serena dared to consider, she might get out of here in one piece after all. She rushed forward, throwing everything she had into a brutal kick to Rachel's midsection. The angel tumbled back onto the floor, still coughing and still smoldering.

The last two rounds burst from the Saiga, its barrel within arm's reach of its target on the floor, and then Serena was out the door.

———

"Fuckin' cop. I know that guy. He gave me a ticket last week."

The police car rolled down Broadway Avenue in the opposite direction. Shannon looked at it in the mirror more out of reflex than rational thought. She had the shotgun seat, her clipboard in her hand so she could keep up with the larger-than-normal load of paperwork after their trip to the ER. It was silly to look in the mirror. How could she even see the guy's face? "So how fast were you going?"

"Not the point," Ian grumbled. He drove on, the bitter frown on his face unchanged since they left the hospital.

"Mm-hm." Despite the continual downer of a day, Shannon managed a smirk at his answer.

"No, seriously," he countered. "I'm just sayin'. I told him I was an EMT and everything. Still wrote me up. Fucker."

"No respect, I guess," his partner shrugged. "God, what a day."

"Yeah, it's pretty shitty. You know Frank's bound to re-shuffle the schedule so we aren't working for the next few days, right? Just so he can say he doesn't have us on the street while there's a complaint pending?"

"It's a bullshit complaint, Ian," Shannon replied. "The nurses all said that guy's in trouble with the hospital for his own fuck-ups and wants to shift blame for this somewhere else. Seattle Fire thought it wasn't a life-threatening call, otherwise they wouldn't have given him to us for transport in the first place, so we're covered there. And we did everything we were supposed to do and nothing we weren't supposed to. We did everything we could."

"That don't mean it won't turn into a thing."

She let out a long sigh. "Yeah."

"Sorry about your boyfriend."

"I'm over it." She paused. "He could've done it a couple weeks sooner, though. I wanted to go to a show on Halloween, but he got all hung up on going to some party with his douchebag friends. Now I'll never get tickets."

"For what?"

"Local bands playing downtown. Throbbing Ennui. Rockerdammerung. Cool guys."

Ian smirked, but said nothing...until he couldn't hold it in. "Seriously?"

Shannon smiled back without looking at him. "Kiss my ass." Then she blinked and leaned forward for a better view. "Hey, is that black smoke up there?" Shannon asked, pointing off to an apartment building a couple blocks ahead off of Broadway.

"What, that building there?"

Then they saw the windows burst as an explosion went off inside the corner apartment. Shannon grabbed for the radio. "Go, go!"

———

She heard sirens as soon as she made it to the rooftop. Smoke from the fire downstairs billowed up around the corner of the apartment building. The sun wouldn't set for hours. All in all, it made for more eyes looking her way than she would've liked, but Serena could escape from mortal vision fairly easily. Angels were another matter. That required serious effort and drained her of power she would need before she reached safety. Evasion was more practical.

The natural thing to do would have been to run out with all of the mortals fleeing the building to the streets below. She could enlist some altruistic fool in her escape or simply blend in with the crowd. The rooftop was closer, though, and she didn't want to compound her problems by letting some random resident's guardian angel spot her and join in the fray.

The rooftop also allowed her a brief use of her wings rather than her feet. It was easy to forget that the succubae had wings; half the time they were concealed, anyway, and even apart from that, the demons rarely flew. Today, however, she was grateful for this much faster option.

She picked a direction, spread her wings, and took to the air. She made it all of six feet up.

The hand that grabbed her ankle exerted enough force to nearly break it. Serena yelped as she was flung back down onto the roof. Rachel immediately followed up with an angry fist that drove into Serena's stomach. Reflexively, the succubus jerked half-upright, bringing her face right into the angel's elbow.

Rachel released Serena's leg, jerked her to her feet by her wrist, and held on tight as she unloaded punches and kicks on the succubus. In a matter of seconds, the fight had entirely turned. Regardless of Rachel's injuries and flagging strength, she had the upper hand and wouldn't lose it now. The fact that the succubus held it together even this long spoke to her high rank in whatever demon lord's court she served.

By the time Rachel let go, Serena was punch-drunk and swaying on her feet. The angel wound up for an uppercut and let it fly, crying out, "Shoryuuuken!"

Then she opened her eyes and saw the unconscious succubus fly in an arc off the roof and down onto the street below.

"Aw, shit."

———

Amazingly, the street was fairly clear when Shannon and Ian came around the corner. Their siren wailed, their horn honked, and their lights flashed, and for once everyone seemed to know what that meant and got the hell out of the way. Their ambulance was the first response vehicle to arrive.

Ian and Shannon looked quickly for someplace to park where they wouldn't block any fire trucks. Consequently, both of them only saw the woman in the trench coat fall from above and land in front of them out of the corner of their eye. No one could reasonably hold Ian responsible for hitting her with the ambulance, but he let out a guilty shriek just the same.

"Take care of the wagon!" Shannon said, jumping out of the ambulance without missing a beat. She rushed over to the fallen woman, making sure to look in every direction and assess the situation. Shannon couldn't really see how the victim had gotten there—nobody could jump from one of the rooftops all the way out to here in the middle of the street— but at least it didn't look like any other women were falling from the windows.

She looked about Shannon's age. Fit. Naked under her trenchcoat. Battered and bloodied, but not lethally so to outward appearances. She smelled of smoke. A big, ugly gun lay beside her. Shannon slipped her gloves on without even thinking about it as she looked over her patient. The woman was already on her back, and thus in a good position to receive care. "Can you hear me?" Shannon asked. She took up her wrist and felt for a pulse. "I'm a paramedic. I'm here to help you. Can you hear me?"

She didn't answer. Shannon felt sure she felt a weak pulse. Nothing indicated she was breathing, though; no chest movement, no sensation against Shannon's ear as leaned over the victim's mouth.

Naturally, she saw, Ian now had trouble with a crowd. He couldn't leave the wagon yet. Shannon drew a crowd, too. She continued her initial exam, but came to the same results. She reached for her CPR mask, but it had fallen out of her belt pouch when she pulled out her gloves. She didn't see it anywhere in reach.

"Hell with it," she muttered. Shannon put her mouth over the fallen woman's lips just as the thousand year-old succubus released her last breath.

Shannon's eyes went wide. Her throat burned while the rest of her body froze. She couldn't let go. Her limbs went weak. That burning sensation went all the way through her, soon chasing away her sudden, inexplicable chill.

Fear and panic would have set in had she not passed out on the spot.

———

She remembered castle walls. She remembered torches, hearth fires, and the laughter and conversation of a feast.

She remembered her dress. It was long and flowing and beautiful, fit for a noblewoman. A woman like herself.

She remembered the smell of beer and the sweat of men. She remembered the power she felt as she seduced them. She remembered feeling of men's flesh, holding her and caressing her and stroking her inside. More than one man, all at once. She remembered lustful laughter, and needful grunts, and satisfaction and hunger for more. She remembered being taken. She remembered liking it.

She remembered that it had been her idea. It had been her deliberate betrayal.

She remembered torches, hearth fires, and flames that roared far higher and hotter than anything seen by mortal man.

She remembered being reborn, and remembered that it hurt, but after that she knew there would be power and pleasure for centuries to come.

———

"Ms. Abrams? Ms. Abrams, can you hear me?"

"Huh? Yeah. Yeah." Her eyes fluttered open. Up above her were grey Seattle skies. Closer to her, but still above, was a handsome face. She liked his green eyes and his short, spiky blond hair. "Wow. You look good in that uniform," she said sleepily.

The officer blinked. Shannon watched him as she became aware of a lot of noise: people yelling, some crying, engines running, and apparently something big burning brightly and loudly not far away. "Uh. Okay. You with us now? What's your name?"

"Shannon. Call me Shannon," she said with a dreamy grin. "Ms. Abrams is my mom." Her smile faded as it all came back to her. "Oh, shit, is she—the woman who fell, is she okay? What happened?"

"Fire's already dealing with the building," explained the cop. He looked to be about thirty and in great shape.

Shannon couldn't stop looking at him. Fit without being bulky. She wanted to see more. Hell of a time to think about that, though. He continued, "Your partner took over with the woman in the street right when I got here and pretty soon… well, anyway, it's under control. I figured somebody should look after you besides random bystanders."

"Aw, that's sweet," Shannon replied. Again, the cop blinked. So did Shannon. "I mean—uh—I mean thanks. Ugh. I gotta get up."

"Woah, careful, slow down," the cop said, helping her sit up as she realized just how stable the world wasn't. "How are you feeling? Does anything hurt besides your head? You obviously took a concussion."

"No, I think I'm okay. I mean I'm a little confused, but I'm okay. I just…I started checking on that woman, and then it all went black. Is she okay?"

The cop frowned. "No, I'm sorry," he said. "She's gone."

"Oh, fuck," Shannon sighed, her hands covering her face. Her voice cracked with frustration. "Dammit, I was trying to help her and I don't know what happened!"

"Hey, hey, don't take it like that," said the cop. He put a hand on her shoulder. "Look, I checked her myself. The whole back of her head was broken in like five different places and you could tell just from looking at her that half her ribs were smashed. There was nothing you could've done."

"What? No, she wasn't that hurt! I didn't see anything like that!" Shannon's hands came away from her face. She looked toward the street to see a black plastic sheet covering

134

the fallen woman. Beyond it, Shannon saw that the apartment building was a full-on blaze. Firefighters worked to contain the mess, but nobody would be able to live there again once it was all over.

The cop relaxed a bit, understanding that Shannon's frustration wasn't to the point of tears or a breakdown. "You might not remember it that way now," he suggested, "but you could take a look at the body over there if you really want to. I don't recommend it. Seriously, she could've taken that fall in the emergency room parking lot and she still wouldn't have made it."

He helped her up when she moved to rise. "Ugh, I've gotta get back to work," Shannon said.

"No, you're good. Think we're all covered here. Plenty of paramedics already. You need to take it easy. Seriously," he reiterated when she tried to brush him off. Finally, he saw her absorb his words and nod. His tone softened. "Listen, did she have anything with her other than the gun?"

"What? No."

"It's just that nobody in this city should have a monster like that gun. If she had anything else and somebody in the crowd walked off with it before we got to you, it could be important."

"No, just… just the coat and the gun. Beside that, she was naked. Gorgeous." Shannon paused as soon as it came out of her mouth. Where did that come from? What would it matter?

He brought her to an ambulance—her own, embarrassingly enough. She accepted his help in sitting her down on the back bumper, though less out of need for assistance than appreciation for his attention. That wasn't normally her style… *but hell, he's cute and he seems really nice, right?*

"What's your name?" she asked.

"I'm Officer Murray."

She smiled up at him. "Does it say 'officer' on your driver's license?"

He grinned back at that. "Kevin," he replied. "My name's Kevin. Look, I'm gonna let your partner know you're okay, alright?"

"I'd appreciate that, thanks," Shannon nodded. She stepped on the urge to flirt more. She wasn't the flirty type at all. If anything, she was normally shy. This was also absolutely not the time or the place. She resolved to get her act together, and then immediately looked back up at him, unfastened the top button on her uniform shirt—just to cool off—and asked with that same girly, not-entirely-innocent smile, "Are you gonna come back?"

"I. Um. I dunno," he stammered. "Listen. Uh… I know this whole scene is crazy," he said, fishing a business card out of his shirt pocket, "but if you remember anything, you wanna give me a call? Anything at all."

"Sure," she said, accepting the card. "If I remember anything about anything." The gun. Right. Something about a gun. That was something a cop would care about, not flirty EMTs. *Stop thinking like you're out barhopping.* "Can I call you if I don't remember anything?"

"…sure?" he answered. He seemed to blush. Then he left, answering a call from someone else on the scene.

Shannon didn't know whether to squeal or slam her head into the ambulance. She'd never made a guy blush before, let alone a guy like him. She still felt out of sorts. Good, oddly enough, but a little confused. The whole situation around her was pretty crazy, too, she conceded. Maybe she was woozier than she thought? Maybe she had imagined all of the cop's promising reactions? Or maybe she read them completely wrong because she'd damaged her brain?

A young woman in a dirty white dress stepped in front of her. She was seriously pretty—and pretty serious. "You're Shannon Abrams," said the blonde.

"Yeah?"

"Your boyfriend just dumped you because he's an asshole," she went on. The blonde's eyes looked her over as if reading something or seeing a scene play out on a television. "He—wow, what a shitbag. Dumped you via text. Didn't have the balls to tell you the real reasons why. Wow."

"Huh? How do you know—"

The blonde shook her head. "You can't worry about that asshole now. He's just a speedbump in your life, Shannon. You've got more important things to deal with. Listen to me: *Don't fuck anyone* until I can talk to you again."

Shannon blinked. "What?"

"Look, for your own good and for theirs: don't fuck anyone. Don't kiss anyone, don't accept any hugs, don't even flirt. Keep your cell phone off. Just get off work, go home, and go to sleep. I'm busy and I can't explain right now. I'll catch up with you as soon as I can, but for the love of God, *don't fuck anyone*, okay?"

She walked around the ambulance. Shannon stood up to follow her, but saw only Ian rushing up to her in the blonde's place. The stranger had vanished.

Ian carried a gear bag, breathing heavily as if he'd been working at a good clip. "Hey, I saw you were up," he said. "How are you feeling? You okay?"

"Yeah, I think so," Shannon answered. "I'm fine now. I think. I'm a little out of it but I don't think I'm gonna pass out again. I feel like such a tool."

"Ah, don't freak out about it," Ian replied. "Shit happens. I mean you should get yourself checked out, but you've already had a hell of a day. Lots to stress about. Listen, they've got plenty of people on hand for the fire. I was told we're released as soon as you're ready to go, so let's just head back to the station, okay?"

He's looking at me differently, she realized. It was a subtle thing; something about the interest in his eyes and his posture and the deeper-than-normal tone of his voice. She felt no mutual spark. He wasn't her type, and after riding with him for the last six months she found a laundry list of her personal turn-offs in his habits and outlook. Working with him was fine; dating him never occurred to her. But she recognized now that there was something there for him, at least.

Ian stepped past her into the ambulance to stow the gear bag. He left Shannon sitting there on the bumper, reflecting on how hard it must be to wear a mask like that. *Must be hard to hide how you really feel all the time,* she thought. *Or to hide who you really are.*

———

It was a good night to live alone.

Freed from her job after entirely too much discussion with her supervisors and *their* supervisors about her day, Shannon all but staggered through the door to her apartment, locked it behind her, and threw the deadbolt. She leaned against the door, inhaling the lingering smells of last night's cooking and the cheap lavender air freshener plugged in down the hallway. She told herself to relax.

She was home now. She would be home for a few days. As Ian predicted, her work schedule had been rearranged, allegedly because of her fainting spell and not at all because of the complaint from the ER doctor. Not one of her bosses thought the complaint held any merit. Nobody blamed her for the death of the woman outside the fire. Nobody wanted to get careless about her passing out, either.

Shannon tugged off her jacket and let it fall to the floor. Her shirt joined it only a second later. Though normally neat and methodical with her clothing, today Shannon shed her uniform right there in the entryway and left it there.

She wanted to be naked. Shannon jerked at the laces of her boots to free herself from them, dumping the footwear on top of her uniform shirt and then tossing the socks as they came off, one toward the kitchen and another down the hall.

Her single-bedroom apartment usually stayed fairly clean. Now her belt went flying carelessly across the living room. Her undershirt fell across the stove, only a few feet away from the front door. She rounded the corner, went into the bathroom and promptly cranked the knob in her bathtub to fill it with hot water. She didn't bother balancing it out by turning the other knob for cold water.

Shannon unfastened her pants and slipped them off her hips, slowing now to touch her legs with her fingers all the way down. When she straightened back up, she found herself looking back in the mirror.

She'd never been fair to herself about her looks. All her life, she'd felt plain, no matter what anyone told her. Every rejection or unrequited crush was enough to convince her she was right. Now, she faced her reflection and asked, "When did you decide you weren't pretty?"

She had been pretty all along. She knew that now. Whether Brad got that or not she didn't know and could hardly bring herself to care. She was clearly better than he deserved. She had a brain. She had a steady job. It wasn't awesome as she'd once thought, and hadn't been for a couple of years now, but it was still a serious job with real responsibilities and she was damn good at it. Shannon was twenty-eight, sane, and stable despite her career frustrations. She'd been a good girlfriend: thoughtful, attentive, willing to give space. And yes, pretty, too, goddammit.

"Can't say much for the underwear, though," Shannon grumbled. She watched herself in the mirror as she pulled the sports bra over her head. Her hands came down to her chest to massage her skin, rubbing the red lines left behind by the edges of her bra.

All of that was normal. It always felt good to shed her bra after work. What wasn't quite normal was the amount of time she took in rubbing her chest, or the slow, sensual pleasure of it. Her breasts felt good. Very good. She'd never noticed it before. For the first time, Shannon felt a little bad about having to restrain her breasts in such an unflattering garment. They looked good. They felt even better.

Her hands lingered. Stress quickly melted away as she touched herself. She couldn't remember ever feeling this sensitive, but she didn't question it. Shannon cupped her breasts, bringing her fingers to her nipples and giving the slightest of caresses, and found herself letting out a deep sigh.

A grin spread across her face, half out of genuine arousal and half out of wry amusement. Like anyone, she sometimes took care of herself while alone. Yet she never liked the thought so much before now. Shannon glanced at the tub, seeing it fill with water hot enough to give off visible steam, and decided she deserved a little playtime. In fact, she deserved a lot.

She shed her panties—dismally plain things, she decided—and allowed one hand to linger between her legs while she slid the flow selector over to "shower."

Scalding hot water rained down from the detachable nozzle, kicking up droplets that partially jumped out onto the floor outside the tub. Shannon hardly cared. She slipped one leg inside, then another, loving the heat that enveloped her legs and sprayed across her body.

How are they so smooth? Shannon wondered absently. It had been several days since she last shaved, but now they felt as if she'd just waxed. Her hands slid up and down her legs, enjoying them almost as much as she enjoyed touching her own breasts, once again didn't question her new sensitivity.

Soaking wet now, Shannon finally slid the shower door closed to avoid a flood in her bathroom before pulling the nozzle from its mount. She ran it over her body, reveling in the heat without considering how it should burn rather than comfort. She brought it over her head. Down across her shoulders. Over her breasts, then under them, and finally down her belly to her center.

She was glad to be home from work. She was glad she didn't have to deal with Brad… and yet she felt a hunger that would best be sated by a man. Still, the shower would do nicely for now, which only seemed surer as she began to tease herself between the legs with the water flow.

The world and all her cares drifted away as the water began to do its work. Shannon lifted one leg up onto the side of the tub to allow better access. She leaned against the wall and sighed while she teased herself further. Arousal built. Heat and pressure applied in small circles quickly banished all of her cares.

Shannon let out a moan as she shook with pleasure. She wasn't normally this quick; more than once, she had run out of hot water before getting off, and that was without filling the tub with hot water beforehand. Today, she didn't feel rushed at all. Were it not for the finite limits of her hot water heater, she would gladly keep at this for quite a while.

Pleasure rose. Her tremors grew more intense. The water felt so good. *She* felt so good. A shuddering breath escaped her as the spasms began. Shannon moaned again, louder this time, shameless and joyful in its announcement of her climax. That, too, went on for longer than she expected. Her center throbbed with pleasure. The sound of the showerhead between her legs changed as she brought it in even closer to prolong her bliss.

Her orgasm abated, only to quickly build into another before she had even pulled the showerhead away. Shannon rode it out, surprised at her body but happy to enjoy it just the same. Water sprayed all around her as her hands shook. Nothing detracted from the sensations of climax.

Relieved and pleased, Shannon lazily assessed the depth of water in her small bathtub and found it adequate. She turned off the flow and left the showerhead hanging from its metal hose as she sank into the tub, immersing herself in water that would have burned any other woman.

Medical training about temperatures and burns faded into the back of her mind. This felt natural. It felt relaxing. She hadn't felt cold before, necessarily, but the heat soothed her. Naked and alone and for the moment satisfied, Shannon felt the last tensions of her day leave her body.

Her mind relaxed. Her worries died off.

When she found herself thinking about much of anything once more, she found her thoughts drifting toward naughty things. She lay in the tub with her legs spread and her knees bent, perfect for the taking if only she had someone here to take her. Or to kneel down and please her. That would be lovely, too. The tub offered no room for either option, of course, but her position was perfect for such fun.

She frowned a bit, reflecting on her bout of self-love. Normally she entertained definite fantasies when she took care of herself. They varied in style and in partners—not that she could ever have told touchy, insecure Brad about her fantasy lovers or what they did for her—but naughty daydreams were always part of the process. Yet tonight she had been turned on without any such thoughts at all. Her own reflection in the mirror had been enough. She had been turned on all by herself—or, more specifically, by her own image.

Her hand was on her breast again. Another drifted between her legs to tease her lips. It felt good... but this wouldn't do. She wanted more.

Shannon slid the shower door open again. Her pants remained in a pool on the bath mat in front of the sink. She grabbed the edge of the mat to pull them over, drying her hands on its fabric. A couple moments of fumbling around allowed her to grab her cell phone without having to leave the tub. Her cell phone and one other tiny, important item.

Her eyes rolled and she let out a sigh as the phone announced an endless stream of texts and voicemails. Friends and family called to offer their sympathies on her break-up.

Several messages asked which of Brad's limbs she would prefer broken. Shannon considered herself shy and socially timid—work was one thing, making friends was another—but even so, she had her support circles.

She didn't need them, though. She needed something different. Shannon checked the time and decided to go for broke. She dialed the number on the card.

"This is Kevin," a voice answered.

"I thought you'd answer with 'Officer Murray' or something," Shannon said, sinking back into the tub with a grin. She felt a bit surprised at how easily she could talk to this man. Normally she found herself tongue-tied around attractive strangers. Now the flirtation came naturally.

"Uh…I'm sorry? Who is this?"

"It's Shannon, from earlier today. The paramedic?"

"Oh, right. Hi. How are you feeling?"

Shannon's free hand wandered back between her legs. "Pretty good," she replied. "So are you at your desk? Or is this your personal phone?"

"I'm still on duty. This is the cell phone I use for work. I have to juggle. Long story," Kevin explained. "Most of it's stupid." Now that she listened for it, Shannon could hear the sound of traffic going by. "Normally I let calls go to voice mail, but I'm parked at the moment. What can I do for you?"

Shannon stomped on her initial bawdy response. That would not do at all. Nor was it even remotely in character for her. Suddenly unsure of what to say, Shannon's eyes darted around as she considered her response. She caught sight of the plastic jack o' lantern on her kitchen counter down the hall, full of candy that she would likely eat before any of the apartment building's children ever came trick-or-treating at her door.

It's almost Halloween, she thought, or close to it. *You can be whoever you want to be.*

He's a stranger. Just met him. Nothing to lose. Probably already attached anyway. Just go for it.

"I was hoping you could meet with me later tonight, if you're up for it. Maybe when you get off work?"

"...this isn't about the mysterious dead woman with the gun, is it?" he asked hesitantly. Shannon didn't hear any particular disapproval in his voice. "You're not asking to meet with me for some professional matter?"

"Does it have to be professional?"

"I dunno. Kind of inappropriate," he teased.

Shannon winced. "Right. God. Sorry, I know, I shouldn't—"

"It's a little before nine now. I'm off at about eleven unless something crazy happens. Probably be midnight at least before I can actually be anywhere. Gotta go home and feed my cat."

"Aw. That's sweet. Late tonight is good for me. I've got tomorrow off. But I wouldn't want your kitty to go hungry."

"Nah, he's a smart guy. If I don't get home and feed him, he'll find a way to get at the food on his own. Mostly I don't want to have to clean up after whatever mess he leaves behind. Anyway. Are you in the city? I live in the north end. Greenwood-ish."

"I'm pretty near Greenwood myself," Shannon smiled. "That'll make things a little easier. Where should we meet?"

"I'm good with anything. You have any favorites?"

———

She didn't normally do much barhopping. More to the point, when she did hit the bars, it was usually as the designated driver. Brad had a tendency to enjoy a bit too much, and for that matter so did the last couple of guys Shannon dated. When Kevin picked her "all-night greasy spoon" suggestion over the bars she knew, Shannon considered it a good sign.

She might have preferred to get him loosened up, but the fact that he would drop whatever plans he had for the night to come meet her hinted that she might not need the edge. Or maybe she should draw a different conclusion; she didn't know. This level of spontaneity was a bit new for her.

Shannon sat in a booth away from the window. The diner clung to its low-brow atmosphere through genuine effort, given that it pulled in enough business and enough cash to become something more if its owners really wanted. Crayon and pencil drawings done by years of customers on plain white paper placemats covered the walls. Some were cute; a few were very well done; most were just silly or witty. Shannon worked on her own picture as she waited with her mug of coffee.

"You look nice out of your uniform," said a voice. Kevin stood by her table, clad in black slacks and a nice but casual blue shirt under a leather jacket. He smirked as he added, "That's not an opening for you to ask if you look bad in your uniform, by the way."

Shannon laughed. Figuring she shouldn't overdo it, she'd gone with a simple black skirt and a lacy white top that allowed for a little cleavage. "You look good out of yours, too, Officer Murray," she grinned back. "Hi. Have a seat."

"Kept you waiting long?" he asked as he obliged.

"Nah. Not too hard to keep myself amused for a little bit in here."

"Yeah... yeah, I can kinda see that," Kevin said. His eyes strayed toward her crayon drawing. A black stick-figure woman with wings, a tail, small horns and a big smile waved a whip over several kneeling stick-figure men, all before a background of tall orange and red flames with bats flying overhead.

Shannon glanced down at the drawing and blushed fiercely. "Oh, this is just... just boredom," she said, and reached to crumple it up.

His hand stopped hers. "No, don't do that. It's good," he said. His hand felt nice. Strong. Warm.

"I don't normally draw a lot."

"Maybe you should. You've got talent."

"Hey, folks, anyone need coffee or anything to get you started?" asked the server, all of a hundred and thirty pounds covered in tattoos and piercings. He offered up a menu for Kevin.

"I could order, actually," he said with a questioning glance to Shannon. When she nodded, he said, "Apple pie a la mode? Just that and water. Thanks."

"Mm. Cherry for me, please. And a Coke," Shannon added. She smiled at Kevin as the waiter left. "Dessert was a good idea. I like to skip straight to the good stuff. So I'm not pulling you away from anything at home, am I? No Mrs. Murray?"

He shook his head. "Just the cat. I can make it up to him later. Never had a Mrs. Murray. Closest thing to that moved out a few months ago. Couple dates since then, but nothing serious."

"What happened there? She have trouble with your job? I know that's a common one for folks like us. Your type more so than mine."

"Nah, just a bag full of crazy. Should've known better. I think the cat tried to warn me, too, but it's not like he speaks English."

"You mean she was a bag full of crazy and you should've known better, or you're the bag and she should've known?" she smirked.

Kevin smiled. As she suspected, he appreciated teasing more than fawning. How she could read him so well, she didn't know, but there it was. He liked her. The more she spoke and the more he looked, the more he liked.

"I shouldn't rip on her. She had her reasons. I'm over it. What about you, though? All I know is your face and your job. How long have you been a paramedic?"

"Few years now. Technically my job title only says 'EMT,' because that lets the company get away with paying me less, but my certifications all say 'paramedic.' I keep hoping to move up to something better. It's turning into kind of a trap."

"You don't have to apologize for your job," he shrugged. "I think it's cool."

"I'm not apologizing. I used to think it was cool, too. It has its high points. I mean you know what it's like to feel like you've rescued someone, right? But after a while it just... it just became a job. I wanted to stay in school and pay for college. Obviously a lot of folks do the same thing, but that's just..." she trailed off. Something inside her said, *That's enough of that. Not the way to attract a man. Keep things positive.* Shannon shook her head and smiled. "Not really what I planned to talk about tonight, anyway."

The waiter came by with their drinks. "You had a plan for tonight?" Kevin asked.

Shannon put her pinky in her soda and swirled it around. "More or less," she admitted with a shrug. "I thought I'd call up this cute guy I met at work today and see what he was doing tonight. See if he's as good a guy as he seems, y'know? And then, if that all checked out, I figured I'd just... see if I couldn't wrap him around my finger." With her gaze locked on his, she pulled her pinky out of her glass and put it in her mouth.

His eyes shined with interest. She withdrew her finger as slowly as she'd put it in her mouth, giving it a gentle suck. To his credit, his jaw didn't fall open. Kevin grinned, appreciating the show but not taking it too seriously. Shannon suspected his interest was greater than he let on. He simply didn't want to seem like a lech.

Shannon wouldn't mind that right now. "Hey, I'm gonna go hit the bathroom for a moment." She slid out of the booth, standing and smiling at him before she turned. She felt his eyes on her backside, and on her stockings with the lace tops that didn't quite come up to the hem of her skirt. She knew he wouldn't take his eyes off of them until she was out of sight.

Others watched her walk, too, just as they had watched her enter the diner. Excitement welled up within her, but she kept a firm hold on it. She kept her cool. She had a mission here, and she meant to see it through.

Her confidence was quite the turn-on for both of them.

———

Kevin pushed her up against the wall beside the door to her apartment. He meant to wait until they were inside, but he just couldn't help himself. She grinned at his firm yet gentle treatment, and grinned further into his kiss. She'd grinned into it outside the diner, too, and beside her car parked on the street outside, and in the garage downstairs, and the elevator.

Shannon slid one leg up along the side of his, bending her knee so she could hook it around his hip. Her companion attacked her mouth without hesitation. She liked that, but she wanted more.

"You're being way too shy," she murmured when his lips moved from her mouth to her neck. His hands on her hips felt good. They'd feel better elsewhere.

"Wouldn't want to make a bad impression," he whispered, his cheek sliding up her neck so his lips could softly attack her earlobe.

"That's all settled. The interview is finished. Now's the practical exam."

"Don't I get study time?" His hands roamed up and down her sides. "Seems like there's a lot to cover."

"Nope. Test time. Better start getting naughtier or I don't open this do-oooohh," she moaned with delight as his hand came up under her skirt and his palm found the warmth between her legs. He skillfully teased her with the pressure and warmth of his palm, their skin separated only by her thin panties. She was surprised at how wet she felt. She knew he had to feel the dampness, too, but he didn't seem at all put off. A week ago—hell, a day ago—she'd have felt scandalized by her forward behavior. Now she couldn't see anything wrong with this at all. Her head rested on his shoulder as she enjoyed his touch. "That's better," she approved.

"You really want me to be naughty?"

"Yesss."

His hand relaxed enough to make her pout. She opened her eyes to find his taunting grin. "Open the door," he told her. Kevin didn't move away as she found her keys in her purse, nor as she unlocked her home. That made her happy. Something about feeling the touch of an aroused, attractive man while she did common things greatly appealed to her. Something about his increasingly open lust appealed to her even more.

"I don't normally do this," she admitted.

"Me neither. I'll cool it if you want," he offered, though he didn't move away. "Should back off? I don't want to make you uncomf—"

"I want you to do something to me that would shame your mother if she ever found out," she told him with a wicked grin. "You can go back to being sweet in the morning." His eyes sparkled. So did hers.

Shannon threw open the door. Kevin refused to remove his hand from under her skirt until they were inside. It made the next few steps a little awkward, but Shannon reveled in his touch. With the door safely shut and locked behind them, Kevin brought her over to the back of the big chair in her living room just a few steps away. She felt him unzip her skirt before he bent her over, hiking the skirt down and then her panties. He did it all with one hand. His other arm stayed wrapped around her shoulders from behind.

When his fingers came back to her wet flesh, Shannon let out another moan of delight. She trembled and gasped and moaned at his touch, loving his exploring fingers and his animal lust. Yet for all his physical power, Shannon had no doubt who called the shots here.

She leaned against the chair, arching her back as jolts of pleasure punctuated the delicious sensations of his fingers sliding over and probing into her sex. Shannon cooperated as Kevin paused to rid her of her skirt and panties. Happy to be toyed with, she gave no thought to the way he crouched behind her, or the shift of his hand, and was all too happy to oblige when she felt him nudge her legs further apart. She bent over further at his wordless instruction.

Then she felt him kneel between her legs. Shannon's breath quickened with excitement and suspense. Could he really be going for that? Brad rarely did anything like this for her, nor had her previous boyfriend after the first time. Kevin didn't hesitate to knee between her stocking-clad legs. She felt his lips trail up the inside of one thigh while his fingers moved up the other and then—"Ooooh," Shannon sighed as she felt the first gentle, probing lick.

His mouth held to the softest, most agonizingly light touch. It only heightened her excitement. Shannon wanted to arch her back as pleasure shot through her, but she knew that would only make the angle more awkward for him. Instead, she made herself give in and relaxed her torso against the back of the plush chair. She let him get to work and adored him for it.

His hands spread across her ass, groping and caressing. Never before had Shannon felt like her butt was particularly attractive, but sometime during her bath or perhaps while she dressed she realized she had a little to show off. She felt better about the rest of her body, too. She was fit, tone, and appealing. Shannon felt sexier than she ever had in her life.

Her enjoyment grew as his kiss went deeper. "Oh, that's incredible," breathed Shannon. "I'll give you about... oh... all night to... to knock that off."

"Hm," he responded. His breath and the vibration of his skin against hers as he spoke drew a shiver of delight from her core. "I might need all night," he confessed.

Shannon's wicked grin returned. He loved the taste of her. She could hear it in his voice and feel it in his touch. She relaxed and let him indulge her. A teasing thought crept around in the back of her brain: *No. He's the one being indulged.*

Her mind wandered to strange places as she enjoyed his attention. Such exquisite physical pleasure clouded her thoughts, but it wasn't as if her brain turned off completely. Shannon could count on one hand the number of men she'd ever slept with. She was shy and slow to trust on this level. It wasn't as if she didn't want a wild sex life. She fantasized about it, but she rarely overcame her personal barriers, and when she managed it, her partners more often than not left her disappointed or hurt.

So what made her so confident all of the sudden? Rebounding from Brad couldn't explain this. Something about her behavior with Kevin felt so easy. Her fears were nowhere to be found. The dirty talk, the invitations and innuendos, and now this intimate service all carried first-time thrills. At the same time, though, it all felt completely natural.

She ceded more and more of her conscious control, and before long it was no longer even hers to give up. Shannon's body trembled and her mouth fell open as she gasped once, then again as she hit a wall inside of her, only to have Kevin's lips and tongue and hands push her through. She moaned loudly, not giving a damn about the neighbors—in fact, she didn't even remember having neighbors anymore. All she knew about in the entire world was her own body, the chair that supported her and the man sending her into orgasm.

It hit harder than ever. It lasted longer, and brought greater satisfaction... but only briefly. Slumped over the back of the chair, still shamelessly exposing herself, Shannon found herself wanting even more. She didn't want recovery time. She didn't want to cool down. She wanted him. Now.

Shannon turned around, leaning back against the chair. She liked the awed look on his face as he saw her from the front, naked from the waist down. "Shoes. Now," she said, pointing to his feet.

His grin told her that he liked her take-charge attitude as much as her previous few minutes of submissive behavior. Kevin quickly slipped off his shoes and socks. As soon as he was finished, she grabbed his collar and pulled him up to meet her face to face. She planted a hungry, deep kiss on his lips, tasting herself on him.

In the back of her mind, she confirmed her initial thoughts. She couldn't blame him for taking his time on her. The lingering taste on his lips aroused her even more.

She tore open his shirt and wrenched it off of him, sending buttons flying. Their kiss only broke off long enough for her to pull his undershirt over his head. Her hands came to his chest, pushing him backward down the hallway to her bedroom until he hit a wall beside the door. She scratched her nails from his shoulders to the top of his pants, then assaulted him with another kiss while she slipped his belt free and shoved down on his pants.

"Gnh!" Kevin grunted. Shannon paused and realized what she'd done wrong. Her rough treatment of his pants had also been a little rough on his erect flesh. Though she nearly gasped and pleaded an embarrassed apology, that particular revelation instantly distracted her. Shannon grinned and slid down his front, keeping her eyes on his the whole way.

"Sorry about that." Her smirking face looked up at him from right beside his cock as she pushed his pants the rest of the way off. Kevin froze against the wall. Shannon only brushed his erection with her cheek, then offered the lightest of kisses on his shaft before rising back up again. "Later for that," she promised with a wink as one of her hands softly closed around it.

His eyes fluttered. She felt the thrill of control and decided she could not let it go. Seeing him completely naked now, Shannon discovered another way in which Kevin represented a considerable step up from her last partner. She guided him into her bedroom, once more pushing him backward until he fell. She looked down with a grin on the fit, attractive man laying diagonally on her bed.

She let him watch as she discarded her top. She held his gaze as she unfastened her lace bra, and smiled as she saw his appreciation for what lay underneath. Then she put one knee up beside his hip and crept in, placing her hands on his chest for support.

Antics out on the living room aside, Shannon normally needed more warm-up than this. Her idea of a good time included much lengthier foreplay. Tonight, though, the thought of any further flirting, cuddling, or teasing seemed like madness. Shannon held his gaze again as she spread her legs over his hips and guided his cock to her center with one affectionate hand.

"Hey," Kevin said, gesturing to the bedroom door, "there's a condom in one of my pants pockets, unless you've got some?"

Condoms? Silly things, she mused to herself, banishing a lifetime of concern for safe sex with a single, completely alien thought. "We're safe," she said softly. Her hand guided him in, giving him just a first taste of the sensations that would consume them both for the rest of the night. She watched his eyes flutter and then open once more. Before he spoke, she said, "Shh. You're mine."

Shannon sank down on him, greedily sheathing his cock within herself. She saw his eyes flutter closed again. His head fell back onto a pillow while her body rose to an all new level of energy and pleasure. Her legs spread wide across the corner of the bed, feet dangling over the sides of the mattress as she rose up on her knees only to sink down upon Kevin once more.

His hips came up to meet her, pushing deeper in response to undeniable need. When his hands came up to touch her, she took hold of his wrists and pushed them back to the bed again. "Relax," she whispered. Shannon leaned forward, bringing her mouth closer to his and rocking her hips up and then down again to stroke him within her. "Let me take care of this."

He let out a heavy, lustful breath. Kevin couldn't take his eyes off of her. She reveled in the look of awe on his face and the ecstasy of having him inside her as she rode him. Taking control excited her. The sensual pleasures of coupling with him excited her more.

Shannon rested her hands on his chest. All the motion seemed to come from her legs and her hips. It wasn't a motion she'd ever tried before; she'd been on top with guys, of course, but never so wantonly or with such confidence. Her motion remained perfect as she came down harder on him, holding him even tighter within herself with each stroke. Shannon bathed in his amazement and knew this was the best thing he'd ever felt in his life. She could feel him thrust up to meet her. That went beyond the spirit of her instructions, but she couldn't complain. Nor could she blame him.

The ride went on. Shannon felt sexier than ever. She *had* him. Kevin was completely enthralled, by her beauty and by her skill and passion in bed. He would never forget this. Nor would she. For the life of her, she couldn't imagine why she wouldn't do this every night.

Well. Let's not get carried away, she thought, her mind capable of such thoughts despite her inflamed emotions. *A one night stand doesn't make us a couple. Still...*

Shannon leaned in on him. Her face came near his. Her red hair dangled around his face. Even with the new angle,

Shannon skillfully kept up the same pace, fucking him as intensely as ever. She heard nothing but surrender in his breath.

"I like you, Kevin," she hissed.

"Oh God," he managed. "I like... I really like you, too... I'm gonna... oh, wow, if you don't slow down I can't... I can't hold back like this."

"So don't," Shannon grinned. "I want you, Kevin. I like you and I want you to get off."

"But you—I don't wanna leave you... unh... hangin'..."

"Shh. Give in to me, Kevin," she whispered before her lips came down on his.

Over a few short hours, Shannon had gotten to know Kevin Murray. She'd taken the measure of the man. Underneath that humble, self-deprecating grin and gentle demeanor, she found the tough spirit of a veteran of war and police work. Like Shannon, he found many frustrations with his job and his co-workers. Still, he persevered. She couldn't imagine him being cowed by any mortal man... yet she now had complete control of him. She heard uncontrolled moans from his throat as she forced him past his point of no return.

She felt him stiffen and watched his muscles tense. He'd never had it this good. She knew that just by looking at him. Kevin had been with plenty of women, but this was beyond his experience. Shannon felt the first intense pulse of his release within her and grinned from ear to ear—or would have if her own orgasm didn't swiftly overcome her, rushing in from out of nowhere to share in her partner's climax.

It slowed her. She still rocked against him, but Shannon relaxed her pace, almost against her will, as if her body forced her to savor every second of the rush.

Shannon lay on top of him, her breasts crushed up against his chest as they bathed in satisfaction together. She felt him throb within her, still getting off well past anything he would have expected. She spasmed right along with him.

The last throbs of orgasm faded, but she refused to let him go. She didn't need to. He stayed perfectly hard. Neither of them knew how much time passed before they stirred once more. Shannon felt his hands rise to her back, and then grinned as they slid down to hold her ass.

"I'm not done with you yet," she warned him. Her voice spoke to her deep satisfaction, but she still wanted more. She knew he'd be up for it, too.

"Not goin' anywhere," breathed Kevin.

"This isn't me, you know."

"Hm?"

"I'm not normally like this. I'm shy. I'm timid. I might crawl back into my shell someday. Maybe even in the morning."

"Well, you can still call me from in there if you want," said Kevin. "I'm not gonna presume anything with you. But either way, I hope this isn't a one-night stand."

"No." Shannon smiled. She propped herself up a bit to look him in the eye. "I'm going to fuck you all night. I'm going to go down on you and taste you and rock your world. And then I *might* let you go in the morning. Maybe. But until then, you're mine. Maybe after that, too."

He nodded. "Yes, ma'am," he said before he kissed her again.

———

She rolled over in bed, frustrated in her half-conscious state by the light in the room and her lack of blankets. Shannon reached out for the sheets, only to find her bedmate beside her. She put her hand over Brad's flat, well-toned abs and smiled to herself.

Wait. No. When did Brad lose the gut? His abs weren't this firm. Certainly not while he slept.

Oh no.

Ohmygod.

It all came back to her. There was no more Brad. She might be in trouble at work. And she'd completely thrown herself at a cop she'd only just met yesterday, taken him home and fucked him all night long like a raging...

Ohmygod. Oh my god I can't believe I did that. This. Oh my God.

Shannon slipped out of the bed with her eyes wide. All thoughts of further sleep vanished from her mind. Kevin lay asleep in her bed, handsome and covered in scratches and bite marks and hickies. Her hands came to her mouth as if it might help keep her from screaming.

No. He's a nice guy. I did this, she remembered, but that did nothing to alleviate her roiling emotions. Safe as Kevin the cop might be, Shannon was not in the habit of bringing people into her home after knowing them for less than a day—less than a month, if she were honest with herself—and had never, ever had sex with someone she'd just met.

Her eyes darted around the room. She grabbed the first thing she saw—a discarded pillow—and promptly snatched it up to cover herself. Then she backed out of the room, nearly leaping with fright when Kevin rolled over and sniffed. She shut the door behind her, kept backing up, moved into the bathroom, shut that door, too, and even locked it for good measure.

Calm down, she told herself. *Calm down and get a grip. You did this. He's just a guy. He's cool. Just wake up and shower and be a good hostess and offer him coffee or a shower or whatever and send him on his way.*

Shannon took a deep breath, then another, and forced her nerves to settle. She was a first responder. She dealt with people when they were at their worst. She could handle this. With an effort of will, she put the pillow down on the floor. Her bathrobe hung from a hook on the bathroom door. She could wear that when she was done in the shower.

She reached inside, turned on the water and dared to look in the mirror. What she saw stopped her in her tracks.

When did she get that swimsuit model figure?

———

"Listen, I know I'm being weird."

"You're not. It's cool."

"No, I am, Kevin," Shannon all but pleaded as she apologized. "You've been so nice to me after I completely took advantage of you and I… God, I can't believe I'm even saying that."

He smiled at her. She liked his smile. "Yeah, I can't believe you're saying that, either," he said. Kevin stood in her kitchen, more or less clothed and ready to go. There were some things he couldn't quite put right before he left.

Shannon winced. "Jeez, you can't even button your shirt anymore." She put her hands on her face for the twelfth time since he woke up. Her cheeks had blushed fiercely from the time he woke up to now, abating only briefly while he showered. And now she stood in her bathrobe, shooing him out of her home and unable to stop herself no matter how much she wanted to.

Kevin was gracious when he woke up. He'd been affectionate at first, then scaled back to being considerate and polite when he saw how awkward she felt. He didn't linger, making a point of showering and dressing quickly. Even so, it felt like an eternity to Shannon. She wanted him to go. She wanted to wish the whole night away. She wanted to bury her face in her couch, because she couldn't bring herself to look at that bed again.

She also wanted to get down on her knees, tear his pants open and go down on him until he could no longer stand. That urge only made her want to hide from him even more.

"I'm sorry," she said for the twelfth time.

"Don't be. Just… listen, I know what it's like to have regrets."

"It's not that I regret anything, except that—"

"Shannon," he interrupted calmly, "let me ask again: did I do anything to make you uncomfortable?"

"No, not at all! It's nothing you did!"

"Okay. Good. Do you like me?"

"…yes?"

"Then call me later. Whenever you feel ready. And if it's like a week or a month from now, I don't care. I mean I'd like it sooner, but if you need time to get your head together or whatever, I understand, okay? You already made it clear that things won't be like last night again. I'm fine with that. I'd just like to see you again. And if you don't call me or if you decide you want to see someone else… no hard feelings, okay?" He shrugged easily. "I had a great time. You seem awesome. Even if you just want to be friends, I'm here, okay? You've got my number."

She blinked. "Just friends?"

"Yeah, I can't believe I said that, either," he confessed. "I may be a little out of it right now. Turns out I had a hell of a night."

"So you *don't* want to be just friends?"

"No. Well." He grinned. "Not 'just,' anyway. But you'll never hear me complain if that's as far as it goes."

His comment nearly triggered yet another apology, but the knock on her door interrupted it. Kevin threw her a quizzical look. She shrugged. "Probably someone looking for the wrong apartment," she said. "It happens." She stepped past him and opened the door.

Shannon had never been legitimately stunned by a woman's beauty before. The woman at her door had long black hair, icy blue eyes, and flawless skin. Her black designer skirt and top fit her like a glove. Shannon's mind ground to a halt.

The woman behind this stranger, though, was at least somewhat more familiar. "Aw, mother fuckballs," groaned the lovely blonde. She slapped her forehead. "What did I tell you? Seriously, you couldn't go one night without fucking somebody? One damn night?"

"Huh?" Kevin blinked. "What?"

The drop-dead gorgeous woman in black sighed. "I apologize for the rude greeting," she said. "Is your name Shannon Abrams? You work as an EMT, and you were outside a fire on Capitol Hill yesterday?"

"Y-yeah?" answered Shannon.

"And is this your boyfriend?" she asked, gesturing to Kevin.

"Uh," Shannon began. She immediately blushed as fiercely as ever.

Kevin shook off his own surprise at the sight of the newcomers. He sensed trouble, or at least discomfort on Shannon's part. "I'm sorry, who are you?" he asked.

The blonde sighed. "His name's Kevin, he's a cop, she met him just yesterday and fucked his brains out all last night," she grumbled. "Looks like he's about to leave."

"I see," said the other woman. She stepped closer to him, putting a hand on his chest. She breathed out in sultry, flirtatious tones, "*Kevin, be on your way. Forget all about the two of us. Pay this no mind.*"

"Okey-dokey," Kevin smiled cheerfully. With that, he slipped past the two women and headed down the hall to the elevator.

Shannon blinked in shock.

"Ms. Abrams... Shannon? May I call you Shannon?" asked the raven-haired woman. "We must speak. Privately. May Rachel and I come in?"

"What... who are you?"

"My name is Lorelei," the woman said. "My...companion is Rachel. You've already met. You had a very strange episode yesterday afternoon. You almost certainly have questions. We hope to provide answers." She paused to let her words process. "Shannon, we're here to help."

Shannon's eyes shifted from Lorelei to Rachel. The lovely young blonde rolled her eyes. "We're on a mission from God."

Lorelei winced, but held her response down to a soft, disgusted breath.

"Okay, *I'm* on a mission from God. She only came along 'cause I nag."

Shannon's first instinct was to close and lock the door. Her natural reluctance to allow strangers into her home reasserted itself. Who were these two women? She'd been able to write Rachel off yesterday as just another Capitol Hill weirdo. Now the blonde stood at her door with a composed, clearly sophisticated woman who seemed to agree with her professed concern for Shannon. Kevin's blithe departure upon Lorelei's prompting unsettled her, too.

She knew she should slam the door, lock it, grab the base-ball bat and the pepper spray and call the cops. Uniformed, on-duty cops who hopefully wouldn't walk right off like Kevin had. She knew all of that.

She also knew that she had never, ever met a woman this sexy. Lorelei wasn't even *trying*. She was calm, collected, businesslike and not at all flirtatious, and yet Shannon found her breath deepening and felt herself lick her lips and shift her posture, pushing her chest ever so slightly forward...

Shannon tried to blink away her strange thoughts about Lorelei—and about Rachel, too. The blonde was undeniably beautiful. But Shannon had never felt attracted to women before. At least, not to this degree. Nothing more than curi-ous wonder, which she had always stepped on before it ran away with her. Perhaps, she might admit only to herself, she was less than bothered by the girl/girl action in her ex-boy-friend's porn movies. But that was all just idle fantasy. Just an appreciation of kink and female beauty...

Wasn't it?

Lorelei's head tilted curiously. "Shannon," she said, "have you caught yourself feeling or acting... out of character at all?"

That was more than Shannon could ignore. Her need for answers overrode her worries about self-defense, but not every other concern that came to mind. "I'm not exactly ready to, uh, entertain visitors just yet," she said.

Lorelei immediately held up her hand to the blonde with-out even turning around to her. Rachel's mouth had opened, but at Lorelei's gesture it closed again without comment. "You wish to get dressed, I imagine. I understand. We'll wait out here."

"Two minutes. Maybe three." With that, Shannon shut the door and threw the deadbolt.

Lorelei turned to a frowning Rachel. "Your one-liners would not get us through the door to talk to her."

Rachel folded her arms over her chest. "Doesn't mean they wouldn't be funny," she pouted.

———

"...so I started rescue breathing, or at least I was about to, but then I sort of passed out," Shannon explained. She sat in her plush living room chair—the one Kevin had bent her over the night before—with a coffee mug in her hands. Blue jeans and an old grey top had replaced her bathrobe. For all the comfort of the chair, her posture wasn't at all relaxed. "When I woke up, something like fifteen or twenty minutes had gone by and there was this cop standing over me. I'd never met him before."

"That's the guy who just did the walk of shame," said Rachel. She sat on the couch beside Lorelei, directly across from Shannon's chair.

Even the way the two sat contrasted sharply. Rachel slumped back against the sofa cushions without a care for ladylike manners. Lorelei exuded the sort of practiced elegance that made perfect posture seem completely natural. There was no prim and proper snobbishness to her, either.

For all Lorelei's masterful etiquette, nothing she said or did put herself above anything in her surroundings—except, of course, for the slight, disapproving frown she turned on her companion.

"Ugh. Yeah," Shannon sighed, putting one hand to her face. "That's about the size of it, actually. I mean I only met him yesterday afternoon, and last night I called him up and... and initiated everything," she forced herself to admit.

"I take it that is not ordinary for you?"

"No! Not at all."

"You should consider that there is nothing wrong with taking the initiative," Lorelei noted, and once more held up a preemptive finger to Rachel's inevitable remark. "You work in a field commonly dominated by men. I'm already willing to guess that you excel at your job. You know you are the equal of any man, certainly. You live independently of family. Surely you don't feel that it is a woman's place to wait on a man when it comes to dating? Or to sex?"

Shannon blushed a bit at the last. "No. No, I know all that up here," she answered, pointing to her head. "But that doesn't mean I'm comfortable taking the lead. At least not usually. It felt totally natural last night, though."

"I realize this must be uncomfortable as a topic," Lorelei prefaced gently. "I will not pry for details, but... was there an unusual energy for you last night with your companion?"

"Yes. I mean I really do like him."

"Not like that," sighed Rachel. "Did you bang him all night long? Screaming awesome sex, literally all night, to the point that you should've both been broken husks?" Lorelei winced, but Rachel paid it no mind. "Did you both get off over and over without having to rest? And you both went at it beyond all ordinary sense, didn't you?"

Shannon stared at the floor. She swallowed hard. "Yes."

Rachel threw a sour look at the woman beside her. "She's a fuckin' paramedic. She deals with blood and guts and puke all the time. You don't have to be so delicate."

"Look, can you just tell me what's going on?" Shannon asked finally. "What's wrong with me?"

"Please understand that we only suspect we know what has happened to you," explained Lorelei. "The details help us create a firmer explanation. Shannon, have you seen any physical changes in yourself?"

"Yes. I don't know. I might be imagining it. But every time I've looked in the mirror since I got home yesterday, it's like I've gotten... prettier. Shapelier. I mean I work out regularly and I've never thought I was ugly, but everything looks different now. I haven't weighed myself yet, but I'm sure I've lost a few pounds, and I've toned up. My skin is smoother. Clothes feel like they fit differently."

"And have you had any memories that seem out of place? Dreams? Visions?"

The answer didn't come right away. "Yeah, kind of. I had some dream last night about being a princess, I think? Not like in a fairy tale, but historical. Something in Europe. I'm not a history buff, so I couldn't tell you when or where it was supposed to be exactly, but it all looked medieval to me." She noticed the obvious interest in the eyes of her visitors. "I was pretty. I was all dolled up. There was a party or something, we had guests, and I think I was supposed to marry one of them. My father or whoever was arranging it. I wasn't happy, but I had a way out."

"What did you do?" Lorelei asked. Her tone hinted that she already knew the answer.

"I… I snuck out of my room, and found my fiancé's… staff? Bodyguards? I don't know. He was a prince or something, too, and he had an entourage. I met with them, and I… I had sex with them. Several of them. We got caught, and it led to a whole huge mess." Shannon paused. "I think there was fighting. People died over it. But not me."

Lorelei frowned. She turned her eyes to Rachel. "Serena," she said.

Rachel leaped out of her seat, looking as if she might shout out, "Touchdown!" until a single, random glance at Shannon quickly clamped down on her elation. The blonde's fists had come up to shoulder level on their way to the sky, but now they dropped back down and merely bounced together awkwardly. She bit her lip. Rather than cheering or howling, Rachel sat back down and muttered, "I am such a badass."

"Shannon, the woman who fell in front of your ambulance yesterday was named Serena," explained Lorelei. "I am fairly familiar with her. For a very long time, she and I had a great deal in common, and none of it good."

"…okay?"

"She was a murderer and a manipulator. She destroyed lives at the bidding of others and also for her own amusement, and she was wholly unrepentant. You should feel no guilt or remorse for her fate."

It hung in the air for a long breath. Shannon asked, "You have all that in common with her?"

"Not the amusement. I am not wholly unrepentant."

Shannon swallowed hard. "Oh." Her hand went to her coffee mug, which she now thought of more as a weapon than a wake-up aid. "So what happened to her?"

"I punched her bitch ass off the roof of that apartment building," Rachel answered with no small amount of pride.

"It is more complicated than that," cautioned Lorelei, seeing Shannon's eyes widen and her jaw clench. "This will only get more shocking, and I apologize for that, Shannon," she continued, "but there is unfortunately only one way to effectively help you understand. Again, you are in no danger from us."

"Uh-huh."

"You may want to put the coffee mug down."

"I'm good, thanks."

"Very well," Lorelei said. And then she changed.

Shannon hadn't blinked. She was sure of that. But in exactly that amount of time, Lorelei suddenly looked very different. Her perfect, smooth skin went almost crimson. Small black horns jutted from just below her hairline. Black, featherless wings appeared at her back, rising up from her shoulders and seeming to fade into the couch and wall behind her in an odd, ghostly effect. Her beauty remained, but now took on a deadly edge.

"Nice," Rachel quipped.

"What the fuck!?" Shannon blurted, rising to her feet. She cocked back with her coffee mug as if to throw it, heedless of the resultant spill across her the wall behind her.

Lorelei looked on placidly. "This is what I am, Shannon. What you saw before is a second form—not exactly an illusion, but not entirely my true self, either. This is my true visage. I will not harm you. But you must understand, Shannon: I am very much the demon you now see. I am a succubus."

"You—um—wait—uh. What about her?" Shannon pointed at Rachel. "Are you…?"

"Pff. Fuck, no," Rachel scoffed. "No way."

"You could show her, Rachel."

"I'm not gonna just show her. Get real."

"Well what the fuck is—" Shannon pointed at Lorelei "—one of those?"

Once again, Lorelei's first response was to interrupt Rachel's inevitably snarky answer with a sharp gesture. "The succubae are demons of seduction and lust," Lorelei explained. "We play on the desires of mortals. We are made to manipulate and draw mortals into their doom through temptation and carnal overindulgence. We are not corruptors—we do not prey upon those who lead virtuous lives—but rather those who have strayed too close to the brink, and those who are overdue in Hell. Shannon, the woman who died under your care yesterday was, like myself, a succubus.

Unlike me, however, she still served Hell. I do not. You are safe from me."

"You don't look safe," replied the shocked host.

"Would you prefer my previous image?"

"Kinda, yeah?"

Even before Lorelei finished her nod, she looked entirely human again. "I show you this because what I must tell you goes beyond much of your understanding about your world. I must explain matters that will sound like superstition and magic to you, but they are quite real. And you cannot afford a lengthy process of overcoming your natural doubts."

"Okay, well... well what the *fuck?*" Shannon demanded. "Just come out with it already, huh? What the hell does all this have to do with me?"

"That demon yesterday died right in front of you, yeah?" Rachel broke in. Her sarcastic tone was gone. "So it turns out, demons don't really die. Not like that, anyway. You were trying to help her. You put your mouth on hers right when she let out her last breath. That was supposed to be her soul fucking off to Hell so she could reconstitute in a new body and come back in another couple decades. Instead, she went straight into you."

None of this settled Shannon's nerves. She remained on her feet, still ready to hurl her mug and lock herself in the bathroom where she could call 911 on her cell phone. She'd have to say there were two crazy women in her apartment. She'd definitely have to leave out the part about Lorelei turning red and demony. Sooner or later, the cops might realize she wasn't telling the whole story, but at least she would have sane people around her.

"So wait, you're saying I'm possessed?" Shannon frowned.

"No," Rachel shook her head. "That sort of thing takes all sorts of preparation and bullshit. And you're too benevolent for it, anyway. You aren't vulnerable to that sort of thing. Besides, you wouldn't be in control now. Possession doesn't allow for co-pilots. You're still calling all the shots. You're still *you*."

"Rachel is correct," said Lorelei. "Possession is not exactly in the repertoire of the succubae. But you do carry her spirit, and it has clearly affected you."

Shannon's throwing arm came down a bit. At the very least, she couldn't ignore what she'd seen with her own two eyes, and she *had* been acting oddly. "So what's that mean for me, then? Am I gonna... am I gonna become one of those things?"

"I assure you, I am not a 'thing,'" Lorelei corrected patiently. "I am not human or mortal, but I am as much a person as you or Rachel.

"Your situation is unique, Shannon. When we tell you that Serena's spirit escaped into you, that is only a theory. It is an inexact explanation for something that neither of us have seen happen before. But when a demon dies—barring certain exceptions—the spirit escapes to Hell, as Rachel has stated. The outcomes are different depending on the sort of demon in question, but in the case of a succubus, that spirit will develop a new body in time. In this case, you seem to have absorbed Serena's spirit as it escaped, or at least some substantial portion of it. You have interrupted the process.

"Again, if this led to possession, you would no longer be in control at all. Rachel and I would see demonic features that you do not bear. However, the changes you have described show that some degree of Serena's *power* is at work. I suspect that as long as her spirit resides within you, her consciousness will remain inert. Her spirit cannot escape back to hell."

"Ohmygod," Shannon murmured. She tried to process all of that. "Can you get it out?"

"That's part of what we need to talk about," answered Rachel. "Listen, I know this is gonna sound crazy, but...putting Serena out of business is kind of a big deal. I mean she's not the baddest succubus ever, but she's a major player in her scene, right? As long as her spirit is stuck inside you, she's off the board. If she'd died normally, she'd have come back in a couple decades like we said. I'd be happy for that, but even so, she'd come back and run around being a murdering, life-ruining twat again. But now, she's off the grid for at least as long as you live."

"Which may be quite a long time," Lorelei added. "Longer than an ordinary mortal might reasonably expect."

That made Shannon blink. "What do you mean?"

"Shannon...you may find that your predicament brings far more benefits than drawbacks. As I said, you are not a demon, but you now carry within you much of that same power."

"What does that mean? What power?"

"Well, you ain't gonna die of disease or from bein' an old fart, that's for sure," Rachel offered. Then she looked away as if staring through one wall. "Fuck. I'm gonna have to bail. Duty calls."

"What duty? Are you a demon, too?"

The blonde snorted. "Fuck, no. Listen, Shannon, I'm sorry if I came off all bitchy. Seriously. I'm just linguistically challenged." For the first time, Lorelei let out a bit of a snicker, but regained her composure when Rachel shot her a glare. The blonde continued. "Just hear Lorelei out, and if you feel like this is too much for you, say so. We might be able to get you an exorcism or something. But as long as she's stuck in there," Rachel said, pointing at Shannon's heart, "she can't do anything to hurt anyone. You're a good person. Practically anything you do with that power is gonna be better than what Serena would do with it. Okay?"

"How do you know all this about me?" Shannon asked.

"I know these things," Rachel teased. "Have faith." She walked straight toward the living room wall, where a window overlooked the street outside Shannon's fourth-floor apartment. Rachel suddenly shined with a white light. Shannon caught a glimpse of her halo and her broad white wings before Rachel effortlessly walked through the wall.

Shannon's jaw dropped. "What—is she really—"

"A grandstanding showoff?" Lorelei smiled. "Yes."

Silence reigned as Shannon overcame her shock. Lorelei waited patiently.

Then Rachel stepped back through the wall and faced Lorelei. "Hey, if I leave you alone with her, are you gonna do what I think you'll do?"

"We have discussed this sort of thing."

"Yeah, I know. That's why I'm asking."

"I will follow my own judgment. You know the rules that bind me," Lorelei reminded her calmly. "You agreed to them. Does any of this change your position?"

Shannon watched without interruption, trying to follow the conversation but finding a distinct lack of context clues. The wings and halo had Shannon more than a little distracted, too.

"No," Rachel answered, though with a reluctant tone.

Lorelei shook her head. "Speak your mind. If you have concerns or objections, voice them."

That seemed to do the trick between the two of them. Rachel nodded. "Guess you gotta be you," she said, more with wry amusement than venom. She tossed a casual salute toward Shannon and then went out through the wall again.

"What does she think you're going to do?" Shannon asked.

"Advise you to explore your new situation, and your power," Lorelei answered. "Encourage you to indulge. Help you adjust. Shannon, I do not blame you for your trepidation or your guarded state, but I will not hurt you. If there is anything I could do to alleviate your nerves, you have but to tell me."

Shannon frowned, more at herself than anything else. She came back around the chair and sat down again, putting the coffee cup on the small stand beside it. "So what do you mean by all that? Indulging? You said you kill men by sleeping with them?"

"Not anymore," Lorelei corrected. "Nor will you. At least, not if you are careful. Shannon, I must be blunt. Your appetites will grow. You will attract the attention and lust of others, and you will find it invigorating. Irresistibly so. This power you now carry isn't something you can simply ignore or hide. Denial will only make you miserable, or worse. You must use it for your own good and for the good of all whom Serena would harm were she to escape you.

"If I am correct in my expectations, you will find yourself healthier and even stronger because of this. As Rachel said, you will never catch another cold for the rest of your life, let alone anything worse. But your real power lay in the desires of mortals. You'll be able to read them. Steer them, at least partially. And you'll derive strength from indulging your own desires."

"What's the catch?" Shannon asked.

"Your hunger will go beyond that of any mortal you have ever known. You will have to adjust and learn to manage it. Ultimately, you may find great joy in all this, but I understand that right now it is unsettling. You are also almost certainly infertile; the touch of Hell has such an effect on the body." She paused, noting that Shannon merely shrugged her last statement off without much trouble. Then she laid out her next warning. "Monogamy may no longer be an option for you."

"Because I could kill whoever I'm with?"

"If you are not careful, yes. This is not a matter of a dangerous touch or some sort of poison. Again, your appetites may become extreme. If you focus them on one individual partner, they may become overwhelming, even if that partner welcomes it. You could potentially run mortals to exhaustion, to say nothing of the distraction you can cause in the rest of their lives if you are not mindful. Passion does not often lend itself well to delicate decisions. Or self-denial."

"How do you manage it? You said you don't kill anyone anymore."

"My situation is unique, as is yours. What works for me will likely not help you. I, too, must be careful… but I have vastly more experience in all this than you."

Shannon wasn't sure she liked what she heard. She wasn't sure she disliked it, either, and that bothered her even more. "So you're saying I'm going to turn into some raging slut?"

"Ask yourself why you use that word. It does not seem natural from your lips."

It stopped her train of thought cold. "Wh…what else would I say?"

"Ask yourself why your society frowns on a woman with an active sex life and multiple partners. There will be no issue of disease. There will be no unwanted pregnancy. Tell your partners that you are uninterested in being tied down and demand that they respect that. If they do not, walk away. If they are harmed, it will not be because you were dishonest with them. It will be because they deceived themselves, and that is not your concern. You need not harm anyone."

Shannon scoffed. "So, what, men are just going to throw themselves at me?"

"Quite possibly, yes. It will not be difficult at all for you to attract men. Women, too, if their desires run toward other women. Shannon, much of this comes down to raw confidence and magnetism. You are already developing all of that without thinking about it. As you said, last night's tryst was out of the ordinary for you, yet you initiated the whole thing, correct? You see your body changing and improving in line with your own ideals of beauty. You will need to get used to being the most desirable woman in the room. It's not a matter of ego; it's simple fact."

Crazy as this story was, Shannon believed her. Moreover, the notion excited her. She clamped down on that, not wanting to let her imagination run away with her, but this was like someone waving a winning lottery ticket at her.

It also seemed too good to be true. "So I'm going to be what people want the most, but they can't have me for keeps? How is that not going to hurt people?"

"You are a person, not an object. No one gets to 'keep' or 'possess' you," Lorelei corrected. "And as I mentioned, you will grow stronger. You have power. Those who push their possessive attitudes on you do so at their own peril. As for the rest?" Lorelei shrugged. "People get hurt in relationships. It happens to everyone. If you are a caring person, you will make what effort you can to be up front with your boundaries. But despite your ability to read and appeal to the desires of others, you cannot dictate their feelings. Nor should you."

It was a lot to take in. Shannon's thoughts drifted. "…I've never been attracted to women," she murmured.

"I think we both know that's not true," Lorelei said quietly. Shannon's eyes lifted toward hers. "I have walked this path for centuries, Shannon. Rachel has her talent for reading people, and I have mine. I have known since you decided to allow us in."

"That wasn't—I mean I didn't—you—uh…"

"You are a very attractive woman, Shannon." Her voice dropped. Her gaze sent Shannon's heart racing. "Intelligent. Independent. Brave. As Rachel said, you are a benevolent soul. I have learned recently to appreciate the appeal of compassion and charity." Lorelei's breathing seemed to deepen, too, judging from the sound of her voice and the rise and fall of her alluring chest. "You did not allow me into your home because of my saintly aura."

Shannon's emotions stirred. So did her desires. Every nerve and muscle seemed ready to throw herself out of her chair and on top of this woman she had just met. She trembled in her seat, unable to admit how good the moment felt.

"We could alleviate the tension between us, Shannon," Lorelei said. It seemed more like an observation than an offer. And yet…

"Is this what you mean by playing on peoples' desires?" Shannon managed to ask.

"Mildly," Lorelei conceded. Her tone grew solemn, but her smoldering gaze remained. "You see that you have a choice, however. You feel that, don't you?" She waited for

Shannon to respond with a nod. "If I make you uncomfortable, I could leave. We could always talk on the phone if you have more questions." She rose.

Shannon all but leapt to her feet. She reached out for Lorelei's hand, saying, "Please, don't go——!" and caught herself. She stared at Lorelei, who waited patiently. "Please stay," she said.

They looked at one another for a long moment.

"Do you want this? Do you want me?"

"Yes," Shannon admitted. She felt nervous. Exposed. Thrilled.

"And what do I want?" Lorelei asked. "Think it through. You have that power. I will not conceal it from you."

Shannon's eyes narrowed. Her hand didn't come off of Lorelei's. "You want me," she murmured. "You could walk away without any worries. You have a lover," she continued, understanding the source of Lorelei's composure and confidence despite her obvious desire. "You have a lover and you're devoted to... him? But he's okay with this sort of thing. Am I right?"

Lorelei nodded. "Yes. With other women, certainly. We share that freedom. My freedoms with other men are not such a simple matter, but he is already shedding that concern faster than I expected. The hypocrisy bothers him, and he knows he will never lose me to another. He knows what I am. He accepts me for it."

Shannon's hand slid up Lorelei's arm. Her skin felt amazingly smooth and inviting. Shannon couldn't deny the thrill of flirting so openly with another woman for the first time. Yet this was more than flirting: she plainly knew where this would lead, and that anticipation excited her even more. "So is this naughty, or is this okay?"

"A little of both." Lorelei smirked. "I may not tell him, or I may derive some enjoyment from taunting him about it. I'll make up my mind later."

"Do I get to meet him?"

"No. I am at least that selfish." Lorelei returned Shannon's touch, tracing her fingers up and down the younger woman's arms.

"Must be a great guy to mean that much to you."

"He is."

"You said we can't limit ourselves to one partner without hurting them."

"I don't believe you can, at least for now," Lorelei corrected. "What I said was that my situation and yours are both unique." Her hand came up to the side of Shannon's head. Graceful fingers slid into her hair, lightly brushing her scalp with their nails. Shannon's breath grew audible.

"I've never been with another woman," Shannon murmured.

"Trust your instincts. I very much doubt I will know the difference," Lorelei said before she drew the younger woman in for a kiss.

Their lips touched tentatively at first, but both immediatcly wanted more. Drawn together, the two repeated the brush of their lips several times, lingering longer and opening more with each heartbeat until their tongues met. They seemed to mirror and complement one another.

Shannon felt the heat between them grow. More than one kind of heat, in fact: her body came alive with arousal, and Lorelei's as well, but she also understood now why she felt so differently about sex after yesterday. Her desire genuinely *burned* inside, compelling her to act. Anything she did to satisfy it—like kissing Lorelei, or seducing Kevin—made the burn comfortable, even delicious. Yet this time she didn't want raw passion and need. She enjoyed the sizzling tension between herself and her new partner and the slow build toward relief.

Lorelei was right about her instincts. Shannon felt the thrill of discovery as her body responded to her partner's touch, and as she explored Lorelei in turn. She felt no sense of timidity, though, nor first time nerves. She knew what to do each step of the way...or, rather, it seemed that everything she wanted to do hit all the right notes.

Gentle, safe exploration by hand accompanied the long bout of kissing, mostly staying to the arms, the shoulders and neck. Wordlessly, the pair agreed it was time for more. Their hands came down and joined together. Their eyes fluttered open. The ritual feeling of it all excited Shannon.

"My room is a mess," she said. "I had someone with me last night. The bed isn't made."

"No apologies," Lorelei replied. "This is what we are. Embrace it. Feel no shame on my account. Take pride in your successes."

Shannon couldn't hold back an excited smile. She knew exactly what Lorelei offered: physical pleasure and intimacy with no presumptions or demands. Open, comfortable acknowledgement of mutual lust. An experience with no price. Sex for the sake of sex.

She could get used to that very quickly.

Wanting to keep the controlled tension going, Shannon calmly led Lorelei into her bedroom. The comforter lay crumpled on the floor. She and Kevin had slept under the top sheet alone, more than warm enough through one another's presence. The outlines of wet spots from the night before stood out on the sheets. One pillow still sat stuffed behind the headboard to mitigate its banging against the wall. Emboldened by Lorelei's advice, Shannon felt no shame over any of it. *I had fun here last night*, Shannon thought. *Check out the damage. Awesome, huh?*

She turned back to Lorelei. The succubus brought her hands to Shannon's shoulders, slipping off one strap from her top, and then the other. Shannon watched her partner's eyes and hands as Lorelei slowly undressed her. Lorelei's touch became bolder, mapping the curves of Shannon's body as she pushed the redhead's top up and over her head and arms. She stood mutely as Lorelei unfastened and unzipped her jeans, and looked down while Lorelei bent and slowly brought them to the floor.

Desire and envy roiled within her. Every move the succubus made enthralled Shannon even more. *Will I ever be able to move like that?* she wondered, but the answer came to her instantly. All this would come naturally from now on. She didn't feel envy. Admiration, yes, but soon it would be mutual.

Her excitement stepped up another notch when Lorelei stepped in and brought her arms around Shannon to unclasp her bra. She felt her breasts up against Lorelei's and let out a heavy breath as the garment fell away. Lorelei paused to stroke and cup her breasts, drawing a moan of delight. Eventually her fingertips slid downward again, this time hooking under Shannon's panties to draw them downward. Lorelei paused there, too, inhaling the scent of her new partner.

Even months into her previous relationships, Shannon felt self-conscious about her body. She knew she had nothing to be embarrassed about, but she'd been raised with a strong sense of modesty. Now she stood naked and openly aroused by a stranger—another woman, no less—and felt nothing but confidence and pride.

Then it was Shannon's turn. Though she did not quite take as much time in undressing her partner as Lorelei had, she took as much if not greater joy in the process. Every revelation of skin made Shannon want more as she removed Lorelei's top to discover a lacy black bra, then unzipped her skirt and left it pooled at the beauty's feet to reveal black lace garters and stockings framing her silk panties.

"You wear these for your lover, don't you?" Shannon grinned.

"Yes. And now for you. But always for me, too. Your body is a treasure. Enjoy it. Enjoy sharing it."

Shannon did nothing to cover her open admiration and lust. "I never wore stuff like this. Didn't want men thinking I was their toy."

"Understandable. You might give it a try some time," Lorelei suggested, stepping in and dropping her voice to intimate levels. "You might like it. Clothing makes you no one's toy. Let no one forget that. But you might find great fun in playing with it from time to time with the right partner."

"I've always been afraid," Shannon murmured, still touching and feasting her eyes on this magnificent woman only inches away. "I was afraid I'd lose who I am."

"Be whoever you want to be, Shannon. All on your own terms. You can change a role as easily as changing clothes. I will show you."

Shannon grinned. "Later?"

"Much later," Lorelei said before they kissed once more.

The embrace felt so much better with fewer clothes. Shannon wanted to slide as much of her skin against Lorelei's as she could. She wanted to look at her and touch every bit of her all at once. As if to emphasize her suggestion, Lorelei took a passive approach; she stood and enjoyed, wordlessly offering herself to Shannon in any way the redhead wished.

Shannon took full advantage. Her hands roamed Lorelei's body, stroking and then clutching her ass as she kissed the succubus. She reached up and kneaded her breasts without removing the bra, eliciting a soft moan of approval. Eventually, this was not enough. Shannon unfastened the garment and tossed it away. Confronted with the beauty of

Lorelei's chest, Shannon took one knee, and then another, and soon kissed another woman's breasts for the first time in her life. Soft flesh welcomed her touch. Erect nipples offered themselves to Shannon's tongue.

She liked it more than she expected. Lorelei responded wonderfully, placing her hands on Shannon's head and shoulders. The older woman exuded submission. Shannon had no doubt that Lorelei could turn the tables and leave her in a pleading, whimpering pile of surrender with little effort. It gave her a sense of what Lorelei meant about playing different roles.

She wanted this. She wanted new partners, new experiences and new roles. If that made her a slut in the eyes of others, so be it—they would not get to enjoy Shannon's charms.

The most beautiful woman Shannon had ever met quivered in her arms and under her kiss. Shannon toyed with her, one hand stroking Lorelei's inner thighs and teasing at her center. The garter eventually came free. Shannon knelt and slipped Lorelei's panties. The intoxicating scent alone felt like a new reward.

She stood, finding the eyes of an equal before her now rather than those of a sex toy. Shannon gestured invitingly to her bed. Lorelei nodded. The two lay side by side in an embrace that indulged both of their welcoming bodies.

Sensual pleasure rose with every moment of contact. Shannon thought she might climax just from that, but then it was her turn to be toyed with. As Lorelei's tongue invaded her mouth, Shannon felt the nipple of her breast pushed and then pinched between her partner's fingers. She had to open her mouth even wider to moan into Lorelei's kiss.

Then Lorelei's thigh came between Shannon's legs. She was impossibly wet, ready for just about anything, and now this smooth, soft, perfect skin began to slide and grind between her legs. Overwhelmed by the sensation, Shannon's muscles involuntarily tensed all over her body. She wanted more. Lorelei obliged.

Eventually, Shannon grew accustomed enough to the pleasure to regain some control. Lorelei's own sex was equally exposed; the redhead shifted, knowing what to do as much from immediate experience as from instinct. She heard Lorelei's breath change and knew she'd found a way to return the favor.

Their first orgasm built as they continued their grind. Shannon's whole body shook. She and Lorelei came together, riding out their spasms together and basking in one another's arms.

She should have been spent. She should have needed time to recover. Instead, "Oh God, it's only worse," whimpered the younger woman. "I need more!"

"Worse?" asked Lorelei, at once taunting and understanding. "Or better?" Her kiss smothered the rest of Shannon's pleas. Her hand trailed down Shannon's center. As she could form no words while occupied with Lorelei's lips, the redhead could only beg with panting breath.

Hyper-sensitive and receptive to every touch, Shannon noticed a change in the feeling of Lorelei's fingertips while

191

they slowly moved from her shoulder to her groin. She was sure, in fact, that Lorelei wanted her to feel it: her fingernails literally shrank. By the time Shannon felt the other woman's touch pass through her thin bush and reach her wet lips, Lorelei's fingertips felt perfectly rounded.

Those fingertips played with her flesh. They teased her, tortured her and left her pleading in soft moans before the first of them finally invaded her. Lorelei broke off her kiss so Shannon could cry out. The succubus knew exactly how to touch her. Shannon felt a thumb glide gently over her clit while Lorelei's finger bent in a hook and stroked the most sensitive spot within.

Orgasm came on quickly, rushed more by Shannon's feelings of complete vulnerability to her partner than by physical stimulation. Lorelei brought her through the spasms, still focusing her attention on Shannon's pleasure. Her expert strokes continued while Shannon cooled down. Her mouth came to Shannon's breast to kiss and pinch her nipple with pleasing lips. All Shannon could do was writhe and moan and enjoy.

Ecstasy obscured the passage of time. Shannon laid there forever under Lorelei's sway, held to only a short, blissful distance from another climax. Perhaps it was only minutes. Perhaps it was hours. Over and over, her eyes drifted open to drink in the sight of her beautiful partner and her own lovely body, then closed once more to focus on the sensation.

"Lorelei," Shannon breathed, "you're ruining me for anyone else."

"No," Lorelei replied. "I'm freeing you."

Lorelei's kiss slid down Shannon's body. Enthralled and pleasured far beyond her experience already, Shannon couldn't believe there was more to anticipate, but now she saw and felt Lorelei's face slide closer to her groin. Their eyes met once more. Shannon nearly opened her mouth to beg for it, but before she could give voice to her need Lorelei's tongue descended onto Shannon's wet flesh.

She cried out loudly. Shannon threw her head back into her pillow and gripped her sheets. Lorelei's first light lick was followed by another, and then by a third, and soon her oral attentions became much more direct and encompassing. Shannon felt herself devoured by the older woman. Again, she nearly crested, but before that satisfaction was reached Lorelei shifted into a new pleasure: her tongue invaded Shannon, thick and dexterous and perfect.

Shannon enjoyed a long, relentless ride until she came harder and longer than ever. Her orgasm rippled through her whole body, from her center to her legs and shoulders and wrists.

Only then did Lorelei allow Shannon any respite. "There is more power in you than I expected," said the succubus. "More of hers...and more of your own."

"What does that mean?" Shannon asked, her voice high and breathless.

"Only good things, for you," Lorelei smiled. "Embrace your appetites. They may seem new or strange, but the more you indulge, the stronger you will become. You are no demon, nor are you immortal, but you have power beyond the natural gifts of mortal man or woman."

"Lorelei, your hands. Your fingers changed. Your nails."

"Yes. I can look quite different if I so choose. Some is pure illusion. Some is actual physical change."

"Can I do that?"

"To some extent, you already do. As you said, you have seen change within yourself. Your abilities will likely not be as potent as mine, but we could experiment."

Shannon grinned. The thought excited her. "You mean I can change what I look like?"

"Yes," said Lorelei. "Still human. Still a woman." Her hands roamed Shannon's body, shamelessly enjoying her breasts, her hips and her thighs. "You can be anyone you want to be."

A shiver ran through the redhead. "Later?"

"Of course."

"I want more of you, Lorelei. I want to taste you."

The succubus smiled broadly. She shifted on the bed. "Then let's see what you've learned," she said, and turned over Shannon to swing one lovely leg over the younger woman's head. The other took up the opposite side, and Shannon reached up to touch those perfect hips and bring Lorelei's sex to her mouth while Lorelei's lips descended on Shannon's own.

Seduction was never something Shannon thought one could taste until that moment. Honey and heat and temptation welcomed Shannon's mouth, and then a jolt of pleasure ran through her body as Lorelei's tongue invaded her again. She knew they would be at this for hours.

Wanting to give Lorelei the same treatment, Shannon thought about shaping her own tongue into something similar and probed her partner's flesh. It was easier than she thought, and the sudden jerk of Lorelei's body over hers told her how effective it was.

Perhaps Shannon hadn't wanted this. Perhaps she would have turned it down had she ever been given a choice. But now that she had this power and these desires, she found that she loved it all.

———

The woman in Shannon's mirror looked very much like her, but she was still a stranger.

Lorelei remained for much of the day. For hours, they made love for its own sake. Shannon didn't really know whether to call it that. Romance would not come of this, but physical familiarity and openness grew into affection of a sort. Moreover, Lorelei coached Shannon on the new conditions of her life. They discussed Shannon's probable abilities, the implications of their use, and the importance of exploring her newfound desires.

Friends and family would still recognize her despite these changes. She looked amazing, but still like herself. None of them would ever see her naked like this, though; they would not see this much of her perfect skin or the exquisite muscle tone she now enjoyed from head to toe. She could make a lot of money modeling with this body. Come to think of it, she would do well in any profession where good looks and charm were key.

Thoughts of family or career concerns didn't feel so welcome at the moment. She wanted more fun. More company. That her mind went to such places bothered her slightly. Lorelei had taken very good care of her—and so had Kevin before her, to be fair—but even with her fires cooled for now, she knew this hunger would stay with her for life. The hunger didn't bother her, though, and *that* was what did concern her. Shannon had never judged others for promiscuous choices. It simply never appealed to her until now. Her attitude had completely changed overnight, and she couldn't see a single drawback—as long as it could be compartmentalized properly.

Her self-worth would not be dictated by how many people lusted after her, or how many men and women she bedded. Shannon was a damn good paramedic. She saved lives. She helped people.

She was also now undeniably sexy. She knew she'd never given herself enough credit before, but now it was very much like a switch had been flipped by magic.

She wanted to show off. She longed to be desired. Needed it, even, as much as she had needed to follow the path that put her in an ambulance tending the sick and injured. This need, though, she could deny to herself... but to what end?

Shannon wanted to explore it, and enjoy it. She didn't want it to become all that defined her.

Lorelei's words echoed in her head: "You can be anyone you want to be."

Shannon's hand reached up to her head. She watched herself as her fingers worked their way to the roots of a lock of hair, and ran along its length from her scalp to the very ends. As the hair passed between her fingers and thumb, it turned from straight and red to wavy and brown and grew two more inches.

Shannon stared at herself in the mirror. Her brown eyes turned blue. "Anyone I want to be," she said to her reflection.

———

"Sexy cop. Ridiculous. Sexy secretary. Cliché and sad. Sexy schoolgirl. Gross." Julie tacked off the costumes in the line both in front and behind her and her companions on the sidewalk.

"I know, right?" snickered Julie's husband. Doug threw his cigarette into the wet gutter. They waited along with a good many others to be let inside the club. "Guess that's why they call it 'Whoreloween.'"

"Oh, whatever," scoffed Patricia. Like Julie, she was dolled up for the show, but not in any sort of costume. Normal street clothes were good enough for the two of them. "People have taken that whole thing too far. At this point, any costume a woman wears on Halloween gets labeled 'too sexy' unless she's covered head to toe like a nun. And people would call the nun outfit a fetish piece, too."

"That's because nuns' outfits are pervy," countered Julie.

"Yeah, I dunno. The schoolgirl outfit always kinda creeped me out, too," agreed Tim. Julie's date leaned over her shoulder to break into the conversation. "I mean it kinda speaks to all sorts of misplaced childhood frustration, doesn't it?"

"Such a line," Patricia said with a roll of her eyes.

"No, seriously," Julie pressed. "You know what kind of fantasies that caters to. Might as well just put up a sign that says, 'Molest Me,' right?"

Unexpectedly, the woman in the lab coat waiting on line in front of them turned around to face the quartet. She wore thin red-rimmed glasses over an exceptionally beautiful face, with her brown hair tied up tightly in the back. A stethoscope hung around her neck. "Hey, if you're going to make a clean sweep of all your slut-shaming, you wanna include me, too?" the 'doctor' asked. "I'm starting to feel left out."

Julie, her husband, and their friends all blinked in surprise..They thought they had been fairly quiet. None of them expected any sort of confrontation out of this. "Uh," stammered Julie, "you don't look like a slut."

The doctor's red lips turned in a frown. She calmly put her hands in the pockets of her lab coat and let their weight push it open. It was only then that the three saw her substantial white bra, her thin, too-short white skirt, and the white garters descending from underneath to hold up her white lace stockings. The doctor's body was nothing short of amazing. All four of her onlookers were stunned.

"So here's the thing: right now, you're all staring at me and deciding I'm a slut," the doctor said. "You have no idea who I am or what I'm like. All you see is that I look good and I've decided to show it off. I'm not here to steal your dates. I've got nothing to do with you at all, but you're bothered by how I dress. You're all adults. You can wear whatever you want. Why can't you extend that to others?"

Julie tried to form words. Patricia didn't even bother. She just turned red and looked down at her feet. She wasn't used to confrontation. Doug and Tim simply kept looking on in awe.

"And if somebody did tell you that you should dress like me," Shannon went on, "is there some reason you couldn't tell them to fuck right off and do your own thing? Or is it just safer to drag down the women who do get a kick out looking like this?"

"I just..." Julie tried. "Look, you can't dress like that and not expect to get that kind of a reaction."

Shannon tilted her head curiously. "Why can't I? Other than the fact that your low expectations of men validate their bad behavior, why should I expect to be harassed? Any guy I'm interested in flirting with is gonna know it. I've absolutely got the right to walk into that club or down that street without anyone giving me a hard time. So does the woman in the schoolgirl outfit."

"Uh, excuse me, Miss? Er, doctor?" called out a guy in a Starfleet uniform shirt standing behind Shannon's stunned audience. "The line's moving."

"Oh. Thank you," she replied with a friendly smile. Her attention returned to Julie and her friends. "Raise your game, people. Seriously. You're not helping anyone." With that she turned and headed off into the club.

The rush of the moment caught up with her. Confrontation had never been high on Shannon's list of hobbies. Two nights ago, she would likely still have bristled at the snarky commentary behind her—shy or not, it wasn't like she bought into that sort of thinking—but turning and telling complete strangers to stuff it wasn't exactly her style. It wasn't anywhere close. Even now, she felt the echoes of her old self wondering if she shouldn't apologize, or at least feel some guilt for her sudden rant and whatever embarrassment those people probably felt.

Then she came to the front doors of the venue and realized she still had neither a plan nor a ticket. The booth had been closed when she arrived; as she expected, the Halloween show was sold out. Shannon came out anyway, hoping for a last-minute ticket release before the show began. Failing that, she figured she could...what? Bat her eyelashes at the doorman?

No. Unacceptable. She carried a demon's lust within her, but that didn't mean she wanted to seduce her way through all her problems. Interested in finding a playmate for the evening though she was, Shannon had no intention of solving every problem through sex appeal.

"Ticket?" asked the muscular man past the door. He held out his hand. Shannon's good looks seemed either lost upon him or irrelevant. She knew she shouldn't be surprised. Bouncers and doormen here probably saw a parade of hot women every night.

"I don't have one," Shannon admitted. "I was hoping... are you going to do a last minute release at all? I couldn't get a straight answer out of anyone over the phone earlier, so I waited in line."

"No," answered the doorman. "No more tickets tonight. Sold out."

Shannon bit her lip. She tried to think of an acceptable approach, but found herself rejecting every idea. She sighed. "It's cool. Guess I'll find another party tonight."

"Ramon! Hey, Ramon!" called a voice from just beyond the doorman. He glanced over his shoulder. Shannon looked, too, and spotted a lovely young woman in a green plaid sexy schoolgirl's outfit. "You should let her in. She just saved a couple snotty bitches from severe trauma outside."

Ramon looked back to her with a cocked eyebrow. Shannon shrugged. "Well," she said coolly, "I *am* a doctor."

—

It couldn't have worked out better if she'd planned it.

Shannon made it into the venue before the first band finished its set. The men she had come to see were only now setting up, with canned music playing over the PA in the interim. Shannon adored Rockerdammerung as much for their music as for their self-deprecating humor. Brad couldn't stand them for reasons Shannon never understood. He refused to go to every show with Shannon and even put on a sullen pity party if she dared to go without him.

Come to think of it, Shannon considered, her ex got sullen whenever she did anything without him. Maybe that was why she didn't feel bad about losing him.

Freed from concern for his fine feelings and ready to enjoy the hell out of the show, Shannon regretted ever having settled for her now-ex. She almost wanted to send him a text to thank him for dumping her before this show rather than after Halloween...but she had better things to do at the moment.

Getting close to the stage turned out to be easier than any task she'd faced all night. Letting her white lab coat fall open once more, Shannon strutted through a crowd that quickly parted for her like the Red Sea. She caught stares and double-takes, knowing all along that the sudden interruptions of conversations or laughter were because of her, and she loved every second of it. No one bothered her, or even approached her.

Every step of the way, Shannon felt the lust of men and more than a few of the women in the crowd. All her life, she'd been reluctant even to go out in a swimsuit. Now she couldn't get enough of this feeling. It was less about her body than about her confidence. She knew that. But she also knew that she had the body to back everything up now. Her presence was such that it actually prevented many men from approaching her. Apparently she intimidated more than a few of them.

That was fine with her. She had only one specific man in mind tonight.

She felt almost giddy with excitement. She felt nourished and hungry at the same time. Powerful and yet wanting more. She felt aroused—deeply, deliciously aroused, by her own intentions as much as the desires of the people around her.

Good God, she thought, *if I feel like this now, how would I feel if I took it further?*

———

They really needed new monitor speakers.

Michael resolved to replace the band's current gear upon his next paycheck. They'd limped along this far, but now the band was starting to headline significant local shows and attract real interest. Even being here tonight was a milestone. They might not be at the top of the bill, but they were only one step down from Throbbing Ennui. A good many people came tonight specifically for Rockerdammerung. It was time to invest in more reliable equipment.

But until he had the money to invest, it was time for duct tape.

The tall, lanky singer and rhythm guitarist stomped out on a mostly-darkened stage to secure the cables into their loose and crappy plugs. Everyone else was about ready to go. He only needed a moment. The music from the venue's speakers rose, letting everyone know that Rockerdammerung would kick off their set soon.

"...these guys aren't even that original," claimed an unnecessarily loud voice from the front. The club was not so crowded that a safety space had to be cleared from the front of the stage. Audience members could practically reach out and touch it. Michael usually liked that aspect of this venue, but suddenly it brought with it unpleasant consequences.

"All the themes in their songs, the chords they play, the tones—they're just another Goth band. They're so stuck in their genre that they're not even anything new within Goth. They're, like, retro-Goth. Only they think they're funny, too, so they're demeaning to their core audience."

Michael almost dropped the tape in his hands. *What the hell? That doesn't even make any sense!* Still bent over the monitor speaker, Michael's eyes rose to look out through his dangling black locks of hair at the crowd at the foot of the stage.

"Well, still," voiced a woman who instinctively spoke as loudly as her companion, "they've got a great name, right?"

"What, Rockerdammerung? It's ironic, but irony's for hipsters, not Goths," came the disdainful reply. "And they're not exactly German or even 'rockers.' The singer and the drummer are just IT guys from Redmond. Not sure how 'rocker' you can be when you're contracting for Microsoft."

There. Michael spotted the critic right near the front of the crowd. Checkered shirt, thick black-rimmed glasses that probably didn't even hold prescription lenses, and a grey wool cap that he wore even in the warmth of the crowded club. And then Michael recognized him; he was part of another band, one not even playing tonight. Explodo. *Check us out, we're so ironic.*

His date wore one of those horrid semi-sexy My Little Pony costumes. That just made Michael hate him more.

Don't take the bait, Michael told himself. *Don't engage. Don't engage. Just ignore him. One random jackass. Focus on your show. Focus on your... holy shit.*

Behind the critic and his date, the crowd seemed to open up all on its own. Michael saw her move with confident grace. The doctor in the lab coat and lace stockings walked up and smiled, leaving even the guitarist from Explodo momentarily stunned.

She made eye contact with Michael. Her gaze held his as she arrived at the foot of the stage. Her quiet smile threatened to hypnotize him.

Someone slapped him on his back. "Hey, Michael, we set?" asked Jared.

"Uh, yeah! Yeah," Michael blinked. He turned his back on the doctor and the rest of the audience, though it required an act of will.

The bassist seemed to understand perfectly. "Jesus Christ," Jared muttered, "I thought doctors were supposed to *treat* heart attacks, not give 'em. Think she's seen us before?"

"Ladies and gentlemen," a voice boomed over the speakers. Michael and Jared looked at one another, shrugged, and turned back to the audience to wait for their cue. The stage went dark, but they could see the crowd perfectly well under red overhead lights. "Please welcome..."

The doctor raised her arms, throwing out goat horns with her fingers and calling out along with the announcer and much of the crowd, "Rockerdammerung!"

Michael grinned widely as he hit the first chords. The doctor's eyes were still on him and threatened to never turn away. He faintly remembered being annoyed at something a moment ago. Whatever it was, he quickly forgot it. He stepped to the microphone to belt out the first lyrics of his song.

Thankfully, he remembered them. The doctor clearly knew the words, too.

———

Shannon watched Michael sway and sing on the stage above her. She found herself appreciating the rocker image as if she'd only now discovered it for the first time.

The singer didn't forget the rest of his audience, but she knew she had his attention. He practically sang the band's only serious ballad to her specifically. Michael played the part of the front man well, engaging with many in the crowd and ensuring his bandmates received plenty of attention from all. He didn't hog the spotlight or grandstand. His words were all for the sum total of his band, and not for himself alone.

When the final song ended, and when the rest of the band all stepped up to take their bow, Michael bent low. Through the curtain of long black hair dangling over his face, Shannon saw his blue eyes staring out at her.

She winked at him. Mirrored his hungry grin. Looked pointedly toward the side hallway. Then she stepped back from the stage. As the lights came up and the band set to breaking down and clearing out for the next act, Shannon slipped away. The crowd's attention shifted toward the club's two bars.

Arriving in the small hallway leading toward the rest-rooms of the club—clean and orderly, unlike many other places Rockerdammerung had played—Shannon considered what she could do to bring things up to the next level if it turned out tonight wasn't enough for her. She wore very little as it was, and this club already invited a bawdy tone by virtue of its advertising and musical selection. What would go further than this? Stripping?

Shannon smiled to herself. That could be fun. She'd never looked down on those who did it, but she figured stripping was the sort of thing *other* women did. She always presumed it was a sort of last resort for those who could pull it off. Sure, some women said they enjoyed it, and perhaps that was true, but how many simply lied to keep up appearances?

Now the thought of it rolled through Shannon's mind and she found it nothing short of delicious. She could have a good time. Feed her needs. And probably clean up financially while she was at it. And nobody even needed to know who she really was…

"Do you know how hard it is to come up with a good pick-up line when you can barely remember lyrics to songs you wrote yourself?" asked a deep, slightly amused voice.

Shannon leaned back on the wall, reminded of her near-nakedness as she felt her lab coat up against her not-entirely-covered ass. Her posture created some difference in their height. Normally she stood about as tall as Michael. Leaning back allowed the singer to loom over her. She wanted that. She wanted him to feel confident.

He had more than a little confidence all on his own, as any good front man for a band must. Even so, Shannon detected a hint of nervousness when he looked at her. He hid it well, but either he didn't actually get much attention from women—which she found unlikely—or he recognized her as someone special.

"I tried to sing along with you to help," Shannon told him. "I'm a fan. I've seen you guys perform a few times."

"Have you? I think I'd remember you."

"I've had a bit of a makeover recently," Shannon replied with a cool, graceful shrug. Her eyes looked up into his again. "But yes. I've seen you several times. Saw you in SoDo. Saw you at that charity thing in Tacoma. And on the side stage for Bumbershoot." Her smile grew sultry. "I saw you bring the crowd control guys onstage with you to sing that Sisters of Mercy cover."

She didn't think she could make him blush, but even in the dim lighting of the club she could see his cheeks grow red. "That was a good show."

"It was a great show," Shannon agreed. "You seem like a good guy. You don't take yourself too seriously, or your band. I like that. It's part of why I wanted to meet you."

"Oh, so you've been stalking me?"

"Only for a couple of hours. Maybe I pay close attention to your blog. Pretty sure it doesn't count as stalking if the victim likes it," she teased, "though I can always take a walk if I make you uncomfortable."

"No, no, keep stalking," he chuckled. "What's your name?"

"Call me Sharon," said Shannon.

"I can do that."

"You aren't here with anyone, are you?"

"Just the band. Sorry to keep you waiting. I couldn't leave them to pack up the gear all on their own. Even if they told me to."

"No, I respect that." Shannon grinned. He had some sense of priorities. She felt even better about this now.

"I take it you're here alone, too?"

"I arrived alone, anyway," she said, reaching out to fondle his black shirt. He'd had a big, beautiful leather coat when he started on stage, but had to shed that before too long. Michael smelled of sweat and energy, yet he didn't stink. He smelled like a man. She liked that. "I'm hoping I'm not really here alone anymore."

"I'd be happy to provide you with an escort," Michael offered.

She smiled broadly. He meant that—he delivered it as a joke, surely, but she understood the subtext. "You're not just *pretending* to be a gentleman because it's Halloween, are you?"

"No. Though that would've been a good costume."

"I ask because I decided not to be a lady tonight," Shannon explained. "At least, not by conventional standards." She tugged his shirt. He moved in closer. One of his hands went up to the wall over her shoulder. "Turns out I need some help to pull that off properly."

Her next line would have been, "So kiss me," but Michael turned out to be just as good at reading between the lines as Shannon. His mouth came to hers. Shannon didn't put up with any gentle lead-in to long, tender kissing this time. Her grip on his shirt turned forceful and her other hand came around the back of his head as she drew him in, kissing back fiercely and goading him into opening up to her more.

Subtle whimpers and lithe body language encouraged Michael to move in. Their lips and tongues grew friendlier as their bodies came together. Shannon welcomed the touch of his shamelessly curious hands on her exposed flesh. Soon, she had to break off from the kiss just to breathe, but the air flowed in and out of her mouth beside his ear in a lusty hiss.

"I'm not usually this forward," he told her. The deep tone of his voice assured her that he had no problem with cold feet. The kiss he planted on her neck punctuated that tone nicely.

"Neither am I," Shannon said directly into his ear, "but I won't hold it against you. Seems like a good night to go out of character."

His mouth came off of her neck. The pair looked at one another with intense, excited eyes. "What aren't you telling me?" he asked.

Shannon grinned again. She could feel how much he wanted her. Most people would buckle under that sort of desire and take anything they could get. Yet Michael could walk away if he had to right now.

"I came here planning to seduce you tonight," Shannon answered. "And I'm not looking for anything exclusive."

"One night only, huh?" he asked.

"I didn't say that," she corrected, "but that's up to you. A man has to protect himself. I understand that. I like you a lot. You're living up to my hopes. I just want you to know there's no white picket fence at the end of this."

She let him sort that out, staring into his eyes all the while. His hand didn't come off her nearly bare hip. His body didn't move off of hers. "White picket fences don't sound very rock'n'roll," he said.

"They don't," Shannon agreed. "Of course, I always figured rock stars were a lot less polite and a lot more fo-ohhh!" she broke off as his hand slipped under her skirt and moved between her legs. She wanted that. She wanted it even more than she realized, and now found him reacting to it. Did he know? Did he read it in her somehow? Was it in her body language, or her demeanor?

It felt far too good to think about now. Shannon melted into Michael's touch, letting him wrap his free arm around her back while his hand worked her through her thin, lacy panties. His mouth came to hers once more, gentler this time as he knew the effect he was having on her body.

Shannon let him take the lead. She liked a guy who could take charge like this. If she felt like seizing control later, she could always do so. For now, she reveled in the fantasy of having a rock star sweep her off her feet…even if he was only a local rock star and both her heels were still on the floor.

She clung weakly to his shoulders. Panted into his mouth. Tensed at the jolts of pleasure that ran through her as his thumb began to tease just the right spot.

Music picked up in the club. Once again, it was all canned stuff, but the music signaled the impending appearance of the next band. Lights around them dimmed. Shannon felt herself grow hotter and hungrier. The distraction, she realized, was exactly what she needed.

"We should get out of here," Michael suggested.

"Nnno," Shannon sighed back. "Everyone's watching the stage now. Not us. Nobody's back here. It's the perfect time."

Michael grinned. "Not something I've ever done," he admitted.

"Me neither." Shannon's voice grew pleading. It was high and breathless and she didn't feel the least bit embarrassed by it. "I'm not…myself…tonight."

Her hands went to his belt. She leaned in and kissed him fiercely as she unfastened it, finding little trouble in freeing him. Then his lips broke off of hers. "We should at least play it safe," he said. "I'm not carrying a con—"

"*We don't need it,*" Shannon assured him in a voice she'd never used before. "*Trust me.*" Her words surprised her, but she knew they were true—and unnaturally persuasive.

His eyes blinked rapidly. Then the touch of his hands became firmer and hungrier. He pushed her up against the wall again as his mouth attacked hers. Somewhere in the distance, fresh, new music hit and appreciative voices exploded into cheers. The opening song wasn't as good as Rockerdammerung's, but neither Michael nor Shannon were there for the music anymore.

She had his groin free of his leather pants. Michael pulled on her lace panties, bringing them down until he realized they had drawstrings on the hips. He shared a knowing grin with Shannon before he took advantage of their convenience and slipped them free.

Their mouths were locked together in a kiss when all was ready. Shannon felt him shift and let him grip her ass with both hands, gladly letting him spread her to hasten the inevitable. She reached for his cock, guided him, held her breath in anticipation…and then moaned uncontrollably into his mouth when she felt him push up inside of her.

She loved him in that moment, though she knew immediately it was more about the act than her partner. Shannon reveled as he thrust in and out of her, alleviating her suspense and anticipation while aggravating her need for release. He was a great partner, and would be so later tonight when they got someplace where they could really enjoy one another. He wasn't just a random lay. He was someone she found genuinely attractive.

Shannon's joy rose along with her pleasure. Monogamy was no longer for her. She carried the unnatural lusts and needs of a woman who was clearly not human. None of that meant she had to lower her standards.

They moved together, grunting and thrusting and loving it.

Distant and all but forgotten already, Shannon heard the customary cheers and applause of the end of the first song. Her eyes met with Michael's. They shifted together, fucking up against the wall and enjoying it on through the next song, and then the next. Neither had anything to say; their needful coupling was statement enough.

Shannon's fingers slipped into his hair. She kissed him again, then couldn't control her breathing enough to continue, and finally leaned her head against his as he brought her to the edge of orgasm. When it hit, Shannon's arms squeezed harder around his shoulders and her fingers dug into his scalp. She let out loud, broken moans directly into his ear. She felt his release hit, too, and enjoyed his voice and the sensations that her partner's climax created within her.

They clung together until their bodies relaxed enough to allow speech. Shannon hardly wanted to let him go, preferring instead to keep him trapped like this. But she knew greater pleasures were to be shared in a different setting.

"I've got a hotel room nearby," he huffed. "Thought I was going to an after party. Knew I wouldn't want to drive."

"Do you still want to go?" Shannon asked with a taunting smile.

"Think I got a better invitation now," Michael grinned.

———

Morning light crept up on them through the sliding glass door of Michael's hotel room. It was a reminder of how little care they had given to planning ahead; the pair had simply tumbled into the room together and begun tearing Michael's clothes off. Shannon's didn't come off right away; she was fully naked now, but for a long time that night she enjoyed playing in her lingerie.

She straddled Michael on the bed, letting him lay back and enjoy a slow ride. His stamina had finally waned some time ago. Shannon was happy to take up the slack. Occasionally, his eyes fluttered closed and he just smiled as her hips moved and as she brought him in and out of her. Mostly, though, he watched her with undisguised appreciation.

"Can't believe we stayed up all night," Michael murmured to the beautiful woman above him. "Wish I had more energy."

"Are you enjoying this?" Shannon grinned naughtily.

"Hell yeah," he sighed. "Never had it so good."

"Then relax," she said. "You put on a whole show. Probably had a full day at work beforehand, right? I'm not holding it against you."

Michael's breath grew shorter and quicker. Shannon's grin spread further. She had him close again. Her own rush would not be long in arriving. "Just don't... wanna... leave you... wanting..." Michael began to pant.

"Shhh, you're wonderful," Shannon assured him. Her eyes fluttered closed. She savored the slow climb to satisfaction. "So good. So… oh. Unh!"

As happened several times already, her orgasm was brought on largely by the first spasms of her partner. Shannon pushed him along by rising up a bit higher and coming down on him a little harder, then remained there as her body was overcome by jolts of pleasure.

She remained on top of Michael in her for several minutes after her orgasm had passed. Warm feelings of satisfaction flowed through her. Despite the pleasure of coupling with Shannon, Michael's endurance had finally reached its limits. He dozed off underneath his partner, having given his all and then some. Shannon smiled. He'd been exactly what she needed.

Her only concern was over what might happen next.

She slipped off of him quietly, pulling a blanket up over his naked body before she moved away from the bed. He was already sound asleep. Shannon felt only slightly tired; she needed to stretch and get some fresh air more than she needed a nap. She found her white lab coat crumpled on the floor and put it on. Then she slipped the balcony door open, drawing the curtains behind her to darken the room for Michael before she stepped outside.

Seattle's skies were overcast as usual this time of year, and dawn had broken only a short while ago. It should have been freezing for her, dressed only in a thin lab coat and with nothing on her feet. Yet she felt fine. Shannon looked out at the great view of downtown and its busy streets flooded with people going back to work.

Where do I go from here?

She still had her job. The complaint from the emergency room would pass without real trouble. Just another speed bump. As she had said to Lorelei, though, her career felt stalled. Brad claimed their relationship had lost its spark, but if anything had gone cold, it was her job. She still enjoyed actually helping people, and she liked the excitement. She just didn't know if she wanted to deal with the low points and all the accompanying bullshit anymore.

Unique conditions steered Shannon's life now. She had new needs to address, and enjoyed them more than she could say. One would think that carrying around the soul of a demon would be a curse. So far, it had been the time of her life.

She wondered how much of her life it would consume.

A gust of wind rushed past. Unconsciously, Shannon turned her head as if to follow it, but all she saw was skyline and rooftops. Then two bare feet came down on the rail of the balcony, and Shannon was not alone.

"Oh! Wow. Hi again. Ohmygod, are you okay?"

The angel's white dress looked fine, but her skin was covered in fresh scars and burns. Rachel's face was set in a scowl. "Yeah," she grumbled, "I'll be fine. Looks worse than it is. You should see what's left of the other dumb fuckers."

"Are those claw marks?" Shannon blinked.

"Hey, it was six against one, alright?" Rachel replied irritably. "I get all dolled up for Halloween and what do I get in return? Werewolves. Fuckin' werewolves, pissing all over my party like it's just a fuckin' tree out in the fuckin' woods. And *they* aren't even what actually ruined my night!"

"What happened?"

"Eh. Long story, ain't got the time to tell it. I just flew by and saw you out here. You might be wearing a different look, but you still kinda stick out for me. The bed-head looks good on you," she teased happily.

Shannon's hand reflexively came up to her ruffled hair. She blushed, but smiled back. "Guess I had a better night than you did."

"Oh, it wasn't all bad. I would've appreciated spending more of it getting laid than I did, but it wasn't all bitches and claws. Anyway, you holdin' up okay?" asked Rachel.

"Yeah. Yeah, I think I'm gonna be fine. Honestly, I'm getting to like this."

"Good. Have a ball. You're doing the world a favor just by living your life. All I ask is that you make sure you're careful with others. Play nice."

"About that," Shannon said, "how...how do I know? I mean, I'm a little afraid I'm gonna start breaking hearts left and right."

Rachel gave a shrug. "Be honest. Be up front." She paused. "Be whoever you want to be. It's your life."

"I just..." Shannon found herself struggling for the words. She jerked her thumb over her shoulder at the room inside. "I like him, y'know? And Kevin. The guy from the other day."

Rachel's mouth turned to a bit of a frown. "Officer ShootsYourAss is a big boy. I've seen him around before. No worries. Tell him your boundaries. He can deal."

Shannon blinked. "Wait," she said, putting her fingers up by her head as if they were fake demon's horns, "you mean *tell* him?"

"Fuck, no, don't tell him *that*. It's funnier if he doesn't know. Just tell him you need your freedom. He'll be fine. As for this one…"

Without ceremony or even a pause, Rachel stuck her head and shoulders through the glass door and the curtain. Shannon saw only her backside, her legs, and her wings; everything else ended at the curtain. Then Rachel stood up straight again and smiled.

"He's cute," she said. "And sweet. But he's not the jealous type. Broke up with his last thing a few weeks ago and now he doesn't want to rush into anything serious, either. You want to make this a one-night stand, he'll be cool. If not? Keep it steamy and mysterious and fuck his brains out, but don't get too comfortable. You'll know when it's getting too serious. When it happens, take a step back. And let him go if he needs to walk away.

"Remember, you gotta play the long game on this. Play the field, y'know? You can stick with some regulars, but it's gotta be plural. You can't stick with the same partner night after night. You'll hurt them."

"I'm more afraid of hurting them if I do play the field," Shannon told her. "The thought of fooling around wherever I go excites me. I'm kind of embarrassed to admit that, but you know what's going on with me, right? Can I really do this?"

"Sure. Believe me, chica, Heaven doesn't give a shit how many people you fuck or how dirty you are in bed. Just play nice with hearts. You'll learn your way. I have faith. Anyway, I gotta fuck off and deal with all my own bullshit." Rachel hopped up onto the balcony rail and spread her wings once more. "See you round!" With that, she dove off into the air and disappeared.

Shannon stood alone, looking out at the city once more. Her hands went into her pockets, where she found her cell phone resting safely. She gave it only a moment's consideration before she pulled it out again and found the number in her call history.

"This is Officer Murray," came the answering voice.

"This is your inappropriate personal call," Shannon replied with a smile. She didn't even consider it before it came out of her mouth. Flirting came naturally now. "Is this an okay time, or are you handcuffing someone?"

"Kinda just got done with that, actually."

"Wow, really?"

"Yeah. Anyway. What's up? You have a good Halloween?"

"I did, but I'm wondering what you're up to maybe tonight or tomorrow," Shannon ventured. "I don't...I'm a little unsure of how to ask. I know I was completely spastic in the morning when you were at my place."

"It's cool. You had company. I understand." He paused. "I could make time for you."

She smiled, felt the joy of anticipation again even despite the satisfaction of her recent conquest—and then remembered exactly that. "Kevin," she said, "I'm kind of complicated."

"Show me someone who isn't."

"No, I mean...I like you. A lot. But I can't do anything exclusive. I mean I *really can't*, and I don't want to lead you on." The eagerness left her voice. Now she felt only concern. She brought a hand to her mouth, clamping nervous teeth down on one nail.

"I wasn't gonna presume anything after two dates," he assured her dryly.

"Yeah, but...what about after twenty?"

He laughed. "Turns out my cat has a strong phobia of commitment, so that might work out well for me."

"You're not just saying that?"

"No. Seriously. You'll have to meet my cat."

Her grin returned. So did the sense of anticipation. "So, your place, then?"

SKIN

"Wait. Your girlfriend had to cut date night short, so sent you to a strip club?" asked Crystal. The blonde leaned over the back of the couch amid flashing lights and thumping bass, giving a "backrub" that focused more on flirtation than muscle therapy.

"True story," said Alex, and it was—apart from everything he left out. He kept his head tilted back so he could look up at her, focusing on her eyes and not the lacy bra under her neon fishnet top.

"Wow. Your girlfriend sounds really cool. Or maybe a little dodgy," Crystal teased.

His eyes widened. *If you only knew*, he thought, but replied aloud, "She can do both."

Crystal laughed. "Then I'm guessing it's more on the cool side. And open-minded, too." She stopped rubbing to grab a sip from the drink he'd bought her, then shifted to running her fingers through his short black hair. "It's too bad she couldn't come along. We see girls come in here with their guys all the time. Makes for a better party when you know everyone's down with all this."

"I've heard that," said Alex, though apparently no such party was happening tonight. Every woman appeared to be a performer or a waitress. The patrons seemed to be exclusively male. He saw a spread of subcultures and styles in the club: some men in business casual, others in sports jerseys, and a handful of guys with Brigands motorcycle club patches on their jackets all seated together. Most of them showed loud appreciation for the dancers on stage.

The club felt clean, spacious, and modern. The crowd was loud and appreciative. Booze flowed freely. So did testosterone. Alex couldn't decide if he felt like this was a safe space or not. Perhaps it was both at once.

Then again, he knew a few things about this particular club that even Crystal probably didn't. "Safe" didn't remotely fit into those secrets.

"So is this your first time?" she asked.

Technically he still had another year to go before he could be in a bar, regardless of what his fake ID said, but she didn't need to know that. "Would you believe I Googled 'strip club etiquette' before I came here?"

"Aw, that's really thoughtful, actually. Guys come in here all the time without a clue of how to act. Or how to dress." She tugged at the collar of his purple dress shirt. "Casual is fine, but looking good is a better way to get attention."

"Yeah, well." Alex shrugged. "I left the house thinking it was date night, right?"

"We'll make up for it," she assured. "You're in the best club in the city."

"That was the plan."

Her eyes turned from his to look around. He suspected she might be checking to see if any of the side rooms were empty. Unexpectedly, she made a plaintive but adorable noise and said, "Hey, I'm being called backstage. Don't go anywhere—the main act's gonna start. And don't bail on me until we've had a private dance, okay?"

That surprised him. Alex held back a thoughtful frown as she moved away. He knew he'd handled the encounter well: he tipped generously, bought her a drink, treated her with respect. Her next move should have been to take him off to one of those private rooms for more expensive entertainment. Wasn't that how dancers made their money? Why wouldn't she stick with him?

His gaze followed her through the club. She slipped around the tables and seats, passing by the front of the stage where flashing lights and men throwing money at the performers made it hard to track anything. It was only by watching her that he spotted the side door near the stage. In the doorway stood a hard-eyed man in the all-black clothes of the club staff. Alex realized the guy was watching him until Crystal reached him, at which point the staffer coolly bent her ear about something or other...and took another glance at Alex before they both disappeared through a door.

Mission accomplished, he thought with a frown. *You've been singled out already. Now watch the hotties on stage and don't look like an undercover cop or some shit.*

Predictably, Alex found the women and the spectacle all too engaging. He had no complaints there. The atmosphere of the club didn't exactly thrill him, but he could easily chalk that up to his fellow customers. It wasn't the first time he'd seen a good show dampened by its audience. No one specific act or culprit ruined things, exactly, but he wished he could be here with fewer men and less booze.

The thought drew his gaze away from the stage once more. Technically, the club required a two-drink minimum. Crystal accounted for his second; the first still sat on the table beside his seat. He'd barely touched it since it arrived.

———

"Did you decide to stop drinking?" asked his "date" at dinner earlier that night.

The question took his attention from the retreating waitress who'd just taken their order. Lorelei paid no mind to his wandering eye. In truth, she was partially responsible for the habit and often shared it with him. At the moment, though, he found her blue eyes watching him thoughtfully. On one side of their table stood candles. On the other sat a pair of nice glasses. Hers held wine. His contained only water and ice.

"You haven't touched a drop since your birthday a couple weeks ago," noted the dark-haired stunner. "I'm not

226

complaining. You never drank much before. A little at parties or when we've gone out. Never to excess. But I've noticed the change."

Alex shrugged. "I hadn't."

The older woman across the table smiled affectionately. "I pay close attention to my man. Is this your decision…or is it someone you used to be?"

His gaze fell to his glass. No curses or necromancy affected the water. Nothing within threatened to drown him in the traumatic memories of earlier lives. Everything in the glass came out of a nice, ordinary faucet. He couldn't say the same for other waters he'd drunk—or been forced to drink. But he was learning to cope with all that.

"I remember working in some rough saloons," he explained. "Saloons and brothels."

"The piano player?"

"Yeah." He grinned as he let out a rueful sigh. "Still can't believe I lived in the Old West and I was a piano player instead of a cowboy. My grandfather would be so disappointed."

"I am not," said Lorelei. "I suspect that piano player was much tougher than most cowboys. We need not speak of it if you wish, or perhaps we might it off until we're alone?"

Alex shook his head. "I'm not bothered. Not like I used to be. And it's all still pretty distant most of the time. I remember working in a lot of nasty places. I remember fights. God, I'm pretty sure there were a *lot* of fights. Enough to get good at it. But it usually happened because someone drank too damn much. Every time there was a punch, there was usually a bottle, too." He shrugged again. "It may have given me an aversion. I might get over it. Might not. We'll see."

"It was a rough time," said Lorelei, "and a rough place."

"Were you there?"

"A little. Nowhere famous. I never made it to Dodge or Tombstone or anywhere else that appeared in the dime novels."

"Dunno if I did, either. The memories aren't that clear. I remember it being rough. Rougher for other people, though. Especially the women. Brothels, like I said." He glanced up to find a troubled look on her beautiful face. "What is it?"

"I had thoughts about something we might do tonight," Lorelei explained. "It's somewhat less romantic than our original plans. I have been unsure of how to broach the subject, and now this talk of brothels and rough lives seems ominous."

Alex held his silence and listened. He knew something was up when they met at the restaurant. She arrived late in a red top under her leather coat, black jeans that looked painted on, and tall boots. Though Lorelei's idea of "casual" was still the sort of image one saw on the cover of a glamour magazine, Alex had reasonably expected more than casual when she suggested a night out. She fed on the attention her sensual beauty attracted, especially from him—more or less literally.

She fed on other fun things, too, but there had been none of that before his classes this morning. Or when he went to bed last night. Even now, she passively avoided his touch. He couldn't help but notice. That wasn't like her at all.

"We have no problem between us," she said as if reading his mind, or at least the look in his eyes. "I am sorry for my distance last night and today. It gets to my plans for tonight." She paused again, this time with an amused smile. "I also thought you might need a full night's sleep for once."

That drew an intimate, naughty grin from her partner. "I'll let you know when I'm worn out. I've spoken up before."

"And then changed your mind ten minutes later, yes," Lorelei teased. "I'll never complain."

"So what's up?"

"I must confess I misled you, Alex. I couldn't tell you of my plans while there was any risk of Rachel discovering them. You know how discerning she can be."

"You mean she might know something's up just by looking at me. Freaky angel-sense or whatever it is," said Alex.

"She has that talent, yes."

"So...?" Alex prompted.

She slid a business card across the table to him. Under the word "Vixens" scrawled in red letters, he saw a picture of an alluring woman in a Catholic school girl outfit that would fail every school dress code ever. "This is a strip club?"

"Yes."

"What's wrong with going to a strip club?" he asked. "I mean, I've never been to one, but I'm pretty sure it'll be way tamer than the places I used to work. Or who I used to be. Whatever. The whole world's different now. Clubs these days probably don't even compare."

"One would think," Lorelei conceded.

His eyes came up to meet hers again. "Only you know better."

"This is more about business than pleasure. I must have private words with the owner of the establishment. It may not be the friendliest conversation."

"Who's the owner?"

"You remember Rob Gorge, the demon you fought after we first met?"

Alex grimaced. "How could I forget?"

"The owner's name is Lester," she explained. "Because I told him a century ago that 'Mr. Luster' was far too obvious."

"Aw, you're kidding me." He pinched the bridge of his nose. "This is a demon strip club? Seriously?"

"Well," Lorelei said with a shrug, "demon-owned, anyway. I doubt most of the employees or patrons have the slightest clue."

"So it's not a gateway to Hell or something?"

"That depends on one's definitions of evil or torture. I expect the drinks will be watered down quite a bit," Lorelei warned. "Also, unlike myself, most demons don't have the best taste in music."

His shoulders sagged. He threw her a look dry enough to match her words. "This guy's another one of your former co-workers?"

"Nothing so close." She smiled at his choice of words. "Lester and I cooperated out of convenience on occasion, but we served different lords. He and his ilk come from a very cold corner of Hell. Like Rob, he works to expand Hell's influence and earn souls for the Pit, and also like Rob, he wears a human form. Rob used wealth to tempt mortals. Lester appeals to more lustful urges."

"Why do you need to talk to him? I thought the idea was to let Rachel and her buddies run all the other demons out of town."

"I prefer to let that run its course, but she must find them first. Lester's human form hides him from the angels and helps anchor him to this world. More powerful demons like myself cannot hide from the angels as easily. I'll explain the complexities another time. Regardless, he'll know where others of his kind may be found. I want to get that information from him, for Rachel's sake. And ours," she added. "Fewer demons in this city is good for us, too. Yet if I tell Rachel about this one, she'll want to know where he is."

Alex could imagine the rest. "And she'll go straight into napalm death mode on his ass and not get any info, right?"

"Nothing will remain but cinders and profanity floating in the wind," she replied. "Subtlety is not her strong suit. On the bright side, as I say, I'm considerably more powerful than Lester. I can handle him if he tries anything stupid. Even a couple of mortal bodyguards should be little trouble."

"So what's the plan?" asked Alex.

"You'll go in ahead of me as an ordinary patron. I'll wait until you're engaged, then slip in as unobtrusively as I can. Lester will have the place warded for his protection and to hide him from the angels. He'll detect my presence immediately. If he has a brain in his head, he'll choose to talk with me rather than doing anything stupid. Then you and I will leave and take steps to ensure we are not followed."

"So I'm the scout?" asked Alex. "Or the back-up?"

"No," said Lorelei. "You're the distraction. Lester works with a temptress. I do not know her name. Not a succubus like myself—a lesser demon, hiding within human flesh like Lester. I'd rather not deal with two demons at once. I hope to divide and conquer.

"You no longer enjoy the direct protection of Heaven. Rachel looks after you, but technically, you have no guardian angel. Demons can sense these things. It will make you an appealing target. This is also why I have not touched you since yesterday. I don't want her to sense my connection to you, either. She might leave you alone if she smells competition." Lorelei favored him with an affectionate, sultry grin. "I want her to see only a vulnerable, attractive young man. You'll be irresistible."

"For what?"

"Temptation. Seduction. She'll want to enthrall you into her service, again like Rob did to others with money. Wealth and carnal pleasures aren't sins in and of themselves, but they offer powerful lures. We've had that talk, though."

"Yeah." Alex frowned. "We have."

"A temptress needs her victim to come back over successive encounters to gain a solid hold over his soul. Her charms cannot do you lasting mystic or spiritual harm in a single night. You may well resist her supernatural charms entirely. You are far more aware than the average mortal, and your will is strong. Besides, even if you should succumb, I will have

232

no trouble rescuing you from her clutches. All you need to do is play along until I come for you. It will not be long. Perhaps half an hour at the very most.

"Or I can apologize," she offered, watching him carefully, "and we can forget this entire matter. I was unsure how to approach this, and unsure how you might react." Her hand stretched out across the table. "We can tell Rachel, let her handle Lester and his temptress her way, and go about our night together. I do not wish to pressure you into anything you don't want to do."

Though much of him wanted to take her up on the offer, Alex pulled his hands back and held them up. "No. No, I want to help. Demons running a strip club can't be a good thing, right?"

"It seems unlikely, yes." She watched him carefully. "You are willing, but what troubles you?"

"How far does 'playing along' go?"

"As far as you choose. Alex, we both understand what our bond does to your appetites. We also know our boundaries. Push her away and I will still have my head start with Lester. Follow her into some private room for much more than a lapdance and you will only empower me further. There is literally nothing you could do with this woman that would make me upset, Alex. You aren't capable of it."

"And if anything goes wrong?"

"Then we'll have to improvise. Errands like this always carry risk. I would not suggest this if I didn't have faith in your..." She stopped, and then smiled.

"What?" he asked.

"'Faith' is not a word my kind use often. But I have great faith in you, Alex. And in us. As I say, there is always risk. I believe it to be minimal here, or I would not suggest it. I believe we can handle whatever may come. It's up to you. I'll not pressure you."

He considered it for a moment more and slowly nodded. "So what's her name?"

"I don't know," said Lorelei. "She'll have a new name and a new face from our last meeting. It's their way. But you'll know her when you see her, or when she sees you."

———

Lorelei wasn't wrong.

Performances and audience interaction followed a clear pattern. A DJ with a booming, enthusiastic game show voice introduced each dancer as she arrived, and the audience showed plenty of appreciation. The newcomer would come out and perform on one of the poles to the left and right of the stage, then move to downstage center for the next song to collect tips from the guys in the pit, while another performer came out to take her previous place. With the tips cleaned up, the dancer would slip offstage, get dressed—more or less—and then circulate through the audience until she found a customer for a lap dance or whatever else went on in the private rooms.

The system made sense to Alex. He thought it strange that dancers came out wearing so little to begin with, often hardly more than a bikini or a costume that covered about as much. He'd always figured a striptease would start with the performer having something to actually take off, but then, his only experience was what he'd seen in film and TV, and it wasn't as if he wanted to lodge a complaint. On the contrary, he found the whole thing all too appealing.

He never lacked for sexy funtime anymore. Alex had better companionship than he could dream of. He had enough of that in his life. Much more than enough. His head knew it. His heart knew it.

The succubus curse that formed part of his bond with Lorelei disagreed in strong, persuasive terms. It often joined in a chorus with his natural libido to declare that "enough" was a damn, dirty lie. Tonight that chorus came through loudly along with lustful hip-hop and shameless rock songs as every single performer claimed his attention.

Alex had little trouble keeping it in his pants as long as nothing encouraged him. One other aspect of the succubus curse, though, was that he found constant encouragement, and that proved true in offices and classrooms and even standing on line at the Department of Licensing. He'd worried at first that it created some sinister emotional influence, but now he understood that it worked more like a magnet for desires that already existed—and it worked in both directions. A place like Vixens made his desires all too welcome, all too strong, and *oh god she's doing splits vertically against the pole this is the best place ever!*

No. Stop it, he told himself. *Demon strip club. Freakin' demons. All these tough guys don't know how small and weak they really are in here. Every one of these chicks could've signed her soul away. Or be possessed. Or be a soul-crushing monster.*

A seriously hot soul-crushing monster. Wow, that ass and that smile, I can't…Stop it! Demons!

As if to prove the point, the lights dimmed and the music faded into steady, ominous bass beats. Alex missed almost everything in the DJ's booming intro, picking up only the tail end: "…blah blah blah Seattle, give it up for Destiny!"

The other dancers seemed to almost bow in deference and then melt away to cede the stage. She strutted out in fishnets, purple lingerie and stiletto heels, her sunglasses creating an air of confidence and mystery over her gorgeous Asian features. Everything from her attitude to the music and the lights marked her as the clear master of this domain.

"Destiny" strutted, swayed, and spun across the stage to a thumping beat and a suggestive melody. Cheers, whistles, and catcalls gave way to almost reverential cries of love and devotion as she began to dance. At first, she seemed to fixate on him, keeping her head turned toward him as her costume corset came off to reveal a swimsuit model belly. A purple lace bra still concealed her breasts. Another minute passed before she threw the sunglasses into the crowd. After that, Alex could see her eyes, and he knew without a doubt she danced specifically for him.

Part of him hated how good it felt to be the deer in someone's headlights. Conscious thoughts reminding him of her true nature and her danger of this place couldn't drown out tempting thoughts of *yeah, but I wish I could.*

His heart beat heavily. A familiar hardness tightened his slacks. Destiny stared at him from across the stage as she swayed, one hand coming to her back to unfasten a clasp and finally reveal her beautiful—*oh God damn it she has another tiny bra under that!*

A minute later, she pulled almost exactly the same trick with her panties: another dancer slipped up behind her to slowly pull them down, revealing more skin but also a tiny thong. Alex saw it coming a mile away. Anyone could. It still only deepened the sense of anticipation through denial.

Men howled in joyous frustration. The music continued. Through it all, Destiny danced and watched the face of one specific young man across the room.

Alex didn't know whether or not Destiny used any sort of supernatural compulsion to draw out his attention or his lust. With a face and body like hers, she hardly needed it. Still, Alex slipped one hand under the table to ensure the iron nail in his pocket hadn't gone anywhere. Molly and Onyx called it a basic occult ward. It required no technique or magical skill. He wondered how he'd feel right now without it. He also wondered if it even mattered.

By the end of the song, he thought less about his fight for self-control or the potential danger Destiny presented. Mostly, he thought about his desires. He wanted her to come over. He'd have gotten up and gone to the stage if he didn't infer from the sudden lack of men standing in the pit that this was forbidden while Destiny performed. *Demon*, he reminded himself, and then, *hot demon*. Smoking hot. Literally.

No. That's not smoke. That's fog from the wings... what?

Another song began. It blended into the end of the previous number with a low, anticipatory beat. Destiny strode to the end of the stage, then slid down and took up a seat on the edge with her lovely legs on display. She watched Alex all the while.

She'd have kept his full attention, too, had it not been for the shapely silhouette that came out onto the stage, stepping into the light in red leather, jet black hair, and a wicked grin.

Aw hell, Alex thought with rising desires and wavering resolve. *There's two of 'em.*

———

They'd pulled this trick before, though Alex didn't know it at the time. Lorelei waited in her car around the corner until she could feel his first real pleasures through their mystic bond. That happened in short order as someone began caressing his shoulders and neck. Knowing nothing more than that, Lorelei stepped out into the night. Most of the neighboring buildings were warehouses or small businesses, all of them closed for the night. Still, Lorelei wrapped herself in demonic enchantments to ensure that no one would see her. The arousal of her prey more than returned the effort spent on supernatural stealth.

Nothing seemed out of place. Cars parked in the back lot largely matched those she'd seen before in earlier scouting. Lights, video cameras, and locked doors all remained in place. No one lurked about. Lester understood the value of mundane security measures. Lorelei also sensed the infernal wards that lined the building. She would feel their wrath once she stepped inside, but nothing Lester could conjure up would seriously harm her. She also had Alex to help with that, as he did the first time they pulled this trick. Then again, Alex took that particular incident much further than he would likely go tonight.

Lorelei wondered if she pushed this plan harder than she'd intended. The succubus still wasn't used to considering other people's feelings, though she got better every day with Alex and his friends. Boundaries weren't so easily measured. Nor were all of her own emotions. All these centuries, yet sincere guilt felt so fresh and new. Unpleasant, but new.

She felt a little guilt along with the sudden rise of Alex's lust. Lorelei knew her cue. Smiling at the rush of desire, the demon strode up to the front entrance without further use for concealment. She couldn't walk through walls, nor open doors without breaking the enchantment. Nor did she have much hope of slipping across the wards without their creator sensing the breach. Best to be straightforward about this.

Immediately inside the building, Lorelei felt the biting chill of the magic that protected Lester's domain. The short, pretty hostess and the dark-toned bouncer stationed in the foyer felt and sensed nothing of the sort, but the wards weren't aimed at mortals. To a demon like Lorelei, the strip club might as well have been inside a glacier.

She had her own powers to keep her warm, though. That and the arousal of her dear victim. Chances were he'd reject the advances of any temptress demon, knowing her for what she was, but that would still leave Alex spun up by the encounter—and Lorelei with him. They'd both need relief soon.

"Hello," Lorelei said pleasantly, unsurprised that hostess and bouncer alike needed a moment for a double-take. "I'm here to see the owner. Privately. Would you *take me straight to him*, please?" she asked, focusing her eyes and a small measure of her power on the bouncer. She watched the big man's jaw slacken as her supernatural suggestion and his enthralled desires overrode any conflicting protocols or loyalties.

"Uh. Sure," he mumbled, shaking his head and then gesturing for Lorelei to follow.

Lorelei noted the hostess's surprise. "Do you need to check my ID or take the cover charge?" she asked politely.

"No, not at all," the hostess smiled brightly despite her confusion. She seemed inclined to follow the bouncer's lead, however unusual this might be. "I guess Jake has you covered. Thanks for coming!"

The demon returned her smile. Nothing about the hostess marked her as bound for the Pit, though one look rarely told that much. Still, Lorelei wondered if the hostess enjoyed Heaven's protection. Either the hostess and all the other mortal employees had lost that blessing, or Lester took constant care to avoid the notice of any passing guardian angel.

Lorelei followed Jake into the club and then off to one side of the main floor. Skirting around the edges, she heard the rhythmic bass and electric guitar melodies of a slow, lusty song. Amid flashing lights on stage, she spotted the temptress in the middle of her performance. Ordinary mortals wouldn't see her wings, her tail, or her little horns. They saw only the beauty of her human guise. Lorelei noted a flashing sign off to one side of the stage that offered the name "Destiny." *Of course you are*, she thought.

She didn't spot Alex, but Destiny's focus suggested he sat at a table somewhere near the middle. He likely wouldn't be there long. Lorelei turned back to her guide.

They skirted the outer edges of the audience, finding a dark hallway with private rooms off to either side. A short flight of stairs rose up not far from where the hall branched off toward a kitchen. Jake led her upstairs without pause.

Her entrance played out according to plan. This took less than a minute. "Thank you, Jake," she said, stroking his cheek as she stepped past him. "You may *leave us alone* now."

Jake grinned at her excitedly. He'd made her happy. Lorelei had seen this reaction before. Her guide turned and left, hoping his helpful service would be remembered.

Alone in the hallway, Lorelei took hold of the door handle and turned it down hard enough to break the lock. She pushed forward, felt further resistance, and slammed an open hand against the door above the handle. The deadbolt broke right through the doorframe.

"Aw shit," hissed a man inside.

Lorelei stepped through the doorway with a pleasant smile that didn't match her show of brute strength. "Hello, Lester," she greeted him.

The good-looking man with the dark goatee stood behind his desk in a suit with no tie. He had a cell phone in one hand and a pistol in the other. Lester nearly dropped both of them as recognition spread across his face. "Oh, *shit!*" he repeated, this time illustrating the difference between being startled and genuine fear.

"What an adorable gun," Lorelei said, striding across the room to his desk—and then stopped.

Lester stared, frozen in place. Through the broken door, they could hear the thumping bass of the club's main floor, but a small speaker set on his desk struck a decidedly different tune: "...*to the place where I belong. West Virginia, mountain momma...*"

She let out a sigh as the music playing in the office clashed with the modern beats from downstairs. "John Denver? Really" she asked. "Ugh. This is how I know your DJ is mortal." She crossed the last couple of feet to his desk to snatch the phone from his hand. "And who are we calling? Anyone I know?" A glance at the screen showed an outgoing call, which she ended with a single touch.

"Wh-what do you want?" asked Lester.

"Any number of things," she answered coolly.

"*All my memories, they gather 'round her...Miner's lady, stranger to blue water...*"

"This is also how one knows a demon in stolen skin from the genuine article," she grimaced. "I don't know if it's a native

242

flaw in those born in the Pit or if it's a problem with your stolen bodies, but something goes terribly wrong with your musical tastes before the process is finished." Lorelei flipped through the phone's screens to open up the music player and cut the song short. Relief spread across her face as the melodic longing ended. "Ah. That's better. Miracles happen to all of us, I suppose." She put the phone in her coat pocket. "I'm looking for information, mostly. The phone should be a start. Thank you for that."

"Lady Lorelei!" hissed an awed voice off to one side. Lorelei turned to see a small red creature in the corner, hiding behind a wastebasket. It had scales instead of skin and a lizard-like head, but its demonic wings, horns, and tail marked it as another servant of the Pit rather than some conjured beast of mortal sorcery. It pointed at her with wide yellow eyes and repeated, "Lady Lorelei!"

The facetious geniality dropped from Lorelei's face. "Do not call me that," she said flatly. The imp shrank back behind the wastebasket. Lorelei turned her attention to Lester once more, hoping to hide her concern at the unexpected sight of a demon in its natural form. She'd simply have to stick to the original plan. "Dear, if you're not going to shoot me with that thing, put it down. Guns make men look so insecure."

Lester opened his mouth again to protest, but gave it up. Defiantly, he shoved the pistol into the pocket of his blazer. "You think you can barge in here, take what you want, and boss me around?"

Her eyebrows rose. She looked back at the broken door, the imp cowering in the corner, and Lester himself. "Yes." She smiled as he scowled. "Oh, don't look so put out, Lester. I'm here to offer you a fair trade for what I want."

His jaw set. "What do you want to know?"

"I'm looking for the other demons in this city. It turns out our kind have become difficult to find in the last couple of months. You're the connected sort. You'd know who is still out and about, or who has gone to ground."

"Yeah, you'd know why it's getting tough, wouldn't you?" Lester sneered. "I've heard about you and Baal. I know you don't work for Belial anymore. Heard who you *have* been running with, too. Word gets around, especially when it comes to sellouts."

"Oh, Lester. I'd have to care about your opinions for that sort of name-calling to mean anything to me. All I want is information. Names, whereabouts, whatever you know. I won't ask you to betray Sammael or the rest of his crew. You'd never tell me the truth about that, anyway. I want to know about everyone else."

He bit back another retort in favor of a question: "What's in it for me?"

"A head start out of town before fiery angelic retribution crashes down on your pretty little face. Make it good and I'll give you several hours. That's more than enough time to escape into the next Dominion over. I hear the angels there are less diligent."

"You call that a deal?"

"I do. Besides, you owe me. Do you remember that mess in Paris, oh, a little over two centuries ago? Remember the whole town suddenly going insane? Public executions left and right, and angels on the hunt everywhere because they blamed the Pit for all the bloodlust and death? You ditched me."

"I had to get out of town!" Lester protested.

"So did I. You were supposed to help me with that. Instead, you ran. Even I couldn't evade all those angels on my own. I had to go through Hell to get out of that city. Literally. I *hate* Hell, Lester."

"Everybody hates being in Hell!" said Lester, holding his hands up helplessly. "That's the point! That's why we're all tryin' to get *here*!"

Her eyes flared. "Indeed." She planted a lightning-fast right cross on his nose.

Lester fell back into his seat, clutching his face. "Ow! What'd you do that for?"

"That's for Paris, Lester. And for dragging this conversation out. Now, you have my offer, and you know why you owe this to me."

"You already hit me for that!"

"One punch doesn't make up for your debts, Lester."

"You didn't bring this up last time we met!"

"No. I decided to save this debt for a rainy day. You may have noticed how often it rains in this city."

The other demon fumed. A small bit of blood dripped from his nose, but the cartilage was already resetting. "What are you gonna do with that info?"

245

"The same thing I'm doing with you. Run every one of you out of town so I don't have to see or smell your kind here anymore."

His lip curled up into a sneer. "Don't you mean our kind?"

"Surely I'll find a way to live with my hypocrisy."

"And what if I tell you to go fuck yourself?"

"Then I won't bother with the angels. I'll deal with you myself. And I'll make sure Sammael hears all about your treachery against him. Oh, don't worry, I'll invent something plausible. By the time you reanimate in Hell, your lord will be so angry with you he may not even stop to ask questions before punishing you for your betrayal." She smiled sweetly. "Or you can take my offer, and no one need know we ever spoke. Your escape from the city will seem like an act of tremendous foresight."

Lester glared. Lorelei waited. Behind her cordial yet steely façade, Lorelei felt Alex's fierce arousal. Someone stroked his shoulder and neck again, this time draping herself along one side of his seat. She could feel the pleasant nearness of her and knew from his reactions that this must be the temptress.

Then she felt another such body slide onto his lap and hook her arm around the other side of Alex's neck. "Let's start with your crew. Since when do you rate more than one assistant?" she asked, gesturing to the imp. "And who are the two temptresses downstairs?"

"I'm Chance," said the woman sitting sideways on his lap. She gently ran her fingers through his hair. Destiny sat on the cushioned arm rest of his seat, caressing his neck. The music kept bumping as the club returned to its previous patterns of dancers on stage and in the audience. "Crystal told us you could use some cheering up."

Once again, his libido shouted all manner of enthusiastic agreement. Every one of Lorelei's enabling comments came back to him in a rush. With two gorgeous, scantily-clad women fawning over him, Alex found that it hardly mattered how good he had it at home. The pair had him well beyond aroused.

Demon strippers! he remembered. The danger they presented didn't turn him off. The absurdity of those words, however, made a slight difference. Humor offered a lifeline. He grabbed onto it and pulled. The names helped.

"Destiny and Chance?" Alex asked with a cooler grin than he would ever have managed before the autumn saw his life turned upside down. "My night got existential fast." *Don't say "sexistential,"* he thought quickly. *Don't say "sexistential." No puns. Don't do it.* "Is there a Karma here, too?"

"Aw, don't make fun," pouted Destiny, sliding her fingers down the back of his collar and dragging her nails back up over the nape of his neck. It gave him a pleasant shiver. "They're only names. I like yours...Alex."

"Didn't mean anything by it," he replied, looking from one to the next as they pawed at him with increasing familiarity. It felt entirely too good, and worked entirely too well.

"I'm glad to meet you. Both of you. Just don't know if this is luck or if it's fate."

"That's the spirit," Chance purred in approval. "Truth is, Crystal told us why you're here. She said out of all the men in this club, you deserve special attention."

"There are other men here?" Alex grinned.

Destiny laughed and shifted around so she could lean her head against his. "None that matter now," she said into his ear.

"We could have more fun in private, though," suggested Chance. Her hands roamed lower toward his groin. "Destiny and I have a VIP room all to ourselves. Care to join us?"

"Wow. Now I feel really special." The sensations continued: nails, caresses, Destiny's breath on his ear, and Chance's pleasant weight shifting in his lap. "How much did Crystal tell you?"

"Only that your girlfriend ditched you like an idiot," Chance explained. "Everything else, we can tell about you all on our own. Her loss. Our gain. Yours, too."

"Trust us, Alex," said Destiny. "We'll make you forget all about her."

Once again, nothing brought him back to Earth like a good dose of absurdity. Forget his girlfriend? No way. Still, he had a job to do here. "Challenge accepted."

With confident smiles and graceful moves, the pair returned to their feet. Each took one of his hands and drew him up from the seat, then led him out of the audience. Alex noted their posture and stride, all of it deliberately intended to show off their tight bodies to any onlooker. They split their attention between him and the other men who called out to them as they left, assuring the others that they hadn't been forgotten while making sure Alex knew he was the most important man in the room...for now, at least.

They led him under the club's balcony into a hall of red lights and doorways blocked only by curtains or beads. He heard more music, along with feminine moans here and there. It all seemed a little too much for him. He wondered if the voices weren't recorded to provide atmosphere. It would certainly get a guy's hopes up. Alex saw a couple of burly men in black t-shirts and jeans in the hallway, too, providing a visible reminder that any transgressions would be quickly dealt with. It made sense to him. Any decent security would put the safety of the dancers first. Real privacy wasn't an option.

Then, at the sight of Alex's escorts, one of those bouncers turned to sweep aside a curtain and open up the door behind it. Alex blinked. It didn't even have a window down the side. This was exactly the privacy he didn't expect. Still fully aware of this club's supernatural secrets, Alex half dreaded what he'd find on the other side of that door.

He kept walking with the women. Alex didn't know how much time Lorelei would need, but he'd only been with Destiny and Chance for a couple of songs. Pulling away now might seem suspicious. Alex resolved to walk away or even run if he saw anything outlandish as they came around the doorway. Instead, he found more red and purple lights, more leather furniture, more mirrors, pillows, and a small bar off to one side.

Okay. This I can do, thought Alex. Then again, maybe that was his libido talking. He couldn't be sure.

Destiny gently pushed him into a chair and immediately straddled his legs. "You're in for the time of your life," she breathed, and he believed her…right up until the private room's speakers came to life with grating pop music.

Alex winced. He glanced over to the bar, where he saw Chance standing with her finger on the small stereo controls and a proud look on her face. "Wait, is this a prank?" asked Alex. "Seriously? You're putting in Justin——"

"Use one of the playlists the DJ made," Destiny cut him off with a grumble. Chance frowned but did as the other woman asked.

Their guest didn't know whether to be grateful for the buzzkill or not. It took the edge off of his desires and gave him a moment of clarity, but still…*Fucking devil music*, he thought. *What's wrong with them?*

———

"She's one of Abbadon's," said Lester. "She's got a little office in downtown a block up the hill from the courthouses." He scribbled out another name and a couple of notes at his desk. "Bail bonds stuff. Ground floor, facing the corner, can't miss it." He snorted. "I think she calls herself Hope 'cause that's how her place smells. If you don't know any better, anyway."

"I believe I've driven past that office several times," Lorelei thought aloud. "What's her real name?"

"Fuck if I know. They usually don't tell me. If someone sets up business and makes sure we don't come to blows where we overlap, I don't get nosey. Her pockets go deep. She's got lawyers on the payroll to make sure she gets the right kinda business, y'know? Some of her marks wouldn't normally get bail out of a judge at any price, but if Hope wants 'em, they grease the wheels."

"Who else?"

Lester made a face, but then turned back to his sheet of paper. "Got some creepers living in some of those condemned hotels on Aurora, north of the bridge. Think they move back and forth. Might spend some time under them buildings, too."

"How many?"

"Never less than three. Doin' what creepers do, y'know? Plenty of homeless and junkies and undocumented types in this town to pick off."

"Lovely."

"Hey, one soul is as good as another," Lester grumbled. "I've heard all about succubi and incubi and your 'prestige' bullshit, but we're all working stiffs up here, okay? Creepers got their place in the ecosystem, too."

Her eyebrow rose. "You're defending the necessity of creepers?"

"I'm sayin' you shouldn't be all high and mighty. It's only luck of the draw that separates us out from you *beautiful people*," he added with a sneer. "Accidents of birth or whatever you wanna call it. And don't kid yourself. I know how often daddy's little princes and princesses wind up on their knees."

"If it makes you feel better, Lester, I started out far lower than you would imagine. Now, less chatting and more writing," she said, putting a finger down on the growing list on his sheet of paper. "I'd imagine someone must have started a fitting room in this city by now. Where is it?"

Lester blinked. "It ain't like this city's that big," he pointed out.

"Compared to what?" Lorelei asked. "I remember seeing fitting rooms in little more than frontier towns a century and a half ago. Don't tell me Seattle isn't big enough to hide one now."

"Yeah, but something like that's an investment," Lester replied, then shrugged. "Anyway, you want what I know, right? Not speculation."

"Indeed."

Lester nodded. "Then I can't tell you about fitting rooms. I can tell you about guy Mammon has in a corner office in a Bellevue tower, though."

"Please do. Your cooperation is noted and appreciated."

The demon looked ready for another resentful comment, but he bit it back and returned to his writing. Lorelei didn't try to drag it out of him. Clearly, he knew when it was time to keep his mouth shut.

———

Destiny gyrated in his lap, expertly massaging the erection in his pants with her groin and grinning wickedly all the while.

He didn't expect full-on kissing. A lot of groping and grind-
ing, sure. He figured their lacy bras weren't long for this
room, and he was right. They hardly spent much time building further anticipation before that big reveal.

Chance leaned over the back of the couch to unbutton
his shirt, kissing and lightly biting at his neck. She was less
gentle with his sleeveless undershirt, though, grabbing at its
low collar and tearing it right down the middle. Alex opened
his mouth in protest. The next thing he knew, Destiny filled
that mouth with her tongue until it was Chance's turn to lean
over and kiss him. He forgot about his complaint.

"Mmm, I like this," murmured Destiny as her hands
roamed. "Nice definition."

Chance didn't stop kissing, but she verified Destiny's
evaluation with a caress. "Mm-hmm."

They were assertive, confident, and even a little rough.
Alex liked all of that. He didn't like the woozy feeling he got
from Chance's kiss, though, or the unnatural echo as Destiny
whispered, "*Give in, Alex.*"

He'd never heard a whisper echo before, let alone directly
into his ear right in the middle of a music-filled room. He
might not have heard it at all if his guard wasn't up and he
didn't have that little nail in his pocket.

Don't even need to know magic for this trick, Molly had
laughed. *You don't even have to believe.*

Simple protection, Onyx had told him. *Like a good coat in a
blizzard. You'll still feel the chill, but it's a hell of a lot better than
going out naked.*

He wondered if going naked wasn't far off. The "private dance" continued through one song on the stereo and then another as he and the two dancers groped, fondled, and kissed one another into a frenzy. Still, Alex had the sense and the willpower to think past physical need. Succubus curse or not, he still cared about context. Fooling around with a flirtatious, eager stranger might be okay—he'd done it at least once—but false pretenses lay well out of bounds for him, at least until now. The compelling voices in his ear, the hands stroking his bared chest, and that wonderful body in his lap steadily eroded that inhibition.

I mean damn, he thought, *it's not like I've never had sex with a demon before. Things worked out great with Lorelei! What's the harm? So what if I'm on my own in a strange place where nobody here has my best interests in . . .*

. . . yep. Like wearing a coat. Still feel the chill.

"We want you, Alex," Chance breathed across his lips. "You're perfect for us."

"Exactly what we're looking for," Destiny agreed, her hands roaming his chest. "*You want us, too, don't you?*" came that echo again. "It'll be so good."

His self-control rallied, carrying him at least as far as ambiguity. "Got it pretty good already," he said.

"That's what you think," Chance taunted. "*She'll never know.*"

Chance couldn't know it, but her suggestion only intensified his conflict. Lorelei would, in fact, know everything that went on. She knew about this right here and would feel every moment of escalation. To make it even harder to resist, she'd already told him she'd be okay with it. And Alex was in no small part down here to help her.

Two sets of lips attacked his neck on either side. Destiny backed off on his groin enough to let Chance unzip his pants and slip her fingers inside. Her grip told him they were beyond teasing now.

"Don't you want it?" asked Destiny.

Words didn't come easily. He found it difficult to hold a steady tone, or even open his eyes up all the way. Honesty fought through the rush of arousal and the clouds in his judgment: "I wish I could."

"You can," Chance assured him sweetly. "No one needs to know."

"C'mon, stud." Destiny slid off of his lap, taking his hands and pulling him up. "Got someplace much more comfortable than this. Secret room," she winked, "right over here."

Alex blinked away the haze as Destiny all but painted herself against him, turning him toward one of the mirrors. It gave him a double reminder of her hot body. Chance crossed between the pair and their reflection, slipping over to the mirror and then putting her fingers to its side. The entire piece swung aside like a door, frame and all, revealing an inviting staircase leading down.

All of his alarm bells went off at once: too much too fast with the sexy stuff, a strange place with strange women, secret rooms, and oh yeah, demons. They had him turned on. No argument. They didn't turn off his brain. *Why do they need a secret room* behind *the private, locked, guarded VIP room?*

Incense beckoned to him as they descended. Destiny kept one of his hands in hers as she led him down the stairs. Chance stuck close behind him with the lightest grip on his shoulder. Perhaps as a small demonstration of resolve and resistance, Alex zipped up his fly again. "*Relax, baby*," Chance whispered. "This is gonna change your entire life."

At the bottom of the stairs, Destiny spun and kissed Alex again before he could see anything of the room besides candles and black curtains. He tried to keep his eyes open, but Chance's lips at the nape of his neck made that difficult. He felt her hands rise up his legs.

"*Don't think about anything but us*," Chance told him. Her fingers even traced up along the nail inside his pocket, but that hardly registered for him. The clouds came back into his mind. He felt only lust and heat and need.

Destiny pulled away. His eyes fluttered open.

Electric lamps hung from the ceiling on black chains. On one side of the room lay a muscular man on a black couch, wearing only a collar and chain attached to the wall. A thick, fresh scar ran up the center of his chest. His eyes glowed with a red light as he sat up, but he said nothing. Along the far wall, a table held unlabeled jars, bottles, and bowls of powders and liquids. Another wall held a tall mirror.

A large, round, leather-covered platform dominated the center of the room, looking like a giant upholstered coffee table with built-in restraints. Faintly glowing runes decorated the platform, and the walls, and the ceiling.

"Ready for the next level?" asked Chance as she came around to his side.

"Nope!" Alex declared, palming her face and shoving her away. "Nope, nope, nope!" He darted out of Destiny's reach as Chance stumbled to the floor. "This shit right here is not a sex-positive scene. I'm out. Ciabatta." He strode over to the man on the couch. "Hey, buddy, you still with us here? What's your name?"

The man snarled. He lunged at Alex, practically clawing at him, but found his chain too short to actually reach once Alex jerked back.

"Woah. Buddy, listen to me. Time for the safe word. Come back to Earth now."

"What are you doing?" asked Destiny as she pulled Chance to her feet. The other woman looked far more shocked than hurt. "What's wrong with you?"

"Aw lady, I'd need to write you a whole novel for that," Alex grumbled. "And a sequel. Okay. Dude. It's time to sober up and go home now." He tried snapping his fingers, clapping and waving his hands in front of the man's glowing eyes. "Are you still in there?"

"Submit or die!" the man sputtered in a rage.

"Okay, I tried." He turned to leave, but found Chance blocking the doorway. Destiny reached under the big platform to produce a pair of handcuffs. "Ladies, we're done," he said. "I'm not down with your kinks. Get out of my way."

"We didn't invest all that time and effort in you for nothing," said Destiny.

Alex made a face. "That was like twenty minutes! Half an hour, tops!"

"You know you want more," Chance offered despite her obvious annoyance. She fixed him with a sultry stare. "*Stay, Alex. Relax.* It only gets better from here. *You'll love it.*"

He felt his eyelids grow heavy as a shudder ran through him, but it went no further than that. He had little trouble resisting now. "You can knock off the demon mojo," he told her, calm and resolute despite the flare of her eyes and the angry curl of her lip. "Mind control isn't consent. It's not a kink. It's assault. Get the fuck out of my way. I'm leaving."

"He knows," Destiny hissed.

"Of course I know!" Alex burst. He gestured to the table. "What part of this room *doesn't* say, 'Freaky Demon Sex Dungeon?' Come on!"

Chance's eyes narrowed. "Then you'll have to stay and explain how you know so much."

Destiny moved in fast, snarling much like the man on the couch as she lunged for Alex. He ducked to his left and swept her away, pushing back mostly with his upper arm so he wouldn't get his wrists anywhere near those cuffs. Alex put his full strength into the move, which turned out to be a good thing. Though she looked no different than before, Destiny felt heavy and solid like a linebacker rather than a lithe, slender dancer.

Still, Alex had leverage, momentum, and technique on his side. Destiny tumbled off balance and sprawled out on the floor. Alex kept moving. Chance looked ready for his attack, but he pushed forward anyway, launching a left hook into her jaw. He followed up with a low, forceful kick to her belly meant to knock her out of his path.

She didn't move. His shoulders slumped. "Aw, really?"

Chance shoved him hard with both hands, sending him stumbling until the ritual platform took his knees out from under him. He fell on his back, but rolled with the momentum to get away from Chance. As she jumped onto the table, Alex brought both feet up at her, kicking her face and shoulders to push her away.

He scrambled off the table, winding up on exactly the furthest spot from the exit. Destiny was coming around on one side. Chance looked ready to move along the other. Alex looked for an escape and found nowhere to run, but he was at least right next to the table full of what he took to be ritual supplies. That gave him a bit of hope. His fists wouldn't get him out of this mess. He needed weapons. The table provided a couple of things he knew how to use. Alex filled his left hand with the neck of a glass bottle. He was about to do the same with his other hand until he spotted an ornate ritual dagger. The dried blood on the blade didn't deter him at all. If anything, it suggested that the thing was for more than show.

Alex moved in to meet Destiny head-on. He thrust the bottom of the bottle under her chin in a wide, underhanded arc, blunting her momentum and setting her up for a stab to the gut with the dagger. As he half-expected, the dagger didn't penetrate much, but as it turned aside it still drew blood and a shriek of pain. Destiny got her arms around him before he could turn her aside. Her nails dug into his skin like talons, forcing him to shout in pain much louder than she had.

Bad. Real bad, Alex thought as he spun, taking advantage of his greater height to lift her off her feet even if he couldn't easily break free. He slammed her into the table as he turned, knocking over jars and bowls. She didn't have the hold locked in yet. Alex spotted the big mirror mounted on the nearby wall. Chance was almost on top of them. Rather than tangle with both women at once, Alex ran straight for the mirror, carrying Destiny with him the whole way. "No!" shrieked Chance.

They hit the mirror hard, with Destiny bearing the full brunt of the impact. It shattered with a louder crash than Alex expected as Destiny cried out in pain, but the bigger surprise came when they fell to the floor behind the mirror. He'd been wrong about it being mounted. His bottle shattered in the mess, too, but he hung onto the blade. Destiny rolled off of him as they landed.

This room was darker than the other. Darker and much smaller, more like a closet than a room, with greenish swirling lights along the walls.

He saw another naked man here, this one restrained upright against the walls, with scraggly hair and a hipster beard—and his chest opened up like someone had popped the hinges on his ribcage. The greenish light was strongest at the gaping hole, where an ethereal, vaguely humanoid shape swirled about as if trying to settle into the man's chest. A similar green glow emanated from the man's eyes and his open mouth.

"Oh, you fucking wretch!" Chance snarled as she approached. "That was a soul mirror!"

Picking himself up off the floor, Alex saw shards of glittering blue glass all around rather than pieces from an ordinary mirror. As if the lights and colors weren't enough, he saw Destiny curled up on the concrete in pain, her wings and tail now showing. Her skin now bore a reddish tint, too. It made the blue shards sticking out of her that much more visible, along with the blood that flowed from dozens of cuts all over her shoulders and back.

He had no clue what a soul mirror was or what it did, but it clearly meant a lot to Chance. Alex switched the dagger into his left hand and carefully took hold of the nearest big shard of debris with his right. "Guess you should've let me go, huh?" he asked.

Chance let out a furious growl as she crossed into the little room, grabbing his shoulder. Alex felt her talons on his skin, but his counterattack was already in motion. He plunged the shard of glass straight into Chance's wrist. She jerked her hand away, screaming in pain. Alex spun around, shoved her aside, and bolted for the exit. He ran right over the cushioned platform and ignored the shouting man on the couch on his way to the stairs.

The door at the top opened up without a problem, giving Alex a slight measure of relief. He found no one in the VIP room, just the same red lights, furniture, thumping music, and discarded lingerie. The door to the hall remained shut. Alex thought fast. Barricading the secret door to the

Chamber of Batshit Crazy downstairs seemed like a great idea, but none of the furniture here looked up to the job. Besides, both of the demon women were much stronger than Alex or any other guys he knew. He ditched that idea and decided he'd have to take the brazen approach. Alex slipped the knife into the back of his belt under his untucked dress shirt, hoped to God he didn't wind up cutting himself or stabbing his own ass like an idiot, and went straight for the door. He took up a bottle from the bar on his way, only this time it was full of vodka rather than whatever freaky ritual stuff they kept downstairs.

He came face to face—or rather face to chin—with one of the bouncers in the dark hallway outside. A second bouncer loomed not far away. "Hi," Alex smiled. "Excuse me."

The bouncer moved to block Alex's sidestep and put one hand on his chest. "Wait. Where are the girls?" he asked.

"Back there. No worries, they're fine," Alex answered breathlessly. "Holy shit are they wild." He kept his right hand low and back to hide the bottle, but almost as soon as he thought of it, he came to the conclusion that only a bouncer on his first day on the job would fall for that…maybe.

"Problem, Donny?" asked the other bouncer.

"Maybe," said the one blocking Alex. He turned his stubbly chin back to the younger man. "Girls come out of the room first, buddy. Those are the rules."

"Wow, really?" Alex blinked. "That's not what they said."

"Yeah?" Donny pushed Alex back a couple steps. "What'd the girls say?"

"Kill him!" came Chance's angry voice, loud enough to be heard at distance and over the ambient music. "Kill that fucking—"

Neither man listened to the rest. Alex stepped back, dropped low and swung the vodka bottle hard against the larger man's knee. His weapon held firm as the bouncer stumbled to one side. Donny's partner saw it all happen and came rushing forward. Alex hurled the bottle with an accuracy developed several lifetimes ago. It smashed as it struck the other bouncer's face, bringing him down hard.

Then Donny caught Alex by the wrist. He twisted hard, putting the younger, smaller man up against the wall. Alex struggled, but knew Donny held all the advantages—except one. That slight advantage jabbed up against the small of Alex's back as the bigger man grappled him. Though he had one hand immobilized behind his back already, Alex slipped the other one around his back to grab the dagger before Donny could do anything about it. He didn't even need to draw it from his belt. Tilting it properly would be enough.

The blade slashed across the top of Donny's leg, causing him to involuntarily jerk back. He didn't let go of Alex right away, twisting the younger man's arm even more painfully, but the break in the hold proved critical. Alex spun around to get his arm bent the right way again as he drew the dagger. He slashed once, this time cutting a nasty gash across Donny's arm.

The curtains over the VIP room's door flew open as Chance burst out into the hallway. With his arm free now,

Alex shoved the wounded bouncer at her and ran. He caught a glimpse of Destiny as she stumbled out after Chance, winding up in a slight tangle with the others. It granted him another second to flee, perhaps two at the most. He almost made it to the end of the hallway, back toward the main showroom full of people and lights and, Alex hoped, cover.

Then Destiny let out a screeching cry louder than any fire alarm.

Alex crossed into the open at the back of the showroom in time for everyone to look back at the noise, and therefore right at him. Heads turned from tables, from the pit, even from the stage. The club seemed to be back to "solo performer" mode, complete with reverential silence for the woman on stage—now interrupted by Alex and Destiny's scream. This dancer was tall and curvy, still wearing a blue lace bra and panty set when Alex arrived. Like the others, she was a strikingly attractive woman, though everything about her from her curves to her jewelry seemed just this side of too much. It was the sort of judgment Alex didn't make unless he suspected anyone around him might be a demon in a flesh suit.

Glittering electronic letters flashing by along the top of the stage revealed her name. His shoulders slumped. "Karma? *Really?*"

Karma's eyes flared at the sound of Destiny's call. She pointed to Alex and shouted in a booming voice, "Seize him!"

Behind him, Alex knew he faced two demons. Toward the front entrance, he saw some more big bouncer types. To his right lay the audience, with a couple dozen men leaving their seats or their spots in the pit. He didn't see any glowing eyes, but the facial expressions and body language suggested other big problems. "Protect the mistress!" snarled out one of the bikers, producing a pistol and leaping onto the stage. Others immediately followed, both from his gang and from completely different walks of life.

"Gun!" someone shouted. "He's got a gun!"

Patrons, performers, and waiters bolted for the exits. Other patrons rushed at Alex. Bouncers and angry demon strippers chased him from down the hallway, too. Alex took the only sensible option: he ran straight for the bar and dove over its side.

Thankfully, neither of the people behind the bar did anything to stop him. The man and woman in black vests and bowties jerked away as he skidded across the top of the bar and then flopped to the floor between them. The woman hustled out of the way. The man found himself stuck when Alex grabbed his ankle. "Where's the shotgun?" Alex demanded. He didn't even notice the change in his own voice. His speech briefly lost its west coast accent as his brain slipped into sensibilities developed in another life.

"What?" blinked the bartender. "What shotgun?"

"You don't keep a shotgun back here?" Alex blinked. "What the hell kinda place is this?"

"This isn't a fucking cowboy bar!" the bartender retorted, jerking his ankle free. He climbed over the counter to get away.

Alex didn't bother to pursue. There *had* to be a shotgun behind the bar. Why the hell wouldn't there be a shotgun? What sense did that—?

A baseball bat. He found a baseball bat in one of the cabinets behind a stack of paper towel rolls. Grimacing, Alex snatched the weapon up in time to meet the first of his attackers as they began leaping over the bar.

In all his lives, he'd never fought with a baseball bat. Alex jabbed the base of the bat into the stomach of the first man to come at him, then reversed to thrust its head into the shin of the next one on the other side. He decided that a club was a club. The next attacker felt the bat come down on his shoulder, sending him down with a howl.

Alex didn't have much room to really swing it, but on the bright side, the bar provided plenty of glass bottles he could throw.

———

"That's about what I can think of, unless we wanna start talkin' about Tacoma or something," said Lester. He let out a grumbling sigh. "Plenty of stuff going on down there."

"I'm sure," said Lorelei. "I've been to Tacoma." Though she presented a patient demeanor, she felt a growing sense of concern. Alex no longer provided her that constant flow of arousal and pleasure, which would be no issue had it not happened all at once. He went from conflicted desires and sensual turn-ons to nothing at all. Such an abrupt end was never a good sign. And there were twice as many demons here as she expected.

"Aw, come on!" Lester fumed, taking her expression all too seriously. "You said *this* city, not others! Look at this list! I've told you all kinds of stuff!"

"Yes, you have," Lorelei agreed. "You've been most forthcoming." She slid the list away from him, folding and tucking it into one pocket of her sleek leather coat. "Suspiciously so, I'd say."

"Wh-what's that supposed to mean?"

"You seem happy to keep me on the subject. Perhaps so we don't stray too close to another?"

"Are you serious? For fuck's sake, what am I supposed to do? You barge in here, you threaten me, you tell me you're gonna set me up to take a fall with my boss. What more do you want?"

"I want to know what you're hiding."

"All kinds of shit!" the exasperated demon replied. "Who do you think you're talking to here?"

"I suppose that's to be expected," decided Lorelei. She stood calmly. "Perhaps it's time I took my leave. I imagine you have packing to do."

"Yeah, yeah," Lester muttered, rising with her. "I'll walk you out."

"That won't be necessary. I know the way."

The other demon scowled. "Oh, but you've been so polite. Ought to at least let me return the favor. Besides, I gotta check on my club, anyway."

"You are the host," Lorelei conceded, or more accurately condescended. "Lead the way."

"You first. I wouldn't want to lose track of you."

Lorelei opened her mouth to respond, but a shrill, inhuman cry from outside the office cut her off. Lester's eyes widened with anger and suspicion. He brushed the mouse on his computer reawaken his monitor and its feed from the security cameras. His hand went into the pocket holding his gun. "What did you do?" he demanded. "Who are you with?"

She didn't give him time for more questions. Lorelei jumped up onto his desk, crouching low to grab his face with her talons extended. She dragged nasty gouges into his skin as she roughly shoved his head back. The bearded man stumbled away hard enough to put a crater in the drywall. She followed up quickly, grabbing the wrist holding his gun to keep it turned away from her. A loud bang split the air as Lester inadvertently pulled the trigger, but the bullet struck neither of them.

"No! Don't hurt master!" rasped the imp in the corner. It leapt up from its hiding spot to stand on the filing cabinet.

"Help me, damn you!" demanded Lester.

Lorelei looked up to see a pained expression on the little thing's reptilian face, but then it belched out a stream of tiny shards of ice. Lorelei dodged the worst of it by stepping off the desk and turning her back to the thing. The imp still drew a painfully frigid line of frost along the back of her coat. The blast caught her wings, too, normally invisible and intangible in mortal environments bout now distinctly painted by magical frost. Despite the pain and the jarring cold, Lorelei kicked the filing cabinet over, sending the imp tumbling from its perch.

Though Lester wasn't strong enough to overcome her grip on his right wrist, his left hand was still free. He sprouted talons and slashed at her face and neck. Lorelei grabbed the back of his head and shoved his face right through his desk, splitting the wood in two with the force of the impact.

"For Sammael!" the imp chirped as frighteningly as it could, coming out for another blast. Lorelei put her arms up in front of her face to shield herself from the next stream of painful frost, pushing into it until she could reach out and grab the insipid little thing. "Ack!" it yelled as she got her hands on its arms and raised it up.

Against Lester or any other demon wearing flesh, Lorelei could rely on brute strength and skill. The imp, though, would bounce back from that too easily. Such an enemy required less subtle tactics. As much as she would have rather held such power in reserve, she had few other options. Lorelei shoved the thing against Lester's office window overlooking the parking lot. "This, too, is for Sammael," she grunted.

The thing screamed, knowing what was coming, but it couldn't save itself from the blast of fire from Lorelei's mouth. The stream of flames instantly melted a hole straight through the plastic white blinds and the glass behind it. In only the space of a few heartbeats, the imp's screams ended. Lorelei tore its charred remains asunder and then looked to its master.

Still on his back and bleeding freely from his smashed
nose, Lester angrily fired his pistol. Lorelei jerked and
grunted as every bullet struck, staggered by the powerful
impacts. A modern pistol or rifle could inflict a terrible beat-
ing on a demon such as Lorelei, but it would take more than
that to kill her. Yet the bullets, the imp's icy breath, and the
oppressive cold of the magical wards over the building all
added up to terrible damage. Lorelei thought in the brief gap
between gunshots that she had clearly underestimated the
dangers here. Even beyond this, the club still held more than
one demon. Lorelei cursed herself for endangering Alex by
bringing him here. She could not afford to prolong this fight
while he was in danger.

Lester got off the entire magazine from his pistol. Most
of his bullets struck. Gasping for breath, Lorelei nearly collapsed against one side of Lester's ruined desk—and then
overturned the whole piece on him with a furious shout.

"Fuck!" Lester yelped, fighting to get clear. Though not
as strong as Lorelei, he pushed the wrecked furniture off
roughly, crawling away his back.

It gave Lorelei a moment to catch her breath. She shook
her head to clear the ringing from the two bullets that struck
her skull and left her hair matted with blood. At first she
thought she could hear more gunshots, or perhaps mere
echoes of those that struck her. Then she realized the sound
came from the hallway.

Alex. The thought banished the worst of her pain and disorientation. Alex needed her.

Lester made it to his feet right before Lorelei spit a small cloud of flame at him, burning his skin and igniting his clothes.

It wasn't a power Lorelei could use lightly or frequently. The attack frightened Lester more than it hurt him. She couldn't work up a second blast at full strength so soon after dealing with the imp, nor did she want to risk setting the building on fire with Alex in it. As Lester screamed and fought to tear off his shirt, though, she felt some measure of satisfaction. He fell to his butt, tripped up by his own feet as he ripped away burning fabric.

Lorelei stepped into a resounding kick against Lester's head, knocking him onto his back once more. Before he could rise again, she brought her foot down hard on his sternum. She repeated the move again and again, each time with all the force she could muster until she could hear and feel the cracking of bones. "Should've brought my own gun," she huffed, stomping again and finally hearing a loose crunch and a gurgle from her opponent.

Wasting no time, Lorelei crouched low. She brought her taloned fingers up through his belly and into his ribs, deliberately hooking in to tear open his broken chest. Lester screamed in agony and fear as she ripped apart ruined cartilage and shattered bones, then went silent as his body went limp.

A wispy green cloud escaped from the vicious wound. It formed a vague head, shoulders, and wings, but demonstrated little control over its rise as it floated through the air. The shape bent at Lorelei and hissed angrily, yet it dissipated noticeably with each heartbeat. The frigid power of Lester's wards faded all around Lorelei, too, confirming that her work here was done.

"Goodbye, Lester," she said to the spirit's last, fading remnants. "Pray we do not meet again."

———

The bar turned out to be a fairly defensible position at first. Alex caught on quickly to using the baseball bat. The skills of his earlier selves leaned more toward blades than clubs, but he had little trouble adjusting. If nothing else, he knew how to fight in close quarters.

The rack of drinks covered his back. The counter didn't completely block attackers, but the obstacle it presented bought Alex time and made it easier to see threats. Guys jumped over the barrier at either end to come at him from both sides, but the narrow passage between bar and shelf meant they couldn't swarm him. Alex moved left, then right, then to the left again, knocking one attacker out of the fight before pivoting to the next on his other side.

Survival depended on staying out of anyone's grasp. His opponents were angry men, and some were bigger than him. Still, few were trained fighters, and this situation didn't come down to a matter of life or death for any of them. A solid blow proved enough to drive back most. No one stood up to more than three hits. Their intimidating numbers didn't ben-efit from any coordination, either. They acted like a mob of individuals all interested in showing off for the woman who sent them into battle. Everyone wanted to be the one guy to bring down her enemy, and that saved him.

He rarely swung the bat, preferring to keep both hands on it rather than risk anyone catching hold of his only weapon and taking it from him. One man managed to do that, sacrificing his ribs to hook the bat under his armpit when Alex opted for a full swing, but the rack of booze right beside them provided an easy counterattack. Alex swept a bottle of gin off the shelf straight into the big man's head. He went down with the ensuing mess of broken glass and wasted alcohol, freeing Alex and his bat as the next attacker behind him made it over the crumpled body of the previous assailant. Alex spun, got his hand on the top of the bat again and jammed the base of his weapon into the new attacker's nose. He stepped back as the new guy stumbled, brought the bat up and swung it down to finish the man off with a blow to his shoulder.

Demons could overpower him, but Alex knew how to handle mortal threats. It wasn't long at all before he lost track of how many bones he'd broken, arms he'd dislocated or teeth he'd knocked out. Desperately fighting for survival, Alex unconsciously blended the lessons and talents of so many previous lives: a veteran legionnaire's experience with a short weapon in crowded fights, the channeled rage that carried him through raids and feuds in colder climes, and above all, the savvy of a piano player who'd worked in all too many of the toughest saloons.

None of that made him bulletproof.

Gunshots boomed as soon as he stood without an upright opponent to either side. Bottles and mirrored glass on the rack behind him exploded with each impact. Alex yelped and dropped low. "They're *all* cowboy bars," muttered one of the men he used to be.

Fortunately, his closer opponents seemed properly averse to bullets despite whatever hold the demons had over them. The bar cleared out with the gunfire as every guy still able to flee did so. One or two of them even had the sense to grab their friends curled up on the floor with concussions on their way.

That left Alex with another thought: by now, the normal patrons—the ones not so enthralled by Karma and the others that they'd leap into a fight—had all bailed on this madness. None of the other dancers or servers remained, either; they seemed to have rushed for other exits. That was the good news. Presumably, someone had called the cops by now, too. Alex didn't know what to think of that, but at least it appeared the club was down to him, the bad guys, and Lorelei, wherever she was.

More bottles broke. A couple of bullets pierced the bottom of the counter. He needed to get out. For that, he needed to stop the shooting so he could make a break for it without being cut down. Alex looked around again at the cabinet shelves and drawers behind the bar for anything he could use. Soon enough, he hit on something appropriately crazy.

Another gunshot destroyed more bottles over his shoulder. He checked his sleeves. Nothing had fallen on him.

Amazingly, his shirt was still largely dry. That was an important consideration, given his plan. This would be crazy, but that seemed par for the course these days. He snatched one of the surviving bottles up off the rack and dropped down again, hoping his remaining enemies still had some degree of survival instinct left in their heads.

The bottle of absinthe broke against the shelf full of dish towels on Alex's first swing. The lighter from the cabinet did the rest. Alex backed off as flames quickly spread. In the space of only a couple breaths, he became sure the bar would catch, too. He didn't hear any more gunshots, but within a few more seconds, he heard guys yell, "Oh shit, something's burning!" and "Fire! We gotta get out!"

"Oh, fucking mortals," said a feminine voice behind Alex. He felt her hands on him before he could turn to face her, and then he was off his feet with the room spinning around him. His attacker slammed him down hard on his back against the bar. Ignoring the pain, Alex swung his bat in retaliation, missed, and then felt the weapon torn from his grasp.

Another pair of feminine hands grabbed his arms and held them back on the other side of the bar, heedless of the burning wood and alcohol. His attackers slid him a few feet away from the flames, but he still felt the heat. They seemed able to resist it. "You can't possibly know how far you've set us back," said Chance. She loomed over him with a cruel sneer on her lips. Beyond her, Alex could see the club was now completely empty except for Chance and Karma, along with Destiny, now slowly walking over from the hallway to join them. She looked worse for wear after her injuries from the mirror, but was still standing and still furious.

"You'll learn, though," promised Karma, looming over him with the bat in her hands. "We'll keep you alive until we've fixed everything you've wrecked. Alive and just conscious enough to wish you weren't." She jabbed his side with the bat. "And then the real fun begins. I can't wait to see who gets put in that cute little body of—"

She stopped cold. Without giving Alex any clue or hint as to why, Karma looked up at Chance in alarm. He saw the other demon look back at her and then glance around the bar with similar concern. "The wards," said Chance.

"Lester!" Karma shouted. She dropped the bat and rushed to a set of stairs that rose from a spot near the entrance to the main hall. The steps seemed to lead to a balcony overlooking the bar, but Alex didn't get much more of a look than that. He had another angry woman in his face already.

"Who are you?" Chance demanded with a growl. She still stood on the open side of the counter, holding his arms back over his head. "Who are you with?"

Lifting his legs, Alex found he could just barely touch the main rack behind the bar from where she held him on his back. Swinging himself up into a curl seemed dumb. Chance easily outmatched him in physical strength and durability. He'd lose that wrestling match. Instead, Alex did the only productive thing he could: he kicked the rack hard once, then again, knocking loose more bottles and finally bringing one of the shelves tumbling down.

It made little difference where he lay. The bottles that fell on the burning end of the bar made much more of an impact on their situation. Flames roared to life as rum and other accelerants crashed down and spread across the counter. If the heat bothered Alex before, it genuinely hurt now. Demon or not, Chance flinched at the sudden change in circumstances, tugging Alex along with her and inadvertently pulling him onto his side. Alex rolled the rest of the way over, bringing his arms into a more natural angle and giving him the counter as a brace. With all his strength, Alex pulled his wrists back hard and tugged Chance face first into the counter.

She let go of one hand. Alex used it to punch her cheek, but her glare reminded him how poorly that worked. Then he jammed his thumb in her eye. The nastier tactic worked out much better for him. Chance jerked back with a grunt, slapping his hand away and releasing his other wrist.

Alex tumbled to the floor behind the bar. He hit his back on the cabinet behind him, finding himself sitting in a cramped stretch of wet floor and a lot of broken glass. He looked up to see Chance staring daggers at him from over the counter. "You still want to fight?"

He coughed from the smoke, shuffling further from the flames to escape the heat. "Sure," he croaked. "As long as I don't have to watch your shitty dancing."

Snarling, Chance rose to climb up over the bar. Then Karma's bloodied body came crashing down onto the counter between them, knocking Chance back out of sight. Karma rolled off to the other side, too. Alex covered his mouth with his forearm and coughed, finding it hard to breathe so close to the fire. Before he could shuffle away, though, another woman came down the counter from high above. This one stuck the landing, with broad, leathery wings sprouting right through her leather coat. Her demon's tail thrashed left and right in quick, angry motions. Flames licked up at one of her boots and her leg. She didn't react at all to the heat.

"Your master is on his way back to Hell," said Lorelei. "Keep fighting and you will join him."

Alex picked himself up off the floor, crouched over and haggard but on his feet in time to gauge the enemy's reactions. Karma was back up to her hands and knees by then. Though she spit black blood and bore scars from Lorelei's talons, she wasn't down for the count. If the other women recognized Lorelei, it made little difference.

Destiny seemed to rally in defiance of her wounds from the mirror. "Sammael won't forgive us if we let them go," she warned the others.

Lorelei tilted her head. "A fair point," she conceded, and then dove off the bar to tackle Chance into the nearest table and chairs. They landed with a loud crash as wood snapped and glasses fell. Destiny rushed into the mess before either of the other combatants regained their footing. She kicked Lorelei hard across the temple as the succubus rose. Chance drove a punch straight into Lorelei's gut, but the succubus swatted her away with a closed fist. The other temptress took advantage of the distraction, getting behind Lorelei to hook her arms under wings and shoulders alike.

Wrestling moves turned out very differently when both combatants had sharp talons. Things got bloody fast for everyone involved. The scene illustrated for Alex why Lorelei wanted to keep their enemies separated. Their slender builds belied their unnatural strength. He saw far less technique than vicious brawling. Lorelei's greater overall power meant less when faced with two opponents, and Alex knew a third temptress still lurked on the other side of the bar.

He staggered away from the spreading flames, coughing with every other step. The big, open showroom offered plenty of overhead space for the smoke to spread, but it would fill up quickly and then Alex would have far more trouble breathing. He needed to get out soon. He also needed to help Lorelei—and for that, he'd need a weapon. A couple of bottles remained on the counter. His bat lay somewhere on the other side. Alex climbed over the side to find it.

Instead, he found Karma. The beautiful, voluptuous dancer from the stage now bled from deep gashes across her chest and down her arms. More blood seeped from her mouth. All of it looked unnaturally dark and thick, but that meant less to Alex than the savage murder in her snarl and her eyes. *Don't try to match her,* Alex thought with alarm as she came at him. *She's shorter but way stronger.*

His body followed the mental warning. He grabbed her leading wrist and turned, kicking back low with one foot so he could throw her over his leg. Karma went falling past him. Alex didn't stop to see her hit the floor, knowing he'd probably only pissed her off even more. He stuck to his priorities: find a weapon, help Lorelei, get the hell out.

The bat was nowhere in sight. Amid the debris on the counter, only a foot away from the flames, lay one last unbroken bottle of rum.

"Fucking! Bitch!" Chance raged, punctuating each word with a blow against Lorelei. She had to be careful not to hit Destiny, who clung to the barest hold on their opponent's arms, but she got her licks in. "All of you stuck-up succubae deserve—oof!" She stepped back with the impact of Lorelei's boot in her gut.

"Don't screw around!" yelled Destiny, who then yelped as her grip on Lorelei faltered. The stronger woman wrenched one arm free and then spun around the other way to slash at Destiny's neck with her talons. The dancer got her shoulder up in time to take the blow there instead of in her throat and retaliated in kind, forcing Lorelei to back up and block rather than press her attack. Lorelei stumbled over debris from the broken furniture. Destiny pounced, once more tangling up one of Lorelei's arms as she fell to one knee. This time, Destiny also managed to yank down hard on Lorelei's hair to expose her neck. The hold left both of her hands occupied, but Destiny wasn't in this alone. "Now!" she demanded.

"On it," promised Chance. She darted in with her talons extended, but never got there. Alex swept in from the side, coming between Chance and her target with a downward swing of his bottle. Though she looked up reflexively, Chance didn't raise her hands in time to block before it crashed into her face. Instantly soaked and annoyed, Chance tore into his abdomen. Alex felt her talons rake through him, one finger scraping his lowest rib while the others dug lower. He screamed in pain as he collapsed.

Chance saw the shock and fear in Lorelei's face. She didn't stop to question such emotions in a fellow demon's eyes. She simply lifted one finger to her rum-soaked face to lick the blood from it in a final taunt. It cost her dearly.

Though Lorelei could not muster up a full blast of flame, she could cough out a slight burst. It lasted only an eyeblink, perhaps two, but the rum helped. Chance's head, shoulders, and chest caught fire instantly. She didn't react well. The temptress shrieked and stumbled back, her supernatural resilience quickly overcome.

"Oh shit," blurted Destiny.

"Flames," grunted Lorelei. "Right."

The other temptress almost let go of her in time. Lorelei grabbed Destiny's leg and a handful of hair at the scalp, hoisting her upward and then rushing for the burning bar at full speed. Destiny had enough time to cry out in protest before Lorelei slammed her down through the flaming wreckage with all her might. The bar collapsed under the impact. Lorelei delivered a final, bone-crunching stomp to keep Destiny down as the temptress howled in agony. Chance kept screaming, too, blindly staggering into Lorelei's reach long enough for the succubus to rake her throat open with her talons. Overcome with pain and panic, Chance thrashed around and stumbled away. She immediately lost Lorelei's interest.

When she turned again, Lorelei saw one remaining foe. Karma moved in to finish off the wounded mortal struggling to rise from the floor until she caught Lorelei's eye. The last temptress needed no further threat than that single gaze. Lorelei rushed at her with a bestial growl. As it turned out, the look in her eyes had already done the trick. Karma turned and fled rather than face the succubus again.

Doubled over in pain and fighting for air, Alex missed most of the battle's end. He managed to open his eyes in time to see Chance drop. That marked progress. Now he had to try moving. He lay on his side clutching the wound, fairly certain Chance had torn open something vital in his guts. Blood spilled out between his fingers as he tried to hold everything together. His lungs weren't doing so great, either. Down on the floor, he escaped the worst of the smoke, but he still coughed with every weak, shallow breath. He had to get out of here before he suffocated. Though he might still be screwed even once outside, fighting for clean air beat fighting for this.

He made it to his knees with his eyes watering and his limbs feeling weak. His predicament recalled the fear and anger he felt at the end of earlier lives. He'd always died by violence before. The memories were never even close to complete, but that detail had come through loud and clear.

"Alex!" Lorelei knelt beside him. He felt her arms around his. Her hair fell across his shoulders. It meant the world to him. "How badly are you hurt?"

Though he tried to respond, all he could manage was a rasping breath and a cough. He looked to her through watering eyes and mouthed out, "Bad," but no sound came.

Lorelei bore numerous wounds, too. Her demonic visage was gone. Alex saw her usual complexion, not so flawless now with all the soot and open cuts. He didn't see horns or wings. Instead, he saw worried, frightened eyes. He also saw spreading flames behind her. Carefully, Lorelei picked him up off the floor to carry him from the room as he coughed.

"Showoff," he managed.

She carried him to the foyer, where they found more gathering smoke but no other dangers. None of the staff or guests remained. "I do not know how to treat this," said Lorelei as she walked with him. "I never had reason to learn before now."

"S'okay," Alex rasped.

"The best I can do is call an ambulance unless we can find—"

The front doors flew open—or, more accurately, flew off their hinges as a body crashed straight through them. She landed a few yards past Lorelei and Alex, struggling to rise and escape from the blur of white light and flames that pursued her.

"Sloppy fucking cunt-captain—" ranted the feminine voice of the glowing figure.

"Rachel!" Lorelei snapped.

"No!" Karma retorted, lashing out defiantly with her talons.

The angel was already on her. She kicked Karma hard enough to lift her off the floor, knocking her against one wall of the foyer. "—bitch ass out of my fucking—"

"Rachel!" Lorelei shouted again. She stood on the other side of the broken doors now on her way to the cleaner air of the night outside. "Alex is hurt!"

The lithe, blonde angel paused in her assault for only a heartbeat to snap a look back over her shoulder. After only one glance, she returned to her opponent. "Nevermind," she told Karma before she swung the flaming sword in her hand up into the temptress, cutting into her midsection and up through her chest. Karma let out a final scream before she collapsed. Faint wisps of green colored the smoke that rose from her smoldering body.

It was all Rachel needed to see to confirm Karma's demise. She spun around to join the pair at the club's doorstep. Her flaming blade vanished. "Oh jeez what happened? Put him down," the angel instructed, still speaking at a mile a minute.

Alex felt better the moment Rachel put her hands on him. Her touch chased the smoke from his lungs. Though Lorelei bent at the knees to set him down, he discovered he could stand as long as Rachel had her hands on him. He essentially went from one woman's arms to the other's. "Guts," he said as he leaned into a hug with the angel. "Feels like it's really bad."

He hardly needed to explain. Rachel put her hand over the wound. "I've got it," she said. "I can fix this. Don't let anyone tear your spleen open again, okay? And what the fuck happened here?" She glanced to Lorelei. "I was at that stupid-assed council meeting, and all of a sudden I had two guardians rushing up to say their guys got chased out of this club with a bunch of strippers trying to murder Alex. Were they all demons in mortal bodies like that bitch?" Rachel tilted her head back toward the entrance.

"Only two others," explained Lorelei. "And their master. All taken care of now. The one you killed was the last."

Rachel frowned. "I knew you were planning a strip club, but fuck me running, y'know?"

Alex rolled his eyes. "Oh, sure, you told *her* in advance," he muttered.

"She needed to know at least that much," said Lorelei.

"Ugh. And this place fucking stinks like hell," Rachel complained. "Seriously. How did none of the angels find this—oh, wait, lemme guess. Wards, right?"

"Yes. Many guardians likely followed their charges inside and never knew any better. The wards fell with their creator." As Lorelei spoke, all three heard the first wails of approaching sirens. "We cannot let the emergency responders find us. I can conceal Alex and myself. This fire must burn away any evidence we were ever here," she warned.

"I can do that," said the angel She let go of Alex, who found himself able to stand on his own now. His abdomen bore ugly bruises and scars, but he no longer bled. "You two get gone."

"Make sure you take care of the basement, too," Alex mumbled idly. "Serious shit down there."

Lorelei paused. "What about the basement?"

"Oh man, there's a room down there with bodies on racks and green ghosties or whatever crawling into 'em. It was behind some mirror that I smashed when the stripper demons wouldn't let me go. That got them fucking pissed. Oh, and there's probably some dude still chained to the wall down there, too. I dunno if he needs help or if he's a bad guy. Big scar on his chest, crazy eyes, and…and I take it that's a big deal?" he asked, watching their expressions.

"Yes," answered Lorelei. "That would be one more bad guy."

"Right," huffed Rachel. "Nuclear option it is. See you in a bit."

Lorelei took Alex by the hand and led him down the steps. "I don't see your motorcycle out here," she noted.

"It's around the block. Figured I shouldn't leave it in the parking lot if this was supposed to be a secret mission, y'know?" He noted her sly, approving grin. "What?"

"You catch on to this lifestyle fast."

As she spoke, they heard a sudden roar of flame. Orange light bathed the parking lot as they walked. Alex glanced over his shoulder at the inferno and sighed. "Not fast enough to get my jacket out of coat check," he grumbled.

———

"How many buildings is this now? Three, right?"

"Hm?" murmured Lorelei. She kept her arms around Alex as they sat on the edge of the warehouse rooftop. She had little trouble keeping him warm in the cold, wet autumn night. All he needed was the demon's touch. He gestured at the conflagration and the firefighters deployed across the street, drawing from her another smile. "Fire seems to be a theme for us, yes."

"Guess I can't think of a better way to cover our tracks," said Alex. "Probably ought to work on that, or every big fire is gonna be a dead giveaway."

Lorelei caught his grin and found herself returning it. "I thought you'd be more upset by all this. Or that you would be more inclined to lie low and avoid these incidents."

"Nah. It's what I get for living with you two. I mean, laying low is good. I don't wanna go out looking for trouble. Maybe space things out so we're not averaging an arson a month," he teased. "But it's like you both said in the beginning. This isn't gonna be an ordinary life. I get that. You're worth it."

"That means more than you know. I gravely underestimated the danger this would present. I am so sorry, Alex," she told him.

He shrugged. "Hey, for all I know, everything would've gone according to plan if I hadn't freaked out at the sight of their sex dungeon or whatever. You told me they couldn't do anything serious to me in only one night, right? Guess I'm not down with bondage. Not on a first date, anyway. Not after the shit that's happened to me in the last couple months."

"We all have our boundaries." Lorelei kissed the side of his neck. "I worried that I pushed yours in even suggesting this errand."

"We're cool." He watched the scene across the street with detached interest. "Guess they're gonna stand off and dump water on it 'til it dies off a bit, huh?"

"Probably. I can't see any guardian angels, but I suspect a few may be discouraging the firefighters from being more aggressive. It keeps them safe in more ways than one."

"Did you get what you came for?"

At that, Lorelei's smile turned rueful. "Yes, though I do not know what good it will do now. Lester gave up names and other information. Unfortunately, his contacts and associates will all likely know about this before the dawn. They will see this for the bad omen it is." Her fingers ran fondly through his matted, smoke-scented hair. "You made the greatest discovery tonight. A fitting room is no small investment. If we had left peacefully, Lester would likely have dismantled it and fled, only to rebuild his operation somewhere else. We would have at best delayed his activities rather than ended them."

Alex shuddered. "That was some freaky shit. I never even imagined." He turned toward her and ventured the question. "Are you…?"

"No. I am something quite different," she reassured him. "It is why I am of a more powerful sort than those we faced tonight. This is my original body, however differently it may be shaped."

"Fair enough," said Alex. "I want to know, if you'll tell me, but maybe not right now. I'm still a little grossed out."

"You ended the whole atrocity when you broke the soul mirror. Such artifacts are not easily constructed or replaced. Without them, bringing an unbound spirit from the Pit is much more tedious." Her lips drew close to his ear. "You did a great deal of good tonight, Alex. You know how Rachel gets when that happens."

"Hey, you did all this, too," he pointed out. "It was your idea to check this place out to begin with."

"I know," she admitted with feigned resignation. "She'll be beside herself with glee. I'll endure it somehow."

The pair fell silent, the burning club providing the same serene spectacle as a campfire or a warm fireplace at home. Before long, the large "Vixens" sign collapsed from its mountings over the front façade with a loud crash.

"So that was the best strip club in Seattle?" asked Alex.

"By reputation, yes."

"Huh."

"Did you at least enjoy yourself before the crazy began?" Lorelei asked.

Alex grinned at her choice of words. She didn't often mirror his speech patterns. "I can't decide. It's not like I could forget where I was or what I knew, y'know?" He considered it a moment longer. "It was a lot nicer than the places I used to work, at least. I used to think these places were all bad news.

Figured it was all morally wrong somehow. I was afraid to try stuff like this. That was before I met you. And it was before all the memories, too. Now I don't know."

"Such places don't generally host demons."

"Yeah." He paused again. "This might not be a fair example for the whole business."

"It may well not be your sort of thing," Lorelei mused. He felt her sly grin at his ear. "But the good clubs are in Portland. And even if they disappoint you, I will not."

"So...weekend road trip, is what you're saying?"

ABOUT THE AUTHOR

Elliott Kay is a survivor of adolescence in Los Angeles, service in the United States Coast Guard, classroom teaching, a motorcycle crash, chronic seasickness, summers in Phoenix, winter in Alaska (only one), serial monogamy, and reading comments on the Internet. He resides in Seattle with his girlfriend and two cats.

Elliott's military sci-fi trilogy, *Poor Man's Fight, Rich Man's War,* and *Dead Man's Debt* are available through Amazon.com. His urban fantasy novels *Good Intentions*, *Natural Consequences*, and the fantasy novella *Days of High Adventure* are independently published and available through numerous online vendors.

Email: elliottkaybooks@gmail.com
Website: www.elliottkay.com
Twitter: @elliottkaybooks

Manufactured by Amazon.ca
Bolton, ON